THE STRONG MAN SURVIVES

KAREN MILLETT

Trigger warnings for talk of suicide
though no actual act and talk of death of parents.

PROLOGUE

CHIEF OF POLICE Jack Raskins stared blankly at the TV screen, watching the interview. He truly wished her adoption records could have remained sealed. He didn't think it was necessary that she learn the particular facts of the day she was born. The Council of Elders let everyone request their birth records at the age of 19, to view them. Under normal circumstances he couldn't have cared less, but considering what had happened that day, 30 years ago, she should not have been allowed to learn that.

"Why are you stirring up shit that should be left buried?" he yelled at the TV. Carol Raskins, his wife of 49 years, came up behind him and put her hands on his shoulders, "What is it, love?"

Jack pointed to the TV screen where an interview was taking place.

"Tessa Carstairs. She was allowed access to her birth

records when she turned 19. She's 30 now and decided to write a book about her family's murder."

"That was so horrible."

"It needs to be left alone. Nothing good is going to come from stirring up the dead."

"I agree, nothing good will come of this."

"When she called me and started asking questions, I thought she wanted it for her own personal information. I told her what she wanted to know. I had no idea she was going to turn it into a book. I poured a lot of feelings and emotions into the stories I told her. I love that little girl, but fuck, Carol, this is not going to end well. I have a strong feeling that I'm going to be hauled into Council chambers when they get wind of it."

"I have no doubt about that. She never told you outright that that was her plan?"

"No."

"Have you thought about canceling her visitation pass?"

"No. I need to deal with this."

Carol heaved a heavy sigh.

"And it's not like we don't have our own issue to contend with, without digging up skeletons."

"Forgive me for saying this, but that's something that should have died that day, too."

CHAPTER 1

TESSA CARSTAIRS WAS nervous. She had never done anything like this in her life. But then again, she had never written a book before. She sat on a rigid, bright blue club chair on the set of "Talk Archives", which was uncomfortable but seemed to match the rest of the set. There was a bright blue chair on her right side with a small table in between them. The backdrop was all shades of blue with "*Talk Archives*" in fanciful script right in the middle.

The host, a young woman with dark brown shoulder-length hair and brown eyes to match, wore a beige twin-set of a cardigan with a short sleeved jumper over a slender frame. Tessa, being of average height and build with long, waist length black hair and deep brown eyes, felt comfortable as she didn't tower over her host nor did she feel small sitting beside her.

The host, Megan, took her place in the other chair and looked over at Tessa.

"Nervous?" she asked.

"More than you know."

"No reason to be. Relax. I'll try not to make it too painful."

"It's going to be painful no matter how it goes, Megan."

Megan gave a sad smile and reached over to give Tessa's forearm a squeeze.

"We're going live in 3…2…" Tessa could hear the director call and could just barely see him pointing at Megan.

Megan painted a huge smile on her face.

"Hi and welcome to another edition of *Talk Archives*. Tonight, we'll be talking to Tessa Carstairs, author of the bestselling book 'Death Hurts—The Carstairs Murders'."

Megan turned slightly in her chair to face Tessa. Tessa turned slightly to meet her gaze.

"When did you find out you were a Carstairs?"

"When I turned 19 and was able to gain access to my birth records. My adopted parents told me of my adoption but really didn't go into much detail about it. It was almost like they didn't know why my birth parents gave me up but they understood when I decided to take my birth family name. I didn't understand at the time, which, I guess, made me all the more curious to find out who my birth parents were. It ripped my heart out when I found out that they had been murdered the day I was born."

"What did it feel like when you started understanding what had happened?"

"It felt like I had been kicked in the gut. Who would do that and why? It still remains unsolved to this day. No suspects or witnesses. The neighbors gave statements but there was nothing relevant that would make them come any closer to solving it."

"What did you think when you found out about Edward Carstairs?"

"I couldn't believe it. It affected him so badly that no amount of therapy could bring him out of his self-imposed mental prison, to the point where he committed suicide at 16 years old."

"Will you be going back to Unicorn Valley?"

"Yes. I have been in contact with the Chief of Police there, Jack Raskins. He was willing to talk to me and gave me all the information that he could. He was best friends with James and John. He became very close to Michael and Steven, treated them like sons. I want to meet him face to face."

"Michael Carstairs was your birth father." She didn't make it a question.

"Yes. He was an omega unicorn shifter. Steven, my daddy, was a wolf shifter. And I know what you're thinking, because, even though I explained it in the book, people still ask me. Michael and Steven were not brothers. They had separate parents, but they were so close, I guess, that it was easy to think that.

"Chief Raskins told me that James and John Carstairs adopted both of them after their parents had been killed because of a drunk driver. James had been expecting Edward when they decided to adopt the boys."

"Can you explain again what John and James were?"

"John was a Council Protector. They are essentially human but have magical abilities. They can cast spells for protection and defense only. They cannot use their magic to intentionally harm someone. They can also send out mental alerts to other Protectors in case of danger. James was a unicorn shifter but he had a black coat of fur instead of white like Michael had."

"That was considered rare?"

"Yes. Which makes Chief Raskins believe that it had been a hunt gone wrong. That hunters were after James because of his coloring but it all went south and they all died."

"I noticed that you never actually touched on what Edward was," Megan commented.

"That's because I really don't know myself. Chief Raskins stated that he didn't know if Edward would show signs of being a shifter like James or a Protector like John. He also made the remark that he thought Edward wasn't up to speed, if I can say that without it sounding rude. That he was a late bloomer. But I guess we'll never know for sure."

"Do you plan to go to Greyson House?"

"I don't know. From what I can understand from Chief Raskins, all Carstairs properties are off limits by order of the town Council of Elders, but I should be able to gain access since I am a Carstairs. At least, I am hoping to. I really don't want to see the other places, I just want to see Greyson House. To see where it happened."

"If you found out about your birth parents at 19, why did it take so long to write the book?"

"I guess it took a long time for the horror and the truth to sink in. That my whole family was gone and I never got to meet any of them. To believe that it was real. I had just started college, enrolling in art history and photography, and I got into the photography side. I loved it and excelled in it. Got myself established and on the road to where I wanted to go. I guess I wanted to put it out of my mind and ignore it because I didn't want to believe that it was real, that it actually happened. That one day I would find them alive and well. But then, about three years ago, it hit like a brick. I sat down in my apartment and just started crying uncontrollably. It was hours before I could stop, pain felt like it was physical. They were all dead and I would never get to meet them.

"I slowly started to gather information on my family. But it's only been within the last couple of years that I started to communicate with Chief Raskins and really started pulling things together. It was only after I had pulled together a significant amount of information from TV reports and news articles and, of course, from Chief Raskins himself, that I decided to write the book."

"Do you think all the answers will ever be known? That it will ever be solved?"

"No, I don't." Tessa tried to set her features to neutral, "But I'm hoping someday...." Tessa let her voice trail off. Taking a hitching breath, she finished, "I don't know why my family was slaughtered when I was just minutes old. Or what Edward saw that drove him to kill himself. "

"From what I understand the town has very tight security and a very low crime rate, especially when it comes to murder," Megan commented.

"Now it does. Unicorn Valley has extremely tight security, all stemming from this incident. Chief Raskins keeps saying something good always comes from something bad. The town security was tight back then but there were still ways to skirt around it. There is the main gate and there is also another gate on the other side of the Valley at the border to Dorhaven. The towers are situated so many miles apart though, and to see people coming they just had binoculars. Now there has been the addition of the 15 foot fence in between the towers. State of the art equipment lets them see practically everything that moves. The Council of Elders requires that anyone visiting has to get a pass from someone who lives there and can vouch for them. There is a two week window unless you request an extension. Anything like deliveries and mail are strictly controlled. I mean, it's not like they don't want anyone to come to the Valley, it's just not a tourist attraction. It's more like a safe haven, I guess, would be the best way I can explain it. It doesn't matter who or what you are."

"We only have a few minutes left. Is there anything else you'd like to say?"

"When I started researching and gathering information, I really had no intentions of writing a book. I just wanted to know what happened. I wanted to play Nancy Drew to see if I could make any sense of it. When I contacted Chief Raskins I never mentioned anything about a book to him because in my mind it really had not yet grown into the idea of a book. I'm sorry, Chief Raskins, I should have told you the minute I knew where I was headed with this. You laid your heart out to me and I gave it to the world. And I imagine right now, seeing this interview, you're not very happy with me. I only want to find the answers, put this to rest forever."

After being cleared, Tessa stepped off the stage. Everyone gave her pats on the shoulders, letting her know what a good job she had done. Going back to her apartment she couldn't believe how wiped out she felt. Laying on her bed, she knew she needed a few minutes to gather herself. Tomorrow she was going to Unicorn Valley, and it was going to come a lot faster than she would like. Her phone pinged and she looked at it. Jack Raskins' cell number popped up with a text message.

Jack: I am not happy with you, little girl. You were not wrong there.

Tessa: I'm sorry, Uncle Jack. I really am. I didn't start out to do a book, it just happened.

Jack: I gave you some sensitive information including the crime scene photos, they had better not be in there. I have not read it.

Tessa: No, most of what is in there is the stories you told me, I did not put any police info that was not already in the papers.

Jack: Good. As it stands, it might be cold but I consider it still active.

Tessa: Do you still want me to come?

Jack: Yes, Tessa, I do. Good night, my dear, I need to rest.

Tessa: Good night, Uncle Jack.

Tessa signed off with a sleepy face emoji then got ready for bed herself. It was going to be a long drive in the morning.

CHAPTER 2

AFTER PACKING ENOUGH clothing and necessities for a couple of weeks, Tessa looked around her small, spartan apartment. She hadn't been back to Unicorn Falls since she had left for college, but she was as nervous as hell. Unicorn Valley was a self-governing town that really knew how to protect itself. It wasn't that they were deliberately trying to hide themselves away from the rest of the world, they were just selective in who they let in. And after such grisly murders, the security of the town got tighter. Chief Raskins had explained some of the reasoning behind the security of Unicorn Falls right from the beginning, but she still wasn't sure she understood. She had done the best she could to explain it on the TV interview and hoped that it didn't sound like she was just rambling and not making any sense.

When she arrived at the main gate, she couldn't help but be impressed. The huge iron gates had high towers on either side that reminded her of small lighthouses. The fences on either side attached to the towers and continued into the distance and out of sight.

She never realized when she left for college just how hard it would be to find her way back to Unicorn Valley. If it wasn't for Jack Raskins giving her directions she would have been looking forever. The people of the Valley liked to keep their anonymity.

A man dressed in camouflage from head to toe came out of one of the towers. He came through a small gate with a clipboard in his hand. Tessa rolled down her window. Jack had told her about the gate guards and he had put her name on the approved visitors list, but she could feel her stomach tying into knots. He leaned in the window to look at her.

"Hello, Miss. I am Protector Davis. How may I serve you today?"

"Jack Raskins said my name would be on the approved visitors list. I came to see him. I'm Tessa Carstairs."

Tessa could see the man visibly pale as he looked at his clipboard.

"Yes, Chief of Police Raskins has you listed as visiting for two weeks. Which is the max unless you require an extension, or are planning to move here, in which case that would have to be approved by Council."

"No, Sir. As of right now it's just a visit. I may not even stay the two weeks. Chief Raskins said that would be fine, he just requested the two weeks."

"Yes, you can leave any time within that period. Any longer than the approved limit he would have to request an extension."

The man turned and walked back through the gate. He

hit a button and the main gates opened. She drove through and stopped as the man approached her.

"Can I give you directions anywhere?"

"Yes, I want to stop off at the police station first before I check in to the Saltwire Motel. I wrote down the directions Chief Raskins gave me but I'm not sure I understand them." She dug a piece of paper from her purse and handed it to him.

He looked it over a few times.

"No disrespect to Chief Raskins but it's clear it's been awhile since he's come in this way. Just a minute." He went into the building and came out a few minutes later with a printed map. "We are located here so you just follow this lane here, I enlarged the street signs so they are easier to see and you should be at the station in about 45 minutes. And from there, you follow this other line and it will take you to the Saltwire." He handed the map to her.

"Thank you very much."

"Enjoy your visit, Miss." He stepped away from the car and watched her drive off.

She watched the main gate close in her rear-view mirror. Jack had not been kidding when he said Unicorn Valley was very well protected. That sometimes good came out of bad.

Tessa pulled up in front of the police station in her car and sat staring at it. It looked more like a two-story house than a police station, with perfectly manicured lawns, rock encased flower gardens, and a brick walkway. She had talked on the phone and video chatted with the Chief of Police numerous times, but this would be the first time she would actually meet him in person. Getting out of the car seemed to take effort. Meeting Chief Raskins was about to make everything as real as it was ever going to get.

Walking up to the door, she stopped. She felt like she was about to walk into someone's home unannounced. Turning the knob, she walked in and a cool blast of AC hit her in the face. The lobby had a desk on the right side and a line of six chairs on the left. There were pictures on the wall of squads and individuals. Noticing that the receptionist was not at her desk, Tessa walked over to the pictures.

She skimmed over the group photos but stopped on the individual pictures. Former Chief of Police Bennett Raskins stood beside a younger man: his son, Jack. A little gold plaque attached to the frame read "First Day on the Job." Tessa smiled. Jack looked so proud of himself.

"Can I help you?" The feminine voice poked into her thoughts. Tessa turned and gave the woman a smile. As she came over to the desk, she noticed the woman looked to be in her 30s or 40s and dressed casually.

"I'm Tessa Carstairs. I don't have an appointment and I know I should have called, but I was wondering if it was possible to see Chief Raskins. He knows who I am."

"Sure, sweetie. He's in the building but I'm not sure where at the moment." She picked up the phone and punched in a code.

"Chief, Tessa Carstairs is here. She would like to see you if you have a few minutes." She listened for a minute then hung up. She stood up and put her hand out to motion to Tessa to go with her.

"This way, dear." She took her down a hallway and to a room at the back. She knocked and opened the door, "Go in."

"Thank you." Tessa smiled at the woman as she went in, and the door was closed behind her. The room was not very big, it might have been a guest room at one time. A wooden desk was catty cornered and two chairs were in front of it. The rest of the room space was taken up with filing cabinets. The room had been painted a dark blue with pale blue curtains. The sunlight that streamed in seemed muted. There were very few pictures on the wall.

"Please, have a seat." Jack Raskins looked better in person than he did when they would video chat. She was amazed at how young he looked for being 66. Although his short hair was salt and pepper, his face showed few wrinkles and his skin was the brown of being in the sun for long periods of time. He stood 6'0" with a firm build. His eyes were a dull green but sparkled as he held out his hand. She sat in the chair after shaking his hand.

"It's so good to finally meet you in person, Uncle Jack." She still felt strange calling him that. They were not related, but James and John had been like brothers to him, and Michael and Steven his adopted godsons. Jack had insisted so that was all that mattered.

"You didn't come all the way out here just to meet me in person, did you? I know this is not a social call."

"No, not entirely. But I'm glad to finally be able to meet you in person instead of a video chat. I know I wouldn't be where I am now if it weren't for all your valuable information and stories. I'm sorry if I damaged our relationship."

"No, you haven't damaged anything, Tessa, you will always be a special person in my life. It just took me off guard. I guess, I really, deep down, didn't want this to come back to the light."

"But you must want it solved."

"I do, very much so. But the pain and memories some-times can be overwhelming."

"Understandable, and, again, I am sorry for not inform-ing you sooner."

Jack waved a hand as if to dismiss it.

"So, did you come straight here or have you checked in and had a rest first?"

"No, I came straight here first. I wanted to meet you before I did anything else and to ask..." Tessa took a deep breath and blew it out through her nose. "It's the reason I wanted to come here, other than to meet you in person. I know, from what you have told me, that all Carstairs proper-ties are basically off-limits, but I want to know if I get access to them since I am a Carstairs."

Sorrow seemed to reflect in Jack's eyes for a brief second.

"I will need to meet with the Council before anything can be handed over. I know you are who you are. I watched you grow up at a distance until you went off to college. But the Council has strict policies that have to be abided by. They have all keys to the Carstairs properties. I will contact the liaison and see when I can meet to discuss it."

"So, why is it restricted to go to the house? Why do you have to go through the Council to get permission?"

"Because technically Greyson House is still Council owned. When the Council moved to the compound that they are at now, they gave Greyson House to the Carstairs'. If "gave" is a proper word. There were three groups of Protectors but the Carstairs' were the main group that protected the Council. The other two groups were more for border secu-rity and town security. The Carstairs' moved into Greyson

House free and clear. It was for all the service that they, as Protectors, provided to the Council. They still had their pay as Protectors, but all bills were taken care of, any renovations done to the house were paid for by Council. All they had to do was put in the requests and invoices were taken care of. They made it into a beautiful home. When the house became John's, they made the basement cold room into a darkroom for James, and when Michael and Steven were adopted they made the attic into a game room.

"The Lizard's Lounge was owned by John's father, but the Council had told him that if he had any issues that he could come to them. J. Carstairs Photography Studio was owned by John. He used his father's inheritance and part of the profits from the Lounge to buy the old Higgins mansion and renovate it."

"I would love to see that someday."

"The land all the way from Greyson House back to Unicorn Falls is Council owned. John's parents built a cabin back by the Falls, it's really nice, too. The Council wanted to preserve it, I guess. I don't know how else to put it." Jack hesitated, a hitch in his voice. "When they died, the Council closed off all Carstairs properties. The fines for trespassing were heavy, not that anyone did. I think the worst of it was when real estate agents started to pester us to contact the Council to find out when the properties would be released to sell. They had no idea about you, but figured Eddie would spend the rest of his life in a mental institution. Since Eddie was blood he was the rightful heir."

"Greedy pigs."

"Yep, they figured Eddie would be too far out of his mind to care. But the Council put an end to it all, stating the properties were under Council protection and would never be sold. That put an end to that."

"Forgive me for asking this but if you were so close to James and John and godfather to Michael and Steven, why didn't you adopt me?"

A haunted look skirted Jack's face.

"The Council would not permit it. I was too close to the case. If the killer found out about you, I may not have been able to protect you. The way it was decided by the Council to secretly adopt you to a family was the best. Plus, I had children and a wife to think of. I could have put them in danger without knowing it, if someone was hunting for you."

Tessa looked at Jack's face closely. She believed what he was saying, but she was certain that there was also something he wasn't saying, something he was holding back.

"When will you be able to meet with the Council?"

"The liaison will contact me with the time. Were you planning to stay long? I know I requested the max time."

"I don't know." She got up, "I guess I'm kind of at a standstill right now."

"May I ask why you want to see the properties?"

"I just want to see the house. I want to see where it happened. I know it's probably not the greatest thing I could be doing, but I just need to."

"I understand."

"Thank you."

"I'll call you as soon as I find out."

Tessa gave a small smile and left him, closing the door behind her. She quickly left the station and got into her car. She sat there for a long moment before heaving out a sigh.

"What are you not telling me, Uncle Jack? What are you hiding?"

Jack picked up the phone and hit the red button on the bottom.

It only rang once before it was picked up.

"How can I help you, Chief Raskins?" The gruff male voice on the other end of the line asked.

"I would like a meeting with the Council. Tessa Carstairs is in town and wants permission to see Greyson House."

There was a long pause on the other end of the line. He could hear the click of the line being put on hold. He held his breath. He knew the liaison was talking to a Council member. Another click and the liaison came back on the line.

"The Council will see you in an hour." The line disconnected and Jack could hear the dial tone in his ear.

"This is going to be a shitshow, I just know it."

CHAPTER 3

JACK WASTED NO time in driving to the Council's compound. It was a remote area just inside the town's border. The compound was a fairly large area hidden by an expanse of forest. It was a two story building with an underground floor. It reminded Jack of a shopping mall, but with fewer windows and doors, and with a whole lot more security.

He pulled up to the main gate and waited for the guard to come out of the gatehouse in front.

"Chief Raskins, the Council is expecting you." He opened the gate, "Drive up to the main building and your escort will take you the rest of the way."

"Thank you." Jack drove in slowly. His knuckles were white from clutching the steering wheel so tight.

He pulled up in front of the main building. Taking a deep breath, he got out. A tall man stood at the main door. He had short brown hair, and skin as pale as a sheet. He was dressed in a blue polo shirt and black slacks.

"Welcome, Chief Raskins, please come with me." He opened the door and stood aside to let Jack pass by him. Jack waited for the man to close the door then move ahead to lead the way. He took Jack down a long hallway to a set of double doors. He opened them then stood aside to allow Jack to enter. Once Jack was inside, the man closed the doors.

He led Jack to stand in front of a solid wooden table on a raised dais with six seats. The main lighting was dim, the accent lighting was evenly spaced around the room.

"The Council will be with you in just a moment." The man left him.

Jack felt his palms starting to sweat. He rubbed them against his pant legs to dry them. He jumped slightly then tensed when four men and two women came into the room single file and took their seats.

Jack bowed slightly and stayed that way until all the Council members were seated. Jack straightened up and his eyes scanned over each of them. They were all dressed alike in black dress shirts and slacks. It made Jack cringe, they looked like a row of judges.

"Speak, Chief Raskins." The man at the far end spoke.

"Councilman Mata, Tessa Carstairs has asked for the key to Greyson House. She wants to see...to see where it happened." Jack felt his face flush with the heat of embarrassment as his voice cracked. "I told her that I needed the Council's permission to give her the keys to any Carstairs property."

"That would be a correct assumption." Councilman Rocha replied from the other end of the table.

"She is a Carstairs." Councilwoman Meadows pointed out, "There is no reason that she should not have access to the properties."

"Does Edward know that she is in town?" Mata wanted to know.

"No, I have not yet told him about her? I don't know what to tell him or even if I should. I don't even know if he remembers her."

"Then he must be told about her." Councilman Hall remarked, "Talk to him about her. He is the rightful heir of all Carstairs properties. It can be his choice if he wants to meet her. She may view Greyson House if that is her desire. That will be all."

The escort appeared and handed Jack a fob with a key on it.

"She has 24hrs to return the key to you. Contact the liaison and he will pick it up from you."

The Council stood, Jack bowed again as they left. He looked down at the key then followed the escort back out to his truck. He got in, pounded his fists on the steering wheel.

"Fuck!!!"

Jack walked into his house and slammed the door. Carol came out of the kitchen drying her hands on a dish towel.

"What's wrong?" Her voice was full of concern.

"Tessa Carstairs came to see me today. She wants to see Greyson House."

Carol paled slightly.

"Why would she want to do that? Doesn't she have to get permission?"

"Yep." Jack flopped down into a chair by the fireplace. "And guess who had to get that permission?"

"Oh crap."

"Yeah." He dug into his pocket and held up the key to show her. He turned his head to give her a strange look when he heard her hard swallow. "What's the matter?"

"What about Eddie?"

"I'm to tell him about her. I don't even think he remembers her. I don't want to think about how he'll react."

"He's at the cabin."

"Eddie?" Jack knocked lightly on the cabin door before he went in. He really hated that the Council thought this was the best solution to keep the boy safe. Safe from what, they really didn't know any more than he did. As far as he was concerned it was a hunter attack gone wrong. He could understand the need for this level of protection if Eddie had been a pure blood unicorn, but he wasn't. He was only half. But the Council's ruling was final and he had to live with it even if he didn't agree with it.

Eddie was curled up on the couch by the fireplace. He had managed to get his 5'6" solid build frame into the tightest ball possible. His deep brown shoulder length hair shone with the blaze of the fire. His eyes never left the fire.

"It's almost bedtime, Uncle Jack."

"I know, son. But I need to talk to you."

Jack went over and sat beside him.

"It's important, Eddie, please bear with me. I don't know how to go about this. I don't want to dredge up nasty memories."

Eddie's eyes were the only thing that shifted to look at him then back to the fire.

"There is someone I would like you to meet, who I think you should meet."

"What if I don't want to?"

"Then that is your choice, but I would like you to give it some serious thought. Michael's little girl. You held her that day in the secret room. You remember her, don't you?"

"Yes."

"I think it would be good for you to meet her. She is in town. Her name is Tessa."

"It is my choice?"

"Yes, son, it is."

"Can I think about it?"

"Yes."

Eddie turned his head slowly to look at Jack.

"I'll think about it....in the morning."

"Of course." Jack got up. It was all he could do to look Eddie in those black eyes. He leaned over and kissed his forehead. "Get a good night's sleep." Jack gently closed the door behind him as he left.

CHAPTER 4

WHEN JACK HAD dropped off the key that morning, Tessa thought she would head right over to Greyson House, but as soon as the door closed behind Jack and she looked down at the key, a whole lot of nerves set in. Her hands shook slightly. Was she really ready to do this? Was she really ready to see the place where her family had died? The place where she was born? She paced around the small motel room. Other than to meet Jack, this was the main reason she had come back here.

She ran to the door and yanked it open. Jack had not left yet, he was leaning against the passenger door of his truck, talking to another person. He looked to be about the same height and age as Jack but his build looked thinner.

"How are things going so far, Adam?" She heard Jack ask the other man.

Tessa could see him roll his eyes.

"I do not understand how some of these men managed to become police officers with the amount of stupid in some of their questions. I don't know, maybe it's because I have studied drugs and their effects on humans and shifters all my career. I don't know why I agreed to this conference."

"Because you are the best at what you do. That is why you are the key speaker."

"I think I'll skip the mingling after the dinner tonight and head straight to the bar."

Jack laughed and slapped Adam on the shoulder.

"Can't say I blame you on that. I've been to conferences here, the food is not what I would call..."

"Edible?" Adam snorted and walked away, heading towards the main doors of the lobby as Jack headed around to the driver's side of his truck.

"Uncle Jack?" Tessa called to Jack.

His hand on the door handle, he turned to face her. She came down the stairs to stand in front of him.

"What do you need?"

"Do you want to come with me?"

"No, sorry. I can't go there right now." He gave her a light pat on the forearm, got into the truck and gave her a small smile as he drove away. Tessa wondered how she should take that comment. His eyes looked so haunted. She could understand not wanting to go back there. The last time he had been in that house was to see the bodies of his two best friends and adopted godsons. She grabbed her car keys then locked the motel door.

It only took a few minutes to park in front of Greyson House. She wasn't sure how long she sat there before she finally got the nerve to make her way to the front door. She had no idea why she needed to see the place where they had died. Was it to give her peace or fire up some desire to continue pushing to find some resolution, some answers as to why they all had been murdered.

Taking a deep breath, she slipped the key into the lock and slowly turned it. It disengaged effortlessly. Opening the door, she stepped in and closed it behind her. The house looked untouched by time. There were no cobwebs or dust to be seen. It was just as if they had walked out and were expected back at any minute. She knew all the utilities had been turned off, so for the house to be clean after 30 years seemed impossible, yet it was. Jack had said that all Carstairs properties were off-limits, so someone had to be sneaking in to keep it clean. There just had to be, but who? It was a question she was definitely going to ask Jack when she saw him again.

She wandered around the first floor, taking everything in. To the right of the front door were the patio doors that lead to the small deck then a few steps down to the in-ground pool. To the left of the front door was the living room with its huge picture windows. The large TV sat to the side of the windows. A coffee table surrounded by two couches, a recliner and a child's recliner. Tessa swallowed hard. Had that small recliner been Eddie's when he was a child or brought for her when she got older? It looked cozy. She looked at the kitchen straight ahead, with its marble island in the middle. She could just bet a lot of fun meals had been cooked there. She turned her head right again to look up the staircase. It was recessed back in the hallway, to the left side. On the right side had been James and John's bedroom, then a half bath, then the guest room, which had been Eddie's nursery. The space under the steps had been made into a closet for storing winter clothing and boots.

Looking up the stairs, she loved the open concept. At the far right would have been Eddie's bedroom when he was able to sleep in a bed instead of a crib. Michael's room was in the middle, then at the end was Steven's. Past that was the stairs leading up to the attic, which had been remodelled into a game room. It looked just as Jack had described it all to her.

Going into the kitchen, she opened the fridge. It was perfectly clean. She smiled, a little box of deodorizer sat at the back on the bottom shelf. By the closed up smell of the fridge the deodorizer had stopped working a long time ago. Shutting the door, she turned her attention to the basement door. She had to stop putting off why she had come here. Between the front door and the patio doors was the basement door. It was open. She forced her feet to move to descend down the stairs. The door at the bottom was closed. With a sweaty hand she opened the door and stepped in. The mid-morning sun streamed in through the small windows with enough light that she didn't have to use the light feature on her cell phone.

In the corner under the window was where it happened. Michael's nest of blankets had been cleaned and lovingly placed exactly as they had been. It looked like it had in the crime scene photos that Jack had shown her. She could see some bloodstains, but they matched the photos exactly. But who had done it? Who had cleaned them and why? It gave her a creepy feeling.

The secret room that they had put her and Eddie in was under the basement stairs. John's parents had made it for him when he was young. He used to have debilitating headaches, so they soundproofed the room and put blankets in there so he would be able to sleep it off all day. The soundproofing worked both ways. No sound came in and no sound came out. The door was designed to look like part of the wall, so there was no knob, just an inset lock with a key. It would have been behind the killers so they never knew to look, most likely had no idea it was even there. She wanted to look inside but couldn't seem to make herself. She turned to look around. There was a door on the opposite wall of the basement. She went over and tried the knob. It opened easily.

Tessa brought a hand to her mouth. It was Michael's at-home darkroom. It, too, looked pristine, well taken care of. Jack had told her that Michael and James had both been great photographers. By the looks of the photos still hanging on the drying line, that was definitely true. It made her heart ache. She would never get to see those smiling faces or hear the laughter. Looking down at the table, Tessa noticed a roll of undeveloped film by a notepad. She leaned over to look at it. Stared at it hard. What was it doing there? If the police were combing everywhere for clues and evidence, why didn't they take the roll of film to see what was on it? It lay there on the table, blatantly ignored. Why? That was definitely something she was going to ask Jack about.

A list of picture sizes were on it. Tessa picked up the roll of film. She wondered if it would be possible to have it developed just to see what was on it. She slipped it into her purse and headed back upstairs, closing all the doors behind her.

"Hey, Tara." Tessa smiled as she walked up to the reception desk of the police station. "Can Chief Raskins see me?"

"Let me ask." Tara picked up her phone and hit a button with the end of her pencil. "Chief? Miss Carstairs is here and would like to see you."

After a few seconds she hung up. "He's on the phone right

now but if you want to have a seat, he'll come and get you when he's able."

"Okay." Tessa went and sat down. She suddenly felt overwhelmed. Tessa sat in one of the plastic chairs in the reception area. She had no idea how long he would be tied up on the phone, but she hoped it wouldn't be long. She let her head fall forward and the tears flow.

"Something wrong, Miss Carstairs?" Tara was looking at her, concerned.

"Why?" Tessa looked over with a tear streaked face, "Why slaughter innocent people? Was it because of money? Money they had or what they could bring in because they were shifters?"

"Hunters are evil people. And evil can do unspeakable things."

"It sure can," Tessa agreed. What else could she do? It was true.

"Tessa?" Tessa jumped when she felt a hand on her shoulder. She looked up at Jack.

"I'm okay. It's just hitting me all at once, you know?"

"I do. Come on back."

Jack led Tessa to his office.

"I'll bring back some coffee," Tara called.

Jack ushered Tessa into his office and sat her down in the chair in front of his desk. He kissed her lightly on the top of her head as he handed her a box of tissues from his desk. Tessa took a few, wiped her face and set the box back on the desk. He loved Tessa. She might not be his flesh and blood, but he loved her like family. It had killed him watching her grow up with adoptive parents and not being able to say anything to her, let alone tell her that her uncle Eddie was still alive.

He watched her move away to college to get into Art History and Photography. When she had turned 19 and was able to access her birth records it had set her feet on a road that he definitely did not like her being on. He was forbidden to tell her that Eddie was still alive when she had been interviewing him, but he continued to question the Council about their decision to fake Eddie's death then hide him up in the Carstairs cabin back by Unicorn Falls.

Jack and Carol took very good care of Eddie, but Jack often wondered if that kind of solitary life had been good for a traumatized teenager. James and John had always argued that there was never anything wrong with Eddie to begin with but Jack could see that there was a slight mental lag when it came to Eddie. Like he wasn't completely up to speed for his age. That certain things he did or said, even his tone of voice or movements did not make Jack feel confident in Eddie being by himself when he became an adult. He also knew that there was a strong possibility that he could be wrong. That maybe it was due to his powers or shifting abilities, whatever he possessed, having not come through yet. That he was a late bloomer. But Jack had always kept his thoughts to himself.

The Council decided that if Eddie felt comfortable, he could meet Tessa, giving Eddie a little control. Eddie had not been comfortable, Jack could see that when he went to talk to Eddie about meeting her. He had not received an answer from Eddie so he took it as a no. Jack knew that the Council really didn't have much choice anymore since the publication of Tessa's book a month ago, and with all the digging she was doing, it was only a matter of time before she found out.

"What do you need, Tessa?"

Tessa started to dig into her purse, but hesitated when Tara brought in the coffee and set the two cups on the desk.

"If you need anything else, just call." Tara left again, quietly closing the door behind her.

Tessa took a deep breath then dug the small canister out of her purse.

"I don't know if I should have taken this but I feel it should be looked at." She handed over the small roll of film. "I went to Greyson House. The inside of the house is so well preserved, Uncle Jack. It was like walking through a museum. Everything is spotless and neat as a pin. It was strange. Someone is taking care of that house. Not on the outside but definitely on the inside."

Jack had to keep his face neutral as Tessa mentioned that the house looked perfectly clean on the inside considering he told her that no one had been given access to the house since the murders. It was the Council's ruling. But the fact that it was clean came as no surprise to him. He already knew. And he knew who was keeping it clean.

He had kept the key that John had given him without anyone knowing and put it in a hidden compartment in his wife's jewelry box. He had told her about it just in case she found it and threw it out without knowing what it unlocked.

Jack had gone ballistic when he found out that Carol had gone over there and cleaned the basement, and washed the blankets Michael had given birth and died on. Had scrubbed the blood off the floor where John, James and Steven had bled out.

It had been even worse when he found out that she was taking Eddie over to the house. Eddie had been resistive at first but started following her when she went over to clean.

She would go to the cabin to get him but he would refuse, then he started to watch her go, following a little distance then stopping. Eventually, he started coming all the way. He would follow her around and clean or just stand in the middle of the living room and watch her. He never went near the basement.

He would get upset when Carol went down, standing at the top of the stairs repeatedly calling until she came back up. With a lot of coaxing she finally got him to go down, and when he saw there was nothing to hurt him, he cleaned with her, but Jack knew that the memories must still be there. Eddie was dealing with it, so both he and Carol claimed that as a win. It was helping Eddie heal in some small way and they hoped that someday he would be able to have his house and his life back. His greatest concern was that someone might have still been watching the house and would find out about Eddie, but nothing ever came of it, so he felt he could breathe.

"Where did you find it?"

"It was on a work table in Michael's darkroom. Beside it was a notepad with picture sizes listed on it. It struck me as odd when I saw it. When the police processed the crime scene, why didn't they take it to see what's on it?"

Jack stared at the film.

"I don't know. I would have taken it. I don't know why Dad would have missed something like that. At the very least one of the other officers should have seen it and asked if he wanted it bagged and developed."

"Is it possible that he didn't take it for a reason?"

Jack turned the film over in his hand but didn't say anything. He didn't know what to say.

CHAPTER 5

JACK HELD THE film in his hand as Tessa left. He wanted to see what was on it, yet he didn't. He wasn't sure if he could handle the pain of the memories. He didn't know who had taken this. Either Michael or James, it didn't matter. The pictures would still be beautiful. It surprised him how they had managed to start off with a few clients then turn it into a seriously successful business. They had been in high demand. He mused that even John hadn't expected it to take off quite like it did, when he had bought the old abandoned Higgins mansion at the edge of town for James as a birthday present, and turned it into a multi room studio.

Shaking his head, he stared at the roll. Why had it been left behind? Why didn't his father take it and have it processed? Was it even there at the time of the crime? It had to have been if Tessa had stated that there was a notepad beside it with print sizes on it. So, why would Bennett have deliberately overlooked it? Wouldn't the other officers there have pointed it out to him? He knew there were photos of the main part of the basement, but he couldn't remember if there were photos of the darkroom. And, if there were, would the pictures show if the film was there or not?

There was only one way to find out. He got up and headed to the file room on the second floor.

It wasn't a big room, but it was cramped with shelves lining every wall and packed with boxes. Passing Tara's desk, he grabbed the sign in clipboard and scrawled his name. She smiled as she took it from him. He tried to smile back but he felt too grim, too nauseated. The last thing he wanted to do was look at those photos again, but he knew it would drive him nuts if he didn't.

He retrieved the box but hesitated before taking off the lid. Why was he doing this, to torture himself? No, deep down he wanted this thing to be over, to be finally solved. He took out the folder with the photos and slowly looked them over. There were photos of the darkroom but only a few, not as many as the actual crime scene. The canister of film was not on the table in the darkroom. But, yet, she said it had been. If it wasn't in the photos but was now sitting on his desk… Shit, he knew. He knew very well how it got on the table. But where had it been in the first place? Putting the photos back in the folder and into the box, he realized his hands were shaking slightly and pain seeped into his chest. Putting the box back on the shelf, he went back to his office and closed the door.

He leaned back into his chair and let the tears come. In the privacy of his office he didn't bother to fight them. He had given up years ago when they had come unbidden. An image flashed in his mind and he let it come. The tears were there so why not the pain.

"Hey, James, grab your camera." Jack laughed. He and John had just graduated from high school, while James had two years left to go. James turned his bright, smiling face in Jack's direction. They were on the deck of John's pool, the sun was just starting to set and the sky was beautiful.

"Pose for me, baby." James might've been 16 but he held himself like an adult with his 5'6' stature and sturdy build. His black eyes sparkled and black hair shone in the sunlight. Jack started going into his best modelling poses.

"Yeah, that's the way to go!" John yelled from another lounger as he sprawled his lanky frame over it. He threw his head back and shook his head, his shoulder length brown hair slapping his face and his lavender eyes gleaming.

The clicking from James's camera got faster. Jack's posing more intense. He slowly slid his thumbs into the waistband of his swim trunks and pushed them down on his hips.

"Oh baby, bring it on!" John howled.

Jack threw his head back and pushed his trunks down just enough to allow the head of his cock to poke out. He went to his knees and let a little more peek out as he raked his hands through his hair.

John's laughter was fierce. James straightened himself up.

"Breathe, Jack, I'm out of film. Have another beer. You know, for a straight guy, you are fucking nuts." James grabbed a bottle from the cooler, popped the top and took a long swing.

Jack laughed. James could knock it back with the best of them and never bat an eye.

In two more gulps the bottle was empty. Legally he was still under age for drinking but in the privacy of John's place none of that mattered.

"I wish you would tell me something I don't already know. And, you know, you need to keep a pouch close to your camera with more than one roll of film in it then you wouldn't have to worry about running out." Jack walked over to a cooler under John's lounger and pulled one out, then handed one to James, who came to stand beside him.

"I know, I know. I'm dense. I just never think about it. I just hope they never decide to try and mess with the film brand. These make the greatest pictures. I'll use it till it's extinct. I just love developing my own pics."

The three erupted into more gales of laughter as they clinked their bottles together.

The laughter rang and slowly faded in Jack's head as he opened his eyes. His breath hitched in his chest. He still had those pictures. James had taken two more rolls of his posing and had made him a wonderful album, and he treasured it. His eyes settled on the film again. He picked up the phone and dialed a number. It was picked up on the second ring.

"Hello, Kyle's photography, Kyle speaking."

"Kyle Burch? It's Jack Raskins."

"Jack Raskins? Well, it's been a while since I heard from you."

"Yeah, We need to go for a beer sometime. It's been a long time."

"Don't I know it. I miss when we all used to get together and have a beer night. It's been what....five or six years?"

"Yeah, something like that. I know the wives still have their card nights, though not as frequently as they used to be, so maybe we'll have to have a poker night sometime."

"Sure, just say when and I'll be there."

"Will do." Jack heaved a heavy sigh. "Look, Kyle. I have a favor to ask but I need your discretion. The highest level of extreme discretion."

"Anything. What's up?"

"I have a roll of film I need developed. It's 30 years old. It's very delicate."

There was silence on the other end of the line.

"30 years old, you say. Any idea what's on it?"

"No. Tessa brought it to me. I'm half scared to see what's on it, if anything at all is on it. She says there was a list of sizes beside it, so there is possibly something."

"You bringing it down or you want me to come and get it?"

"I'll drop it off after work."

"No problem."

Jack hung up, gently set the film on his desk and stared at it. His drive to work and train of thought were gone. Going to the washroom, he splashed cold water on his face. He stared at his reflection in the mirror. The young handsome town sheriff was long since gone, only to be replaced by an ancient Chief of Police. The years had not been kind to him at all. He liked living but not as long as some of the pack elders, who shifted regularly, lived. He thought the average age a human would pass away at would be good enough for him and Carol had agreed and stopped shifting with him. He would deal. Going back to his office, he grabbed the roll of film.

"Fuck this shit," he growled to himself.

"I'm taking the rest of the day off!" he growled at Tara, as he grabbed his jacket from the coat rack by the door. Tara only nodded her head as she watched him leave.

Jack pulled his car up and parked outside of Greyson House. He sat there staring up at it. It looked so dilapidated on the outside but according to Tessa it looked pristine on the inside. The once immaculate lawn was a shambles and he had made sure that the pool had been drained, but suspected that it was full of 30 years worth of debris and possibly the odd animal carcass.

It dawned on Jack that after 30 years, taking a fresh look at the case was opening new questions. How did they know to hide Eddie and Tessa when the front door was broken open? Was there anyone else with them at the time? It was always standard practice to have a nurse or midwife present for at home births, especially for a unicorn. It was Council law in that regard. He had been certain that Michael and Steven had someone on call for when it came time to deliver, but he wasn't sure who. He didn't think that they had given him a name.

Something he would definitely have to look into. It wouldn't be hard to find out who had been there, or who was scheduled to go, and what time they logged out of the hospital to go to Greyson House.

And if there had been someone there, why didn't they report it? Had they reported it? He didn't think he had remembered reading their statement the last time he accessed the files. Were they even there when all hell broke loose? Did they even give a statement? Were they one of the killers? Where did they go?

Why just walk in and start shooting? He always thought hunters were a lot more cautious than that. They had been in human form when they died, which didn't make any sense. Hunters usually forced their victims to shift, most times with drugs. Bennett had told him once that there was a good stash of the force shift drug in the chemical locker of the evidence room that he had taken off hunters that had managed to get in. Most kidnapped their victims, took them somewhere secluded, harvested what they could while alive, then killed them. Body parts were so much more valuable when the victim was in shifted form.

Unanswered questions, too many of them all of a sudden. Jack knew he was going to have to go back through the evidence box again. A lot more carefully this time. He had given it a cursory look when he had collected the information that Tessa had wanted. Not really paying attention to what he had been looking at. Trying not to let the pain overwhelm him if he dug too deeply. It had been enough when he had looked at the crime scene photos to send him to the bathroom to puke his guts up. Numerous times he had been glad that the upstairs bathroom was just across the hall. Now he had to swallow it all back down and go through that box again, inch by inch.

He had been sheriff back then, and too full of pain and rage to process anything. His father, the Chief of Police, took control right away, made Jack take a week off. He would have been in no shape to conduct a proper investigation. He knew that much for sure.

His stomach suddenly bottomed out and he felt like he was going to throw up. There was just no way his father could have been involved? Could he? No! He refused to believe it. He shouldn't be entertaining such thoughts. It was horrible to even think it. His father would have done no such thing. But now, all of a sudden, his mind was accusing the man of being a dirty cop and a murderer.

Bennett had known that Jack was too distraught to work the investigation, so he had taken over. There was no way he would have been so sloppy or careless in the investigation to let anything slide. Or had that been the reason all along? Get Jack out of there so he could hide crucial evidence that would point to him.

He would have gone over everything with a fine tooth comb and questioned everyone and anyone he thought that might have a shred of evidence to pass along. And where they were shifters and one Protector, Jack knew the Council would be breathing down Bennett's neck to make sure they were kept in the loop about everything.

Jack started up the car and took off. He pulled into the parking lot of Kyle's photography. He'd known Kyle since high school. Kyle had been quiet and shy. He had no idea what he had wanted out of life. He tried numerous jobs but couldn't seem to keep them. When old man Hagan gave Kyle a job at his photography store, Kyle seemed to come into his own. When Hagan decided to retire, he gave the store to Kyle. Jack went inside.

"I came early. I just couldn't sit on this any longer."

Kyle looked up from the catalog he was looking at.

"Are you saying that film came from where I think it came from?"

"Tessa went to Greyson House. She found it on the table in Michael's darkroom. I have no idea what is on it or who took it. I just know it's 30 years old and possibly very fragile."

"I can probably get a set of prints off it. I take it you don't want this to get out."

"No, I don't. Not now, maybe not ever. I'm not sure. Don't want to open old wounds unless I have to."

"Agreed on that." Kyle gingerly took the roll." I'll give you a call."

Jack gave him a weak smile as he left.

Jack sat in his chair in front of the fireplace. From the creak of the floorboard in the back hallway, he knew Edward Carstairs was there.

"Uncle Jack?" A dark gravelly voice asked from the shadows behind the chair. He heard the soft footsteps and he tensed as he felt strong masculine hands on his shoulders.

"What is it, sweetness?"

"Do I have to meet Tessa?"

"No, that is entirely up to you. I told you last night that the choice was yours."

"I don't want to meet her."

"Why don't you want to meet with her? It would be good for you to meet her."

"I don't know why."

Jack gripped the arms of his chair tightly,

"Is it because she is the last link to your adopted brothers who loved you like you were actually their own little brother with unconditional love? Or is it that, seeing her, you'll see

Michael and Steven and that could take you to a place you don't want to go?"

An unearthly scream ripped through the house and Jack could hear something break behind him. He jumped out of his chair and turned to face his charge.

It had never occurred to him or his grief-addled brain at the time what the Council had been telling him. But now he understood why he could never have cared for Tessa. Not only would it have put her at risk with him working all the time, but trying to help a mentally disabled boy and care for an infant would have been like mixing oil and water. And with two young pups of his own. It just would not have worked. If she had been found out, then that would have led to Eddie being found out, which could have led to more bodies, his and Carol's and his pups included.

"I won't go back there, you can't make me."

Jack took a step toward Eddie only to have the back of Eddie's hand connect with the side of his head. He hit the floor hard and knew nothing more.

Jack looked up from staring at his beer bottle. It was the fourth... fifth or possibly sixth one he'd had since he had gotten up that morning, with quite possibly a few shots of vodka mixed in. He had gotten up early from the nightmares. It had not been a good night. He couldn't get the image of seeing his dead friends and adopted godsons out of his head. He was sure it would drive him insane.

His father was standing in front of him.

"Carol came by the station on her way back from taking the

pups to school, wanted me to check on you. Hoped you would talk to me since you seem unwilling to talk to her."

"I don't need her analyzing me. Where is she?"

"She's with your mother. I told her to stay there as long as she needs to."

"She won't. She'll come back to make sure I don't drink myself to death.

"Is all you've had today is just beer?"

"No, I had a couple of vodka shots somewhere in between when I got up."

"When was that?"

"Around five."

"Have you had anything to eat?"

"Yeah, Carol managed to force some breakfast into me around 7:00. It came back up around 7:30."

Bennett Raskins sat in the chair across from his son.

"Talk to me, Jack."

"What do you want me to say, Dad? The nightmares are crippling. I don't get much sleep. Every time I close my eyes I go back there. I see everything in crystal clear clarity."

"Son..."

"Dad," Jack cut him off, "I feel like I'm losing my mind. My childhood friends, my two best friends in the whole world are dead. Their adopted sons, who I came to love like my own pups, are dead. Brutally and senselessly murdered. How am I supposed to get over that? How does one just forget and move on? I know you've seen some nasty shit, how do you deal with it?"

"You don't get over it, you never will forget but it gets easier with time. Maybe counselling...."

"You think I'm nuts?"

"No, son, I don't. Even I've needed to sit down and talk with

*a shrink a time or two because shit got to me. But this is such a
tragic shock to your system that you don't know how to handle it."*

*"How can you just sit there and be so blasé about it?" Jack
yelled, throwing the beer bottle he held at the fireplace.*

*"With incredible difficulty, Jack. It hurts bad and I can't tell
you how I feel because I just don't know myself. I watched those
boys grow up with you. All the stupid shit you used to do. It's like a
knife in my heart that I cannot pull out."*

Jack let his head hang,

"I was too late."

Carol Raskins came in the kitchen door with bags of gro-
ceries in her arms. Shopping for herself, Jack and Eddie did
not make for light work. As soon as she set the bags on the
kitchen counter, a cold chill went up her spine as if something
wasn't right. She shook it off as she went to check the answering machine.

"Jack. It's Kyle. It's ready. It was easier than I thought
it would be. You can pick it up any time," the message said.
Carol looked at the machine strangely as another chill went up
her spine. Not being able to ignore it this time she went into
the living room, her hands flew to her face and a gasp escaped
her lips. She ran to her husband and Eddie, who was curled up
on the floor beside him.

"Eddie?" Carol lightly shook him, she could see tears had
dried on his face.

His eyes flickered open.

"I think I killed him, Aunt Carol. I didn't mean to. I didn't
mean to hit him."

"Why did you?" She checked for a pulse by placing her

fingers on Jack's wrist then breathed a sigh of relief when she found it.

"He said bad things, things I didn't want to hear. I won't go back to that place. I won't. I can't."

"Shhh, it's okay. Why did you come to the house, anyway?"

Eddie slowly got up,

"I'm running low on supplies and Stuffie needs to be fixed again."

She took him to her and Jack's bedroom and laid him down. "What's wrong with Stuffie?"

Eddie reached into the inside of his jacket and brought out a small stuffed black unicorn. It had a split seam on one side. It had been mended many times and had seen better days but it was the only thing he had left to remind him of his adopted brothers Michael and Steven. At 45 years old, Eddie was a handsome man with a strong healthy body but not the mind to match.

"I'll take care of him. Do you want a shower before your nap?"

"I don't want to meet her, Aunt Carol. Not yet, not now. I don't know. I'm scared."

"Not to worry, baby, it's up to you. You'll make your mind up properly when the time comes. I brought extra stuff home for you. You go shower if you want to then I'll get you some dinner. And don't you worry about Stuffie, I'll take very good care of him."

Carol left the room and went to get a mug from the kitchen. She gave a quick glance in Jack's direction before going to the wet bar. He still hadn't moved. She poured a teaspoon of brandy into the cup then went back to the bedroom.

"Here, baby, take a few sips of this. It'll help you sleep."

Eddie took the cup from her and took a drink, he grimaced at the taste.

"I know, I don't like it either." Carol gave him a quick kiss on the forehead before leaving the room. She looked back to see him laying down on the bed before she closed the door behind her.

She felt so sorry for the boy that never had a life. His death had been faked by the Council in case someone came after him as well, but neither Carol nor Jack could understand the rationale in the Council's method. The Council argued that if they didn't do something to hide him, the hunters might not stop looking for him to shut him up or find Tessa, more bodies to bury. The Carstairs house and properties were closed and sealed. They were not allowed to be sold. The Lizard's Lounge and J. Carstairs Photography Studio had been included in that order. The Council had basically ordered Jack and Carol to teach Eddie how to take care of himself and learn to live in the Carstairs cabin out by Unicorn Falls. They took care of him as best they could but they knew the happy carefree lavender eyed little boy was gone, only to be replaced by the black eyed young man with limited mentality.

Jack had no idea how much time had passed when he slowly opened his eyes, and heard his name being called softly. It was Carol. He turned his head but the pain made him wince.

"Holy fuck!" he ground out.

"He said he hit you. Looks pretty hard, too." The understatement of the year.

"Was he here when you got here? I'm going to smack that little shit."

Carol gave her husband a sad look.

"Yes, he was. He was laying beside you, he had cried himself to sleep. He thought he killed you."

Jack, suddenly, felt guilty as hell.

"What did you say to him?" she asked.

"One of the worst things I ever could. I asked him if the reason he didn't want to meet Tessa was because it would take him back there to that day or if he would see too much of Steven and Michael in her."

Carol hung her head.

"Jack, how could you?"

"I know, I'm a fucking idiot. Where is he now?"

"I didn't have the heart to send him back to the cabin so he's sleeping on our bed."

Jack pulled himself to his feet, the side of his face swollen, turning black and blue.

"I had better go talk to him."

"Be careful what you say. I gave him a few sips of brandy before he would relax enough to lay down." She said as she went to the bathroom.

Jack nodded his head and instantly regretted it. When she came back she gave his good cheek a light kiss though her eyes were sad. She handed him a couple of ibuprofens and a glass of water. He looked at them for a second before taking them.

"I can see his point in a lot of ways."

"Yeah, so can I. It hits me in the gut every time I look at Tessa. She's the spitting image of Michael."

"But she has Steven's smile."

That brought a smile to Jack's lips.

"She sure does. I just wish it was all over. Fuck, I wish it never happened to begin with."

"Don't start that again, Jack. It's not your fault. It never was your fault."

"Yeah, but try telling that to my heart," Jack muttered as he headed towards the bedroom.

"Jack."

He turned to face her.

"There was a message on the machine from Kyle. He says you can pick it up any time. Whatever that meant."

"I'll show you when I get it," Jack replied cryptically as he continued towards the bedroom.

Jack sat down on the edge of the bed and lightly brushed the soft brown strands of hair away from Eddie's face.

"Oh, rodent, my sweet little godson, how I wish I could see you just one more time happily chewing those cheese balls. You hide in fear behind those black eyes. What I would give to see those sparkling lavender ones just to know you're in there some place."

Eddie stirred and opened his eyes and for just a split second Jack was sure he caught sight of the old Eddie before the blackness took hold again. He sat up but wouldn't look Jack in the face.

"Eddie," Jack put his finger under his chin and raised his head so that Eddie was looking at him, "I'm sorry. I shouldn't have said that. It was wrong. I'm just frustrated." He heaved a sigh, "I just want to know where my sweet little godson went. Is he still in there somewhere? I don't understand where that darkness comes from that reflects in your eyes."

"Maybe you weren't meant to know," he growled, but then tears suddenly spilled down Eddie's cheeks and whispered. "I miss Da and Daddy."

"I know you do, we all do. And you end up suffering the most. Locking you up in that cabin all those years was not the best thing for you. I know the Council was only trying to protect you but there should have been a better way. Even keeping you here till you were older was a serious risk for me and Aunt Carol, if the Council found out. But even that, I don't believe, was the best solution either. You needed to get back out into society and try to move on from there even if you had to have a Protector assigned to follow your every move. If you could have gotten out and gone to grief groups, anything like that, you might be different now. I miss the little boy who used to pound the shit out of me at chess or had cheese ball fights with me. Much to the dismay of Da and Daddy of course."

A small smile crept over Eddie's face then vanished.

"I need to go home now." Eddie got up and started to leave the bedroom, with Jack sitting on the bed watching him go.

"No, Eddie. Stay here, son. It's better for you here. We're closer that way."

Eddie turned and looked back at him. "Aunt Carol is in the kitchen. She'll make you anything you want for supper."

"Hot dogs?" A smile crept across Eddie's face.

"Sure, baby. Anything you want."

"On that thing she got that makes it like a BBQ."

"You want to get a little more rest? Aunt Carol said she gave you a little stuff to help you sleep."

"No, I'm okay now."

Jack suddenly felt his stomach grumble, and by the little giggle that came from Eddie's lips he had heard it too.

"Okay. You're making me hungry now. Come on."

Jack got up and put his arm around Eddie's waist in a simple gesture to urge him forward. It didn't take much, Eddie was out the door and Jack could hear him in the kitchen asking for hot dogs.

CHAPTER 6

JACK WALKED INTO Kyle's Photography early the next morning. Kyle smiled at him from behind the counter.

"I figured you wouldn't take long to get here once you got my message."

"How did they turn out?"

"Not the greatest quality, but we're talking 30 years. Even if this is the highest quality film you could get back then there is still going to be degradation. But even still, the pictures are wonderful. I would have loved to have been there."

Jack took them out of the envelope and quickly scanned them.

"This was when they went to Barbados for a week. They told me stories of how wonderful it was. Thanks Kyle, what do I owe you?"

"Nothing, Jack. Just to see it solved someday will be payment enough. Oh, and maybe, a poker night and steak dinner would work, too." Kyle chuckled.

Jack smiled grimly.

"Thanks, Kyle." Jack left to head home.

Tessa slowly opened her eyes, trying to figure out where the music was coming from until she realized her cell phone was ringing. She grabbed it and swiped the screen.

"Hello?" Her voice was full of sleep.

"I'm sorry if I woke you."

Tessa looked over at the clock on the night stand, it was 8:30.

"No, Uncle Jack. It's okay. I'm surprised it's so late. I'm usually up around seven most mornings."

"I don't know if this has any relevance or bearing but I got the pictures back. They were of their trip to Barbados. If I remember right, Michael was five months along."

"I would love to see them. I can be down at the station in an hour or so."

"That's fine, my dear, take your time."

After hanging up, Tessa quickly showered and dressed in jeans and a thin sweater and sneakers. She ordered breakfast from room service of scrambled eggs, bacon, toast, and orange juice. After going through a coffee shop drive-through and getting coffee, she pulled into the police station. She smiled at Tara, who motioned her to go back to Jack's office. Tessa smiled and walked back to the chief's office.

"Uncle Jack?" She knocked as she came in.

"Come in, Tessa."

She sat in the chair in front of the desk, took one of the coffees from the tray, and handed it to him. She took the other coffee then tossed the carry tray into the recycling bin by the desk. He slid the pictures across to her. Setting her coffee down, she slowly looked at them and tears welled up in her eyes.

"It's not hard to see you have Michael's looks," Jack teased. "He was five months along. Starting to show, as you can see there are no pics of him below the chest. He hated pregnancy pics just as much as James did. Only Michael was not quite as anal about it. He would let you take some pics, but, as I say, not below the chest."

"Yeah," Tessa choked out looking at a picture of a 15 year old Eddie sticking his tongue out at the camera. "It's still hard to swallow that that happy little boy would survive a massacre just to end his life a year later."

Jack opened his mouth but closed it again. He wanted so desperately to tell Tessa about Eddie but knew his hands were tied. The ball was in Eddie's court. If he agreed to meet her then Jack would tell her about him and set it up from there for them to meet.

Jack slid the last two photographs he'd held back across to her.

"You see that guy in the background of these last two? He seems familiar but I can't place him right now."

Tessa studied the photos again.

"Why does he seem to be staring at them?"

"I'm going to do some digging and hope we'll be able to find out."

Jack lounged back in his chair by the fireplace, looking at the photos. His chest ached with the pain of emotion. A small smile creased his face. They all looked so happy. He could only imagine all the fun that they had had. James and John had just wanted some time away and to have fun with Eddie. Michael and Steven had only been married two years and thought it would be a great early second honeymoon. They had been life-long friends that eventually grew into a loving relationship. They had all agreed that Barbados was the perfect choice.

Carol came up behind and looked over his shoulder.

"They all look so happy."

"Yeah," Jack shook his head. "Tessa found it on the work-bench in Michael's darkroom at Greyson House. She brought it to me and I took it to Kyle to have it developed. I still can't understand why it was not picked up in the original inves-tigation. I don't understand how Dad missed it. The photos show that it was not on the workbench but it might have been on the floor and someone picked it up and laid it there after, I don't know. But if it had been an officer I can't figure why they would be so careless and not bring it to Dad's atten-tion. Why just leave it there?"

"I'm impressed at how well they came out, considering the age of the film."

"Kyle said the pics wouldn't be great because of the age but I'm just glad he was able to get a decent set off it. Sure does look like they had a really great time. They asked me to go but I couldn't. That kind of heat makes me sick, so they brought me back a vial of sand. I have it tucked away in my fire safe so nothing will ever happen to it."

"I think you showed me." Carol smiled as she kissed the top of his head. "Will it ever be solved, Jack? Will we ever have closure?"

"I don't know." Jack's shoulders suddenly tensed. Carol put her hands on Jack's shoulders and started to massage.

"Running out of supplies, Eddie?"

Eddie came out of the shadows of the back hallway to stand beside Carol.

"No, I was bored."

Carol turned and took his hand,

"You want to play a game?"

"I want a story."

"Okay." Carol tugged Eddie toward the couch but Eddie stopped when he saw the pictures in Jack's hands, "I remember that."

Jack, startled, looked up at him.

"You do?"

"Yes, it was sunny and warm. We had so much fun. Michael was going to make albums for all of us."

"You remember that well but other things, not."

"I was happy." Eddie moved to the couch and laid down. Carol sat and put his head on her lap.

Jack smiled as his gaze went back to the photographs. He stared hard at the two photos with the strange man. He furrowed his brow in concentration but nothing came to him.

"Who are you?" Jack muttered to himself, "And why just these two?"

Carol and Eddie looked at Jack strangely,

"What is it, dear?"

"There are two photos this one guy is in. He looks familiar in a way and in a way not. He's at a distance but he seems to be staring right at Michael, and it seems like he doesn't realize that he's being photographed. It's like he's watching him in this one. In the other one, it looks like he's staring at

James. They both must have been using the same camera to take pictures and happened to get this guy in the pictures, but just these two."

Jack got up and went over to the couch.

"Eddie," He held the picture down so that Eddie could see it. "Do you recognize the guy in the background? Does he seem familiar to you?"

Eddie took the photo and stared hard at it. Jack watched Eddie's eyes flickering back and forth across it, his brow furrowed. There was a slight flicker of recognition in his eyes.

"I know him." Eddie sat up and Jack watched a light sweat break out on his forehead. He was racking his brain to come up with a name. His black eyes searched Jack's face for an answer.

"Da! Da knew him. He was there a lot. He...he came over..for..aaahhh." Eddie dropped the picture and grabbed the sides of his head. Carol reached over and brought him into her arms.

"It's okay, baby." She kissed his temple. "It'll come."

Jack picked up the picture.

"Someone that used to come and see James, was it business that brought this guy over?"

Eddie nodded,

"I think so. Business. Yeah, it was like I saw him all the time. Not always with Da but sometimes he would be parked outside. Like he was waiting to go inside, always had a sad expression like he was afraid to go in. Mostly in the morning when I was getting on the bus." Eddie looked up, his eyes still flickering, still searching.

Jack went back to his chair and flopped down.

"Now that is strange, but whoever it was, if they were

an employee, they would have had to have been from the Studio. That still makes a big list of photographers he was renting rooms for shoots out to, the secretary and, I think, he had, three or four who cleaned up every night."

"Not really," Carol said from the couch, Jack turned his head to look at her. She had Eddie laying down again with his head on her lap. "The only ones that would really need to come and talk to James would have been the photographers. And as for hanging around all the time, you have me on that one."

Jack quietly nodded,

"Yes, but trying to get names now or even photographs is probably next to impossible."

"Why? Wouldn't there be a staff list in the case file along with statements?"

He nodded his head slightly.

"Yes, there should be. Damn, my head is tired and my brain numb. All the employees that were interviewed should. Dad did all the leg work on that. I was still in the bottle. I'll look tomorrow."

Carol looked down at Eddie. He had fallen asleep. She stroked his hair and pulled the quilt from the back of the couch over him.

"I just wish we could end this. Give him some peace. Give him freedom."

"I wish we could too, love."

"Has there been any progress in getting through to the Carstairs boy?" Councilman Walters wanted to know.

Jack made a slight bow as he stood beside his father in Council chambers.

"No, Councilman. He has not spoken a word. The nurses tell me he either sits in his chair or in bed and just stares at nothing. They cannot get him to speak. The only time he moves is to go to the bathroom and they say it's like watching a zombie. It took them almost a week to get him to understand to go to the bathroom and to eat. It was like teaching a child potty training. The same thing with eating. They didn't want him constantly on an IV so they started by feeding him baby food and got him to eventually feed himself. But that has been the only sign of independence they've gotten from him." Jack shook his head slightly to ward off the tears that were threatening to come. "That lavender-eyed happy little boy that I know seems to be gone, possibly forever. When he looks at you, he sees right through you. His eyes have gone completely black. I do not know or understand what that means. The doctors have no idea what it means either. They even called in Head Protector Cain but he has never seen anything like it."

Bennett Raskins made another slight bow,

"Council, what of the child? Michael's daughter? Has she ever been given a name?"

Councilwoman Teva spoke,

"Yes, her name is Tessa Marie. We are quietly making arrangements for her to be adopted. Her new parents know nothing of her background or where she came from. When she turns 19 they will be allowed to tell her that she is adopted. If she pursues the matter, then the files will be open to her to view. If she wants to go further, then that will be her choice."

Jack's father almost choked,

"Do you think that would be wise? Considering her family

was just butchered for an unknown reason, even at 19 she could still be in danger."

Jack cut in,

"Why would I not be allowed to adopt her? I can also protect her."

"You are too close to the situation. We cannot afford to let anything slip. She may yet still be in danger, that is why this is being done in absolute secrecy and her background foolproof. We understand the validity of your statement, and at 19 if we find that there is still a danger then the files will remain sealed and her adoptive parents will be denied permission to tell her."

"What about Eddie? He could still be in danger at the hospital," Jack ground out.

"We know that as well," Councilman Walters agreed, "We are planning to move him to a more secure facility."

"What kind of treatment will he get there?" Bennett wanted to know.

"The best there is."

"Will he be there for the rest of his life if he does not improve?"

"If it is deemed a safe place, then, unfortunately, yes. If he does not improve anymore than what he is right now, he will have to remain there. However, other arrangements are currently being looked at should he show signs of improvement."

Jack and his father bowed again and left Council chambers. Once they were in Bennett's truck, Jack slammed his fists on the dash.

"Fuck!" he screamed. "I might not be family but I'm the closest thing she's got."

"I understand, but you must remember you have two young pups at home. They might be watching you, your house, work, or anywhere you might go to see if she turns up. We still have no idea *what went on in that house. We don't know if they wanted her for some reason or if they planned to kill her or even Eddie. They knew about a baby coming and Eddie, if they were watching the house then there is no way of knowing. They just don't know where they vanished to. If they found out she was being raised by you, you could be adding more bodies to the count."*

Jack bent over in the seat and could feel his father's hand on his back.

"Why, Dad, Why?"

"I wish I could tell you, I really do. But I don't have any more answers than you do."

"I was so close, but I couldn't get there fast enough. I knew he was due any day and I chose that day to go backpacking."

"Don't start with that line of thinking. You had no idea. When you really think about it, they could have come the day before or the day after. And even if you had gotten there, the killers could have shot you, too. I don't like the thought that I might have had to bury my son."

"Do you know the last words John said to me?" Jack whimpered.

"No, I don't."

"'Soon,' he said. 'He's eager to make his appearance.' The pride, the love, the joy in his voice was so undeniable. He swore up and down it would be a boy. He wanted a grandson so bad."

Jack's father chuckled,

"Guess not. Turned out to be a girl. Even fresh out of the womb she was beautiful."

The words echoed in Jack's head as he sat up in bed. His heart pounded in his chest and he found it was hard to catch his breath. Sweat poured down his body. He started to tremble slightly from the cold the sweat produced on his body.

Carol stirred slightly and opened her eyes. She sat up quickly when she realized Jack was sitting up and had pulled his knees up and put his arms around them. She reached out and tentatively put a hand on his forearm.

"Jack? What is it?" She moved closer, and it frightened her when she could hear his sobs that he tried to muffle with the blanket.

"He was there. He was there, Carol, he practically admitted it to me and I was too stupid at the time to catch it. He practically admitted to watching them being shot."

"What do you mean?"

"I don't remember how long it was after, but Dad and I went to the Council with an update on Eddie. It wasn't as if the Council couldn't do it themselves. I thought it was because the Council wanted to keep a low profile. The doctors talked to me because I was the sheriff. Dad could have gotten the information just as easily. But Dad insisted that I do it.

"We were in his truck, I was pissed that they would not allow me to take custody of Tessa. That I couldn't protect her like she could be with adopted parents and anonymity. And that I had my family to think about if whoever tried to come after her. I told him the last thing John said to me about the baby being a boy. You know what he said to me, Carol?"

"No, I don't think you ever told me."

"Dad said that even fresh from the womb she was beautiful. How would he know that, Carol? There was no way he could have seen her just birthed unless he had been there. She had been cleaned up when we took her and Eddie out of the hidden room. And how did he know it was a girl? He had to have been there to see her. Because he wouldn't have known until he saw her when I opened the secret room door."

Carol went pale.

"Oh, Jack. Then it's possible that he knew the shooters. The only reason he got out of there with his skin on...."

"Was if he set it all up. And the reason Dad told me the Council wanted me to get the updates on Eddie was because he was afraid that Eddie would call him out. That he was there and let them all be killed," Jack finished for her, his voice cracking. "My father was a dirty cop and a fucking murderer. He let them die."

CHAPTER 7

JACK STOOD IN the file room. He heaved a sigh. Every time he had to come in here to get that box it was like opening the wound all over again.

When he had agreed to help Tessa he was sure he could handle it, but once he started looking at the photos it had hit him like a knife in the chest. He had given her the information that she had wanted but it didn't make it any easier to look at it again. On more than one occasion he had felt like he was going to puke his guts up.

Taking the box from the shelf with sweaty hands, he set it on the table and realized his hands were shaking as well. Taking a deep breath, he took the lid off. Avoiding the folder with the photos, he took out the folder with the statements. Right on top were the lists of employees for both The Lizard's Lounge and J. Carstairs Studio. Could there really be a connection? Could someone in their employment at the time have set them up? And if so, why? What was the reasoning?

It seemed too over the top to be a disgruntled employee. His only hope was if Eddie could remember a name. A light bulb went off over his head. He'd take the lists to Eddie with the picture and see if his mind would click and give him a name. He photocopied the two pages, put them in their folder and started to put the lid back on the box and stopped. Something made his chest feel tight. He stared at the contents of the box hard. Something was missing. He started taking the folders out, looking at each one, and as he did the tightness in his chest got stronger. He laid everything out on the table. The pain in his chest got to the point it felt like he might be having a heart attack. Then it hit him. The ballistics reports were gone. The bullets were gone. He went over the files again. Even the coroner's reports were gone. How long had they been missing; a long time or just recently? Why did he just notice it now? Why had he not noticed before when he had the box open collecting stuff for Tessa. Tessa had asked for those items but Jack preferred not to give her that information. But he still should have seen it then. Had his grief really made him so stupid that he was just now cluing in that something was not right? That things were really missing? Was it because he was actively digging into the case again? He stuck his head out the door and called for Tara.

She stood at the bottom of the stairs and looked up. The file room was the first door on the right. Jack held the door open as he looked down at her.

"Has anyone other than me been up here today?"

"Let me have a look." Tara turned back to her desk and picked up the sign-in clipboard. "Just Adam."

"What was he doing up here?"

Tara looked back at the clipboard. "He has in the reason box; 'Filing papers on closed cases'."

"Do you know if he was in the Carstairs box?"

"No, not to my knowledge. The box number is not listed. Is something wrong? Is something missing?"

"Yeah, something's missing alright, and I don't know how long it's been gone."

"What's missing?"

Without answering her, Jack went back into the room, letting the door slam behind him. He dropped into the chair and scrubbed his hands over his face. He was letting his imagination run away with him. There was no way Detective Adam Doherty was involved. He had no reason to suspect the man of taking the reports and bullets. So, why was he? Just because the man had been up here didn't mean anything. The reports could have been missing long before he came up or went missing after. His head started to pound, what was going on with him? He was seeing suspects in every corner now. Just because Adam had his squirrely moments didn't mean he was up to any wrongdoing.

Adam had signed up at the same time he had. He had been tall and lanky, but hard training and a lot of gym time had filled the man out. He had come into a healthy build for a wolf shifter. At 5"9" with deep brown eyes and dark brown hair, Adam was not one to mess with. He was quiet and single. He spent most of his free time studying and learning. His speciality was drugs. Hence the conference he was stuck at. He never really wanted to be involved with the pack, but he did stand with them when needed. He rarely, if ever, attended the monthly meeting or runs. Jack knew Adam paid his dues in other ways. Volunteering, charity work and donating to fundraisers were just a few of the things he was known for helping with.

Jack thought they got along well, Adam was always willing to go that extra mile. They never really quarrelled about anything. No, this case had him paranoid, there was no way Adam was involved. But he often wondered why Adam hadn't retired yet, he spoke of it often but never seemed to follow through. It was like he was waiting for something. Was he waiting for this case to be solved like Jack was?

Jack closed his eyes, Adam had been at Greyson House that day as well, and had looked positively green, though he did a better job of keeping it in than Jack had. It was not exactly something either of them had wanted to see nor hoped to ever see again. But Adam's eyes seemed to have the same haunted look as his father's did. No, he was not going down that rabbit hole, not today.

"I am fucking losing it," he hissed, as he pounded down the steps.

He stopped beside Tara's desk.

"And, Tara?"

"Yes?"

"I want to know who's been in the file room for the last, let's say, three months. I don't care whatever reason they were up there, I just want to know who they were."

"Sure."

"Thank you."

Going back to his office, he shut the door and used the landline to call Carol.

"Is he there?"

"No. I sent him home this morning after you left, with leftovers and some goodies."

"Damn. He didn't say anything more to you, did he?"

"No, but he feels bad."

"I know. I've got some names. I'll go up to the cabin after supper and see if he recognizes any of the names on here. And I'm going to ask him about that film. Tessa says she found it on the workbench but in the photos it's not there. I want to know if Eddie found it and put it there."

"Good idea."

Jack tapped on the cabin door before he let himself in. He knew Eddie knew that he was there long before he knocked.

"Hello, Uncle Jack." The tone was measured.

Jack closed the door behind him.

"Sitting in the dark again, are we?"

"I was thinking. I heard you walking up the path. You didn't have to knock."

"I know. Just being polite."

Jack saw a match, then a candle being lit.

"Generator off for the night?"

"Yes, I was going to bed but something made me wait up."

"I'm sorry. I should have come before supper instead of after."

"Doesn't matter." Eddie made room for him on the couch. Jack sat beside him.

"Were you able to remember a name?"

"No," Eddie snapped, "My brain is stupid."

"No, Eddie, don't say that. It's been a long time. You should have no reason to keep names in your head that are really of no relevance to you."

Eddie heaved a heavy sigh. Jack reached over and pulled him close.

"I brought a list of names and the pictures. I want you to have a look at them together. Maybe something will jump out at you. If Da mentioned his name around you, maybe your memory will float it to the surface."

Eddie took the list and photos. He stared at them hard, his eyes flicked back and forth from one to the other.

"Yes!" Eddie exclaimed as he pointed to a name on the list. "This name, it fits that face. The first name. Da never said his last name but the first name fits. I know it does. I'm sure of it. It seems right."

He looked up at Jack,

"Is it right?"

Jack hugged Eddie.

"I'm sure it is, baby. You did good. Is there anything else you can remember?"

"He was nervous. Always nervous. Like I said, he seemed to be parked outside a lot, though he did come in. "

Jack took a pen from his pocket and circled the name. Cody Mitchell. He was assistant manager at the Lounge. He had been hired a year before the murders. That seemed odd, if he worked at the Lounge why would he be coming to see James all the time? If he had business to discuss, he should have been going to see John.

"Do you know why he would come over, Eddie? Can you remember?"

Eddie shook his head slowly,

"No."

"Eddie, I also want to ask you a couple more questions. I

know you and Carol have been going over to Greyson House to keep it clean."

Eddie moved away from Jack on the couch slightly, his body tensing. A look of fear slid across his face.

"No, Eddie. I'm not mad. I'm glad you've been doing it, keeping it clean so that, maybe, one day you can live in it again. Though I was scared for a while that someone was still watching the house and would see you. "

"Aunt Carol said if we went through the woods and in through the back gate no one would see us."

"Not very well that way, true. But I was still worried for you two. But I have seen over the years that it was all for nothing."

Eddie shook his head slowly.

"Da would be mad if I let it get real dirty. Da was always cleaning."

Jack chuckled slightly.

"I know he was. Eddie, do you ever go to the basement and clean or does Aunt Carol go down by herself?"

"At first, she just went down alone 'cause I was scared. I kept calling for her to come up in case something happened and killed her down there. When I saw nothing did, I started going down with her. She was really happy about that."

"Do you clean Michael's darkroom?"

"Yeah. I make sure it's clean."

"Did you happen to see, at any time, a roll of film on the table?"

"Yeah, but it always wasn't on the table. I found it on the floor behind the leg of the microwave stand he was using for his chemicals. I was never allowed to touch those but they were taken away and Aunt Carol said it was okay for me to clean there. So, I pulled it out from the wall and there it was, back against the wall behind one of the legs. It must have gotten knocked off the table and rolled away. When I started cleaning I found it and put it back on the table beside the notepad."

"Did you know that was the roll of film that had your trip to Barbados?"

Eddie was silent for a long time.

"I do now. I probably did then, too. Michael said it got lost. He looked but couldn't find it. He thought it got misplaced somewhere even though he kept saying he was sure it had been on the table all along. But he kept getting called away from the darkroom for other stuff and really didn't put much time into looking for it.

"I never was allowed in there without Michael or Da so I never looked for it then. I think Michael was just too tired, the baby made him tired and Da told him if it turned up we would get to see it then. He didn't want Michael stressing, Michael's baby was starting to show, make his belly big, so he was uncomfortable."

"He was around five months, I think, when you went on your trip."

Jack leaned over and kissed Eddie lightly on the forehead.

"Thank you, Eddie. You have been a very big help."

Eddie got up and walked towards the back of the cabin. "Blow the light out when you leave."

Jack stood up as he heard a door close. He was quite impressed about how much Eddie remembered. It was a good sign. He blew out the candle and left.

Jack almost spilled his coffee at the unexpected knock on his office door. He had been waiting for it all morning but wasn't sure when it would come. He set his cup down.

"Come in."

Tara poked her head around the door.

"The intel on Cody Mitchell came back. And the list of names for the file room, too." She stepped in to set the file on his desk.

"Thanks."

She smiled as she closed the door behind her. Opening the file, Jack took a long drink from his coffee. Looking over the list of names from the file room clipboard. Adam, Dale and two other officers besides himself had been up there. He stared hard at Adam and Dale's names. The other two really would have no reason to be in the Carstairs box, they had only been there less than a year. Unless someone had told them of the murders, he saw no reason why they would go looking in the box, let alone remove anything. So, it was just down to Adam and Dale. But just because they had been up there still didn't mean anything.

Dale was a by-the-book man, he had always had Jack's back no matter what the situation. They had been friends for a long time. Jack had met Dale at Twelve Oaks University and knew Dale wanted this case solved just as badly as he did. It had brought them so close they were almost like brothers. Though Dale had not been at the scene due to his illness, he still took it personally. There was just no way that Jack could see Dale being a part of something so brutal.

"Do I want this over that bad?" He stared at the paper.

"That I'm accusing everyone all of a sudden? Fuck! This is bullshit!" He slammed the paper down on his desk. Forcing himself to take a deep calming breath, he picked up the other piece of paper from the folder and scanned it over.

Cody Mitchell was still alive, that was good. But he no longer lived in Unicorn Valley; he had moved to a nearby town, NorthRiver. Roughly a two hour drive away. He worked as a cook and lived in a small apartment building.

Jack set his cup down and stared hard at the paper. He had moved there about a week after the killings. Why leave so suddenly? He had been assistant manager at The Lizard's Lounge, which would have set him up for any number of good paying jobs around the Valley.

Jack could see him being upset over their deaths, even really shaken up, but not devastated to the point that you pack up and take off to another town only a week later. He really wished Eddie could remember why Cody had been over to see James so often. Provided he had been present when James and Cody were talking. He had no doubt in his mind that Eddie was telling the truth. He had most likely blocked a lot of it out, but if he could start to remember, even the slightest snippet about Cody's visits would be helpful. But he could see from Eddie's point of view why remembering brought back the pain.

Jack looked at his empty coffee cup and got up to refill it from the coffee maker that he kept on a shelf on the back wall. He liked to make his own, the cheap crap from the break room tasted like dishwater. He had no idea where Tara got that stuff, but it tasted like it was salvaged from the local dump.

Sitting back down, he knew what he was going to have

to do. He was going to have to pay a visit to Cody Mitchell. Something didn't sit right. It was as suspicious as fuck. He was the only one of all the staff that had left town. That in itself wasn't really strange but something nagged at him. There was more to this story. He wanted to know what it was.

Tessa sat at Dottie's Diner having a nice lunch. The burger was huge and the fries plenty. She loved diner food. When she was in college, she found that she ate out more than she cooked for herself. And she was definitely savoring this. She didn't realize how hungry she had been until she stepped in and the smell of the food had hit her. She loved to eat out, especially at new places. She was willing to give a new discovery a chance and Dottie's Diner seemed like the perfect choice. It was decked out in 50s style, complete with a jukebox.

It wasn't a big diner, with a row of six booths on one side and a long bar on the other side that had about a dozen stools in front of it. It had 50s and 60s memorabilia covering the walls. The seats were a bright teal that matched the walls with a black and white checker-board floor.

She smiled grimly to herself but looked up quickly when the waitress, in teal colored short sleeved shirt and skirt to just above the knee with a white apron and saddle shoes, came over asking if she wanted a refill on her coffee. She was an older lady who looked tired.

"Yes, thank you." Tessa moved the cup over so the waitress could easily fill it.

"You're new in town, haven't seen you before."

"Yes. This is such a beautiful town. I hope to get a chance to do some exploring before I leave."

"Oh, here on business?" The waitress's face took on a guarded look.

"I don't know if you could really call it that. Visiting my adopted uncle and tying up some loose ends." Using air quotes around the word 'adopted' Tessa shivered a little. "It's a little overwhelming."

"Are you alright, dear?"

Tessa looked up at the woman.

"How long have you lived here? If you don't mind my asking."

"All my life. Born here. Going on 56. I'm Dottie, by the way. Been working here since I was a teenager. Then when Paul Osborn, the owner, died, I took over. His wife had wanted nothing to do with the place and I was the only one who showed interest so she gave it to me, lock, stock and barrel as they say, and wished me luck."

"That was generous of her."

"Yeah, she moved not long after, don't know where. But I had gotten the feeling she thought I would fail and come after her. But I kept it going and it's still doing a good business."

Tessa pointed to her nearly empty plate.

"With food this good how could you not succeed? But that can't really be why she left?"

"Naw," Dottie chuckled, "There just wasn't really anything to keep her here. Her children were grown and gone, her husband died and she got rid of a business that was a stone around her neck. Probably moved to where she could be closer to her children."

Tessa nodded her head slowly in agreement.

"I can see that."

Dottie started to move away when Tessa reached out and touched her arm,

"Can I ask you something?"

"Sure."

Tessa hesitated, suddenly not sure if she should ask or not, not knowing how Dottie would react.

"You don't recognize me, do you?"

Dottie stared hard,

"No, not really. Am I supposed to?"

"That depends on how much or what you read."

"Don't have much time for reading."

"I wrote Death Hurts-The Carstairs Murders."

Dottie's face paled.

"I remember that. It was so horrible. I cannot believe or even understand why anyone would do that. What the reasoning was. I hope you're not here to open old wounds. It's sad that it'll never be solved but sometimes it's best just to let the dead rest in peace."

"Opening old wounds is the last thing I want to do but when I turned 19 I was told I was adopted. I went looking for my birth records and found out that I am a Carstairs. That my birth parents were Michael and Steven Carstairs. I wrote the book, but there are still so many unanswered questions. I wrote it as an outlet for the pain and grief that I felt when I found out what had happened and to see if it might bring in some new leads even after all these years." Tessa blew air out her nose, "Uncle Jack has been giving me information, helping me. He's Chief of Police now."

"Jack Raskins? How can you be his niece? Jack was an only child."

"I know, but it's more of an unofficial title."

"Well, I hope you find the answers you're looking for, honey. Jack is a good man and I know he'll do all he can to help you."

"Do you have a minute to talk?"

Dottie looked at her watch then at the near vacant diner.

"Sure, rush is over for a while." She slid into the booth opposite Tessa.

"Do you know what happened that day?"

"Yeah."

"I mean, aside from what was in the papers."

"Yeah, I can tell you a little more. I used to live on Hawthorne Street. It intersected with Greyson Drive. I was at the corner, right across. The trees that were there are gone now but you could see decently between them. Not 100% clear but decent enough that I could see who came and went." Dottie chuckled. "Though there were times I really didn't need to see to know what was going on when the wind blew just right."

"What do you mean?"

"When James and John were in high school Jack would come over. Loud talk and loud music. Sometimes John's parents were home, if I was outside I could hear her telling them to keep it down, and they would immediately comply. When his parents were not home then you could really hear them but it was nothing anyone ever called the police over. They knew James was a photographer so they assumed he was doing a photo shoot, probably. Never actually paying attention to what they heard. I could catch snippets sometimes by the way the wind blew. Let's just put it this way; if I didn't know that Chief Raskins was straight and seeing Carol I would have said he was gay. I will not embarrass him by repeating what I heard."

Tessa felt her cheeks flush.

"You mean...."

"I will only say that I believe you younger kids call them dick pics."

Tessa's blush went redder.

"I don't know if I'll be brave enough to ask about that."

Dottie laughed, then got somber.

"I know they had a lot of good times until Chief Raskins went to Twelve Oaks and he had his kids. James and John had Edward then Michael and Steven came to live with them. They were such beautiful boys. If it ever comes out who did it and they're not dead I hope the Council puts them so far into the ground even the worms will never find them."

Tessa felt her eyes prick with tears, she grabbed a napkin and dabbed at them.

"So much evil," she whispered more to herself than Dottie, though Dottie nodded her head in agreement.

"I was outside that day, can't really remember exactly what I was doing. Pruning the rose bushes, I think. It was quiet so I wasn't really paying any attention to the goings on over there. James was at the studio, I think John would have been at the bar. Edward was in school. Michael would have been the only one home, he had stopped going to work. Steven could have been at the studio or somewhere, I'm not really sure.

"The moment I knew shit was going down was when I heard that first shot. It was a hell of a crack and brought my head up. I looked in between the trees just in time to see Adam Doherty hightail it out of there. I was pretty sure there was blood coming from his shoulder. When I heard four more cracks that's when I beelined it into the house and called the police. I didn't know what the hell was going on but I sure wasn't hanging around outside to find out. I do remember Jack arriving. The way his brakes squealed and tires howled as he pulled up in front of the house, you could have heard it for miles. And the way he tore into that house; I will never forget it."

"I couldn't see well from the window I was at, but I knew by the truck it was him. Then his father arrived a few minutes later along with everyone else."

"Did you see anyone else leaving?"

"No, if they did they must have used the back gate, I couldn't see that from the house. As I said, the only person I saw leaving was Adam Doherty."

"Thank you so much for taking the time to tell me this."

Dottie gave her a sad smile as she got up and collected Tessa's dishes.

"I gotta get back to work. Take care."

"You too." Tessa smiled as Dottie moved away.

Tessa sat in her car for a few minutes mulling over everything that Dottie had told her when her cell phone went off.

"Hello?"

"Hey, sweetie."

"Hey, Uncle Jack. what's up?"

"How would you like to go on a fact finding mission to NorthRiver?"

Tessa pulled her phone away from her ear and looked at it then put it back.

"Why?"

"I found his name. It's Cody Mitchell. It took some time to run a check and get any information back on him."

"Count me in."

"I'll pick you up in the morning."

"Uncle Jack, I have some interesting information," Tessa quickly said before Jack could hang up.

"Like what?"

"I was having lunch at Dottie's Diner and had a little chat with her."

"She lived across the street. I swear she knew every move we made. I have never seen anyone so nosy. She should have worked for the newspaper instead of that diner."

"She said she could hear some interesting things coming from their yard."

"Yeah, I bet she could. There were a lot of things we weren't exactly quiet about when John's parents weren't at home. And, no, I'm not bi. We did, however, do a lot of nude photo sessions. At first it was just John doing it but I had a few and showed them to Carol. After that I did a lot more for her."

Tessa felt her cheeks grow red.

"I would have had to be pretty drunk to do that in front of my best friends."

"A lot of the times we were. It wasn't all the time we did them, though. For me, it was enough to make a couple of really wonderful albums for Carol. While I went to Twelve Oaks we hardly got together at all. Every now and then on the odd weekend we'd get drunk and have some fun with the camera. James made me another small album. The difference between a teenager and an adult. He knew how to work the camera. But when Eddie came along and Steven and Michael came to live with them, we stopped doing things like that completely, the, ahem, dick pics were shelved permanently. I didn't mind. It was a fun thing we did, then we stopped."

"I wish I could see some of his work."

"If this ever gets solved and you decide to keep the studio, I will show you what he could do with the camera."

CHAPTER 8

EDDIE SAT AT the kitchen table eating his meal as he listened to his adopted aunt and uncle chatter about nothing in particular. His head was starting to ache. He knew it tended to ache for no reason. Maybe this was one of those times, or maybe he was just pushing himself too hard to remember things that he was fighting himself not to remember. He needed to relax. His mind needed to calm down.

"Cartoons?" was the first thing that popped out of his mouth. Jack and Carol turned to look at him.

It took a second or two for Carol to shake herself out of her look of confusion. "Of course, sweetheart."

She led him from the table to the living room. He curled up on the couch and pulled the quilt from the back of the couch over him. Carol turned on the TV to his favorite cartoon channel, then went back to the kitchen. Eddie watched for a while then his mind seemed to drift. He tried to concentrate on his show but it wasn't working. The flashes in his mind were like lightning, there one second then gone the next. He gripped the quilt tightly and squeezed his eyes shut to fight back the tears. Why were the memories coming back now? He had worked hard at keeping them away. Uncle Jack was keeping things from him and he knew it had to do with Tessa. He didn't want to see her. He said she looked like Steven and Michael. Jack may be right but he just didn't want to face it. He didn't want his mind to go back there to relive that day all over again. It hadn't seemed real then and it still didn't, even though he knew that it had happened. Then it was as if it hit him like a shovel to the face.

"Da....!!" The scream tore out of his throat so loud and hard, his voice cracked.

Jack and Carol came running from the kitchen. Carol came to sit beside him and brought his trembling body into her arms. She held him tight and he felt comforted by it. Jack crouched in front of him, he stroked the loose strands of hair from his face.

"What is it, baby? What's wrong?"

"Da's dead," he managed to choke out. "They're all dead."

"I know, baby, I know." He could see tears forming in Jack's eyes. "If I could've kept you from seeing that, I would have. I could've told you in a gentler manner."

Eddie felt like his heart was being squeezed so tight that it was going to explode. The flashes in his mind grew stronger, to the point it was like watching an old grainy movie in black and white.

"Eddie?" Carol's voice whispered in his ear, "What do you remember?"

Eddie could feel his body collapse onto Carol. She sat

back further on the couch so she could lay Eddie's head on her lap.

"I'd just gotten home from school……."

"DA! DADDY! WHERE are you?"

He could hear a faint voice reply, "In the basement, son. Come down quick."

Eddie threw his stuff on the couch and ran down the stairs. Michael lay on his back on his nest of blankets with a light sheet covering him. He was sweaty and panting. His eyes looked wild and pained. Steven was beside him, holding his hand. James came out of the darkroom with a wet rag in his hand and gave it to Steven, who applied it to Michael's forehead.

John sat on the other side of Michael, as he smiled at his son.

"Won't be too long now, son. You get to see if you have a niece or nephew."

Eddie's smile grew big as he kneeled beside Michael.

"Is it really coming?"

Michael could only smile and nod. The birthing nurse watched intently but said nothing. Michael squeezed his eyes shut and grunted.

"You're doing good. Won't be much longer." The nurse moved the sheet.

Eddie watched, fascinated.

Michael tucked his head down to muffle his crying, but Eddie could also see the rapid breath he took before taking a deep gulp and then holding it.

"That's it, keep it up. I can see a head."

Michael let his breath go. Eddie reached out and took Michael's other hand and whispered,

"It's a girl."

Michael's teary eyes glittered as he smiled at Eddie,

"I know." Then he buried his head down again to push, the nurse rubbed his arm.

"You can do this."

"Fuck, it hurts." Michael gripped both Eddie's and Steven's hands as he took a deep breath and pushed as hard as he could. Eddie gripped Michael's hand tight to give him reassurance.

"You can do this," Eddie whispered. His words were met with a grunt and a cry. Eddie went to let go but Michael held his hand tight. He watched in fascination the efforts of Michael's pain.

Eddie couldn't believe his eyes as he watched. The baby was no more than a few seconds old when, to Eddie, all hell broke loose. He could hear the front door bang open and close quickly, then Chief Raskin's voice.

"Where are you?"

"Down here," John called out. "Something wrong, Chief?"

"I am so glad I was able to get here first. I figured this was what was happening when one of my sergeants saw Jack speeding past his checkpoint at top speed. Damn, even fresh out of the womb she is beautiful."

"What's going on?" James asked in a sharp voice.

"I will explain all that but first we need to get that boy and baby in a safe place where they will not easily be found. Jack told me one time about a wall room big enough to fit a person down here?"

James's eyes went wide.

"What are you saying, sir? Are we in danger?"

"Yes, and you don't have a lot of time," Bennett snapped, as

he watched the nurse clean up the baby and make sure she was breathing okay. "Where is your gun, John?"

"In the wall safe in the darkroom."

"Get it."

John tore into the darkroom. In less than a minute he was back with his Glock 17. His eyes flashed, sending out a mental alert.

"Bennett." Footsteps sounded on the basement stairs.

John brought the gun up and fired. A yelp came from Adam Doherty as he fell against the wall. A squeal came from Eddie as he clamped his hands over his ears.

"Hurry up," Adam ground out as he headed back outside.

"The darkroom," James hissed. "The door can be locked."

"No, they'll look there." The look on Bennett's face showed that he was losing patience.

"The room under the steps, put them in there. It's sound-proof. Practically invisible if you're really not looking for it. You can't hear anything either way," John said.

"Do it!" Bennett's voice went up an octave.

James got up and grabbed Eddie, he quickly pulled him to the door and opened it.

"In there, Eddie."

Eddie crawled in and turned to look at his father, a confused look on his face.

"How long?"

"Not long, baby. It'll be okay. We'll get it straightened out."

John came over with the baby wrapped up in blankets. He handed the infant to Eddie.

"Keep her wrapped up, Eddie. It's just going to be a short time. Be as still and as quiet as you can. You'll be alright."

Eddie held the baby tightly as he moved to the back of the

room. There was no light, but he was not afraid of the dark. He watched as his father shut the door. Eddie could hear it latch, then silence.

"And then I don't know what happened until you opened the door and took me out."

Jack kissed Eddie on the forehead. "So, Dad really was there."

Eddie nodded slowly.

"He had his gun out but he looked scared. He wanted to protect us but I never saw the danger. I didn't hear or see anything after the door closed. I only know what I saw after."

"And you shouldn't have had to see that."

Eddie closed his eyes, his head aching. He felt strange, his whole body felt like it was humming. He felt shaky.

"I don't feel good, Uncle Jack."

"You going to be sick?"

Eddie nodded, he knew it was only a matter of seconds. Jack pulled him up and got Eddie into the bathroom. Eddie dropped to his knees and flung his head over the toilet, vomiting. His body wracked with each heave. He could faintly hear Carol saying she was going to get him something. After a minute he sat back on his haunches. Jack handed him a glass of water.

"Rinse, baby." Eddie took a big mouth full of water, swished it around and spit it into the toilet, then Jack flushed it. Carol was suddenly at his side.

"Here." She handed him a small pill. "Take this, it will settle your stomach so you won't get sick again."

Eddie took the pill and drank the rest of the water.

"Let's get you to bed." Jack and Carol eased Eddie to his feet and took him into the basement apartment. They stripped him down to his briefs and covered him with warm blankets. Eddie snuggled down in the bed.

"You want a story?" Carol asked.

Eddie nodded his head as Jack turned the nightlight on and the overhead light off. Then turned on the bedside lamp for her to read by. He kissed the top of Eddie's head.

"I'll leave you two to it." He headed back upstairs.

Eddie focused his attention on Carol.

"Okay." She picked up a book from the shelf, "How about Pooh Bear?" Eddie nodded, he was starting to feel sleepy before she even had time to start the story. He only heard her turn the page twice before he found himself fast asleep.

Eddie wasn't sure how much time had passed before he had woken up. He lay in his bed, his face buried in the pillow to muffle the screams. He pushed himself up and ran to the bathroom and vomited. The nightmare had been so real. Why had his brain suddenly decided to start hashing things up again? He didn't want to see it again. He was tired of seeing it and feeling the pain that came with it. His family laying on the basement floor, so still and lifeless, covered in blood. They were gone. All gone.

He flushed and sat on the cold floor, his back against the shower door. He was sweating, and trembled slightly. What was happening to him? Why were all these memories coming back to him now, and could he trust them to be the truth? But it had to be the truth. He staggered back to bed and got under the warm covers. He wished he was in his Da's strong arms where he knew he would be safe. The world was such an evil place.

Why couldn't it be the way it was when he was a kid? Because evil people took that away from him. Evil people that were never caught or punished for taking his whole world from him. Tears slid down his face. He wanted so badly to help Uncle Jack, but he didn't know how or even where to begin. If only his brain would work right.

CHAPTER 9

JACK LAID DOWN in bed and pulled Carol close. She sighed and snuggled in. He kissed the top of her head.

"I'm taking Tessa and going to NorthRiver in the morning, see what we can get out of Cody. He worked at the Lounge as assistant manager, not the Studio. Which seems strange to me because if he wasn't at the Studio why would he be at the house all the time to talk to James? James stayed out of Lounge business just as John stayed out of Studio business. What would they have to talk about? And for them to see each other so much?"

"The only thing that would make sense would be an affair but there is no way in hell I can see James doing that."

"No, not a chance. They could never stay out of each other's pants long enough to have an affair
with anyone."

"Hopefully Cody will tell you."

"I hope so, too."

"You two will be careful. Please, Jack."

"We will. But I don't think there will be any trouble."

"You don't know that, you big oaf. Please." She smacked him on the chest.

Jack grunted but smiled at her.

"I promise. We'll take care. I'll take my gun and shoulder holster if it'll make you happy."

"Yes." She traced a finger down his chest. "Very happy. I love you, Jack. You are the only one I have ever loved. You are my everything and I don't want you taken away from me."

Jack huffed.

"Even when you thought I was ripping you apart, taking your virginity?"

Carol playfully swatted Jack on the chest.

"Shut up."

Jack held Carol tighter.

"Jack?" She moved to whisper in his ear. "Make love to me."

"You know, I would never say this to any other guy but you, James. You look radiant." Jack laughed as he grabbed his beer off the stand by the lounger, then took a swig.

"Fuck. Off." James sneered as he tried to make himself more comfortable on another lounger. Jack had to smile, James was almost 8 months and hated not being able to do anything.

"No, seriously. You look good for a pregnant dude. Have you decided if you want to know the sex yet before you deliver?" Jack asked.

"No, don't want to. They've asked a couple of times but we

decided we don't want to know until the kid is out; but I have a feeling it's a girl." He reached over to the stand beside his lounger and picked up the glass of lemonade. He took a sip then looked at it. "Damn, I swear John doesn't believe in sugar."

Jack got up and went to the edge of the pool, sat down and put his feet in, wiping sweat from his forehead. He shielded his eyes and stared up at the sky.

"What's wrong?" Jack could hear the concern in James's voice.

"Mom and Dad came over last night for supper. Mom was asking how you were doing and I told her you were dealing. Then she wanted to know what was going to happen to the kids that were orphaned because of that crash that killed both their parents, the ones that worked at the Lounge and Studio."

"You mean the Hamiltons and the Andersons? Marla Anderson, worked at the Lounge as a waitress, her husband was thinking of applying at Crowell and Wilson as a general counsellor. Jason worked at the Studio setting up sets and the like. Twila was a stay at home mom, but she thought if they all were approved to move here by Council she might be able to get hired on at that used book store, I think it's called Turn The Page. "

"Yeah."

"Their kids were both boys, Michael Anderson and Steven Hamilton. I don't think you got to meet them. They were only working for us for a month or so. They were here through the council work program. You work here a month then the Council requests an update. If you want them to continue on, they are approved for another month. After that, you need to decide if you are going to move here; if not, the Council will not renew your work permit. They were in the process of requesting a move here. They loved their jobs."

"Sounds like a good program. But, no, I don't think I did get to meet them. But Dad said if no relatives were willing to take them then they would remain in the orphanage until someone adopts them. I would love to adopt but we have our hands full with Tucker and Haley. They are hellions right now, they listen to their mother but not me. It would be chaos and, with everything that has happened to them, they would need a quiet, stable environment right now. I know that is something I cannot provide."

He could hear James's voice hitch.

"That is nasty. Those boys grew up together, just like we did. It'll kill them to be torn apart. I can't even begin to imagine what my life would be without John."

Jack hesitated before he spoke,

"Even though you're going to have a baby, would you consider adopting?"

James was silent for a long time.

"It would be so overwhelming getting used to an infant and a couple of pre-teens. But the thought has crossed our minds since the accident."

"It would be at first, but you would adapt. You're good at that. It would be something to seriously consider. I would hate to think of those kids languishing in an orphanage not getting a loving home because they are older."

"John and I have had a lot of discussions about the accident but, none, really, about adopting them. Just more like random statements. He feels as guilty as fuck and I can't seem to beat it into his thick skull that it was not his fault that they were killed. It was that fucking drunk driver who decided to get behind the wheel. If that asshole hadn't of died in the crash, I would have fucking killed him with my bare hands."

"Why would John feel guilty? I can understand being upset

that you lost valuable employees and new friends, and regretting the kids losing their parents, but it's not his fault."

James heaved a sigh.

"Unfortunately he doesn't see it that way. He told them to go that way, that it was a short cut. Cut their driving time. They lived over in SnowKeep, on the other side of us and were planning to move here if they got Council approval. He feels like he sent them to their deaths."

"That is fucking bullshit. Anyone could have given them those directions that night. If anyone feels guilty, it should be me. We were the ones chasing the fucker. Me and Dale. We were out patrolling when we got the call of a reckless driver. It's a wonder that shitface didn't do more damage or kill more people than what he did. John is nuts for thinking that."

"Did I hear my name being mentioned?" John came out the patio door with a beer in one hand and another glass of lemonade in the other. He sat in the lounger beside James, putting the glass on the stand. James grimaced.

"Yeah," Jack snapped, "I was just telling James you are a fucking asshole for blaming yourself for the deaths of those kids' parents."

"I sent them that way."

Jack turned to look John square in the face.

"Anyone could have sent them that way. It is not your fault. You need to stop chewing yourself up over it."

"Just as you need to stop blaming yourself, Jack. Not your fault either." James snapped. John opened his mouth to speak but James cut him off. "The fucktard who slammed into their car is the one who is to blame, not you. What it boils down to is that those boys are suffering far more than you ever thought of. They've lost everything they have ever known. They may even be

separated if a family wants to adopt one and not the other one. Or they may be stuck there until they're 18."

Jack grabbed his beer bottle and chugged the rest of it down. There was dead silence. No one spoke for the longest time, then it was John who broke the silence.

"I have been on the phone with Colin Marritz."

"Your lawyer?" Jack asked.

John's voice was a whisper when he spoke again, Jack had to strain to hear him.

"Yes. I asked about adopting the boys if the relatives refuse to take them."

Jack and James stared hard at John. James reached over and took his hand.

"John, why didn't you say something sooner?"

"I don't know. I just got off the phone with Colin. The guilt got me so bad."

"So, why didn't you talk to me?"

"I don't know. I didn't think you would want to or be able to. If they came to live with us, Colin couldn't guarantee when it would be, depending on if the relatives didn't take them and how much paperwork would be involved. Plus Colin would need to request Council approval."

Jack looked at John questioningly.

"What would the Council have to do with anything?"

"Because they would be moving here permanently. It's stupid but all rules apply whether adults or children."

"Oh for fuck sakes..." James spat out.

John heaved a sigh.

"I didn't think you'd want that extra burden. But I wanted to call and ask just the same."

James brought John's hand to his lips and kissed it.

"It won't be a burden. I can deal. I'll learn to deal with it."

"But...."

"John, we will make it work."

Jack got up and went back to his lounger.

"What did Colin have to say?"

"He said he'd look into it for me. It's been eating me alive, and today it just got to the point I couldn't take it anymore."

"Before you got pregnant did you think of adopting?" Jack asked.

"We talked about it a couple of times if James couldn't get pregnant."

Jack got another beer from the cooler on the other side of his lounger, popped the top and took a drink.

"If you don't mind my asking, why didn't you think you'd get pregnant?"

James shifted his eyes to his belly and gave it a light rub.

"Not so much getting pregnant as keeping the baby. I had two miscarriages prior to conceiving this one. I wasn't that far along with either of them, two months and four months, but incredibly heartbreaking and painful. I'm still not out of the woods with this one. I have to be extremely careful. I can't work and am supposed to rest as much as possible. After the first two miscarriages I never thought I would get this far."

"You never said."

"I couldn't. I wanted to but every time I tried I choked up and the words just refused to come. John supported my decision to tell you and understood when I couldn't. I know it was too hard for him to talk about it as well."

"If you come to full term with this one, will you still adopt those boys or decide not to?"

John spoke up,

"I definitely want to but it will be up to James."
"I will, as long as John is by my side."
John took James's hand and kissed it.
Jack took another drink.
"I love you guys."

Jack felt exhausted. After making love to Carol, he had drifted into a restless sleep, the night being swallowed up by dreams. He hadn't dreamed about James and John in years and now they were coming back. He felt like his body was made of bricks and it took every effort to move. He had not left his office since he had come in and was pretty sure he had dozed off a few times. He picked up the phone and called out to Tara.

"Yes, Chief?"

"Can you have Dale and Adam come to see me when they are able to."

"Dale is taking his lunch at Dottie's but I can shoot him a text to have him haul ass back here."

"No, that's fine. Don't rush him. Food that good should not be rushed."

"Adam is still at the conference. But it should be over soon. Today, I think, is just closing comments and lunch."

"I'm glad it's not me. I have had more than my fair share. Send him a text that he can see me when he's through."

"Sure."

Jack hung up the phone and stared at the ceiling. He brought his hands up and rubbed his eyes. He jumped when he felt his phone vibrate in his pocket. Looking at the screen he saw Dale's name and a text.

Dale: Tara said you wanted to see me. I'm at Dottie's. I'll try to finish up and be back in half an hour.

Jack: Don't hurry. Get back when you can but you had better bring me a piece of her chocolate pie.

Dale: LOL. You got it.

Jack was pretty sure he had dozed off again when a knock came at the door. He jumped and snorted.

"I'm getting too old for this shit." He straightened himself up. "Come in."

Dale came in and closed the door behind him. He had a plastic take out container in his hand with a fork. Jack almost started to salivate. Dale grinned as he sat it on the desk then sat down.

"No." Dale raised a hand when Jack reached to pull out the drawer where he kept a dish of change. "You pay for lunch next time."

"Fair enough." Jack took the container and opened it up. It looked heavenly. Thin crust, lots of chocolate and very little topping. Just how he liked it. He took a bite before looking at Dale.

Dale smirked as he watched Jack eat.

"What's going on, Jack? You don't seem yourself. You haven't since Tessa came to town. We've known each other for way too long. I know you, talk to me."

Jack sighed, he knew Dale was right. They had gone to Twelve Oaks to take the police courses together, graduating in the top ten of their class. They had grown tight when they joined the force. Always had each other's back. But that day, 30 years ago, Dale had been lucky, he had been off with pneumonia. He had been saved from seeing the carnage. Though

Dale had seen the photographs, it had not been the same as actually being there.

"I'll admit I'm a bit squirrelly. Who wouldn't be? Tessa pops up out of nowhere all of a sudden and writes that book, and now it feels like it's 30 years ago all over again. The dreams are coming back and it's all I can think about. Some new evidence has come to light, Dale, and I think it could give us some new insights." Jack shifted his eyes to the closed door and back again. "This does not go any further than this office."

"Of course."

"Tessa went to look at Greyson House; there was a roll of film on Michael's workbench and she brought it to me. I had it developed. There are two pictures with a guy in it that I couldn't place but I can now. Cody Mitchell. He worked at the Lounge. He left town about a week after the killings. Tessa and I are going to see him and see what he has to say."

"Sounds like a plan."

"Dale, I have reason to believe Dad was involved."

Dale's mouth opened and closed like a fish but no sound came out. He sat forward then leaned back trying to get enough of a grip on himself to speak.

"Are you fucking kidding me?"

"I wish I was."

"What makes you think that?"

"The ballistics reports and bullets recovered from the bodies are missing from the box."

"But that doesn't sound like enough to put him there at the time of the killings."

"That might not, but this does. It never occurred to me then, I was too deep in shock and grief for it to register. There were two things he said to me. I used to dream so much about that day, I can hear every word in crystal clear clarity and it makes sense now. ”

"What?"

"He said that even fresh from the womb she was beautiful. How would he know that? If he supposedly didn't see her until I did when we took her out of the secret room, how would he know that it was a girl? And the other key point; when he called for the officers to look for Eddie and Tessa, not knowing they were in the secret room, he made another slip up. His exact words were: 'Attention all units: search the grounds and surrounding area for a 15 year old boy and a newborn infant girl.'"

Dale paled. Jack thought he was either going to faint, puke or both.

Jack sat his face in stone when he heard a light knock at the door. He knew it had to be Adam.

"Come in."

Adam came in Closing the door, he sat in the chair in front of Jack's desk.

"You wanted to see me?"

"How was the conference?" A small grin appeared on Jack's lips.

Adam rolled his eyes.

"I swear if I never do anything like that again it will be too soon. I don't know why I agreed to it in the first place."

"Because you are an expert around here."

"Only because I am continuously studying. Taking online courses in my free time."

"It's your field of choice. But to a lot of other officers, it's not. They have other interests. They only do this to keep on top of things. Most officers really only need to know what drug counters another, not what makes each drug tick. That's why they have these things. Believe me, I've been to my fair share of conferences. You just want to be glad all you had to do was speak and teach. Be glad you weren't the go between for the organizers and the Council to arrange permits and lodging."

"Oh fuck, I never thought of that. Every single one of them would have had to be issued a visitation permit."

"Yep." Jack leaned back in his chair. "I used to have to do that too, for some of the conferences that were held here."

"I don't mind attending conferences, not really. I mean they can be a pain, especially if you get a speaker that drones on for hours in that voice that bores you to sleep. But to be the main speaker. I'm not used to that."

"Fun, isn't it?" Jack's grin became a full on smirk.

"Fuck, no!"

Jack laughed, then grew serious.

"But getting to why I wanted to see you. I need you and Dale to keep an eye on things here. Make it go as smoothly as if I were still at my desk. I should only be gone a couple of days, three at the most."

"May I ask, why? Where're you going?"

"This stays in this office between you and me."

"Of course."

"I think Tessa and I could be onto a lead that could

bring in some new information that, we are hoping, could be enough to reopen the Carstairs case."

Adam's eyebrows raised as he leaned forward, his face going pale.

"Are you serious?"

"Yes, I've been warring with myself on how much to tell you and Dale."

"Dale was sick the day it happened, wasn't he?"

"Yes. When he was better and I was out of the bottle I brought him up to speed on everything that had happened from what I had heard over my radio to the time I got there. I thought he was going to puke when he saw the crime scene photos."

"Yeah, they are quite different from actually being there."

"It took a long time to get that out of my head."

"No surprises there. I saw you when you left. You were as pale as a ghost carrying that little kid in your arms. You never saw me when I went down to help secure the scene."

"No, I was too focused on getting Eddie out of there. He should never have had to see that."

"None of us should have."

Jack shuddered slightly.

"But...getting back to the reason I'm leaving."

"You know I'll never say anything."

Jack took a deep breath keeping his eyes straight on Adam.

"Cody Mitchell."

Adam stared at Jack with a blank look.

"Should I know that name?"

"He worked at the Lizard's Lounge. I really don't want to get into how I came across this information. Not just yet anyway. But he was the only one on either employee list for both businesses who left town roughly a week after the murders."

"And this has relevance because....."

"From what I have recently been able to find out, he also frequented Greyson House. Why? I don't know. But, I'm hoping I'll be able to find out."

Adam's face showed no emotion. Jack wondered if he was making a mistake in his line of thinking. But he needed to be sure. The reports and bullets could have been missing long before Tara gave him the names in the time frame he requested. Just because Adam had been up there didn't mean a thing, Dale had been up there too. For all he knew his father could have taken them back out after filing them as evidence. Jack felt his heart slam into his chest so hard he had to force back the grimace that threatened to take over his face. That had been an insane thought but a, suddenly, strong possibility. So why he suddenly thought Adam might have taken them at any point in time, or,even been in on it, was ludicrous. He had to put a stop to this shit line of thinking.

Adam nodded slowly.

"Don't worry about it. Everything will be fine here."

"I know it will."

Adam lounged back in his chair for a minute, eyes cast down as if he was thinking. He got up and headed to the door. Turning back he looked at Jack, his face neutral.

"Why dig this up again? Tessa's book is just a fad. Before long it'll be in the background and forgotten like all the other true crime and unsolved murder books out there. Opening old wounds can sometimes be very painful, and it's better to let the past be the past and the dead rest." He closed the door quietly on his way out.

Jack stared at the door. Was that just some friendly advice, a threat, or one hell of an admission without actually coming out and saying it? He knew that, eventually, he would find out one way or another.

CHAPTER 10

JACK PARKED OUT front of Greyson House and stared up at the dark house. He had a lot of good memories here. A lot of fun times. Getting out, he went to the back gate. He was amazed that the Council had not put a lock on the latch. He would have, but he knew most people in this town would not come near this place with a ten foot pole, knowing the Council laws regarding the Carstairs properties, and no one really wanted to risk high fines and long jail sentences. Plus, he figured, people in this town were extremely respectful when it came to the Carstairs, so they stayed away.

Unlocking the gate, he slipped in. Closing it, he walked to the edge of the pool. He, James and John had a lot of drunk, often nude, photo sessions here. Carol only knew about one, maybe two, that resulted in the albums he had gifted her, but the rest of them he would keep to himself.

He had no doubt that the negatives were still in the lock box in the bottom of James's filing cabinet in his darkroom, as Jack had the pictures in his small safe in the back of the closet that Carol did not know the combination to.

He squatted down to look in the pool. Where pristine blue water once was, there was now only dirt and debris.

"We'll solve it, guys. I know we will. We're taking good care of Eddie. I just know that once this is all over with we can get him the help he needs." Tears streaked Jack's face. "It's not fair. It was senseless, and for what? Money? Dad was involved, so is Adam. I feel like the world I know is crashing down around my shoulders."

For a split second Jack felt sure he felt the pressure of strong hands on his shoulders. He turned sharply but nothing was there.

"John? I will find the answers, John. I know I'm not going to like it, though. But I will so I can give you guys peace. We'll get it done, and Eddie will be safe. You guys will be able to rest and Eddie will have the life he deserves."

He got up and wiped at his eyes. Looking at the key in his hand, he thought about going into the house but changed his mind. He left quickly, making sure the gate was latched tight.

When he picked Tessa up from her motel room he prayed she didn't see the bags under his eyes when she got in the car. She had a carry tray of delicious smelling coffee and a bag of pastries.

Tessa handed him one of the coffees and he took a long drink.

"Oohhh, that's good."

"Walked to Mug Shot Joint down at the corner. Got some goodies, too."

"They make the best stuff."

Tessa was silent as they got on the road. She could see him white knuckling the steering wheel. This was not going to be a comfortable adventure for him. This could dig up more than he wanted to hear, but knew he had to.

Tessa had started second guessing herself about all of this. She didn't want to stir up trouble or open old wounds, but the ball had started rolling and there really was no way to stop it now. She wanted to know why her family had been murdered and she knew Jack did too, but what would it cost to finally find out?

"Take me back there, Uncle Jack. I know what all the articles say and what I saw in the pictures. But I want to know what you saw. What your point of view is. Give me some history."

Jack finished his coffee in a couple of gulps then tossed the empty cup into the backseat behind her.

"Garbage box back there," he mumbled as he took a shuddering breath. Tessa gave a small smile.

"I met John and James when I was seven years old. John and I became fast friends. The Conners came to Unicorn Valley for protection when James was 5. They had lived in Portland, but when they were found out by hunters, the shifter police told them to come to the Valley. Most shifter police know about the Valley, and if they feel it is a last resort for protection, they will get in contact with the Council who will make arrangements for them to move. Sort of like witness protection for shifters. It's not like we keep the town invisible, but it's become a safe place for shifters mostly now. They know that once they are here they are safe. The security and protection that has developed over the years has made sure of that. The cases of hunter related attacks here have dropped to practically zero. You've seen the towers and fences. There are at least two Protectors to a tower at any given time. Plus anyone coming and going will need permits from residents or the police if they plan to stay awhile. For all deliveries and mail, the Council approves the drivers. Never had a problem that way. It's not like the world doesn't know about us, but we're not exactly a tourist attraction that people will go out of their way to come and see. Just an average little town like any other, only difference is we're mainly shifters.

"Those that come here seeking protection are given a whole new identity and their old one is completely erased. All bills and bank accounts are deleted and new ones made. A lot, though, just prefer to keep running until their time runs out. But most do live out full lives in relative safety because they have nothing hunters want.

"It's the rarities that come here, like unicorns, but as far as I know there are very few out there that live in populated areas. The Conners were the last unicorn shifters to come to the Valley. Now we have none."

"What about Eddie? Wasn't he..?"

Jack cut her off.

"No, he was only part. John was a Protector. A human, for the most part, with an enhanced ability for protection spells, and mind contact with other Protectors. Eddie really didn't have either, it never showed. He couldn't shift and never showed any magical talents. If he did, he was a late bloomer. Protectors usually start showing their talents when they are 12 or 13.

"The Conners moved in across the street from Greyson

House and John's father was assigned to them as their Protector. They were in his sector, after all. When James started school he was scared to death, so John and I took it upon ourselves to make sure that he was okay and helped him to adjust. John decided to form a Protection Society at school and we had nine members including ourselves.

"James was the only full blood black male omega unicorn in the whole school, for the whole Valley, and that made us proud. He made friends quickly and everyone loved him. He was two years younger than John and I, but I could still see something in John's eyes that was more than just best friends love.

"It was a strong and true attraction that, over the years, grew into love. And it was hard not to notice. Everyone could see it. And that's another great thing about Unicorn Valley, it doesn't matter if you're straight, gay or bi, or whatever, it just doesn't matter. You are who you are.

"There is no racism or bigotry or anything else. I mean, there most likely is to some degree, but I mean full scale enough that it would cross my desk and we'd have to respond with putting people in jail. It's not completely non-existent. No place is ever completely free of anything, there is no perfect paradise, but I like to think we are pretty close to it in a lot of things. But we do have crime, I'm not saying we don't.

"Anyone that comes to the Valley is completely checked out and has to abide by Council law. If they want to live here they need to understand that evil in any form will not be tolerated. That we want to live and be at peace. When the unicorns and Protectors came to the falls, they brought with them their laws and value systems and instilled them in their offspring who, in turn, carried on those traditions.

"And I know what you're going to say, how can that be with the Carstairs murders hanging over our heads? There are some things, sometimes, unfortunately, that are just beyond our control. There always will be hunters and evil out there but I like to think that because of that we have learned a harsh lesson and have bettered ourselves at protecting our valley. Sometimes good comes from bad."

Tessa was silent for a long time. Jack kept snatching glances her way, not sure if she wanted him to continue or not.

"Please, go on." Her voice was barely a whisper.

James and John were rarely apart, always together. Even though James was younger, John always managed to find a way to include him in everything we did. I did, too, if it was possible."

"And you never felt like a third wheel with James being so close to John?"

"Actually, no. I was proud to have James around. Who wouldn't? Having a rare unicorn as a friend. And I protected him fiercely just like John did.

"But when Carol and I started dating when I was sixteen, I guess that's when I started slipping away. I didn't see them quite as much on the weekends or sometimes after school as I once did and they understood. They were happy for me. John and I still had our moments and shared our secrets. He was sixteen when he confessed his love for James and was pretty sure that James was in love with him but he had to be careful. James was only fourteen and he had to tread lightly."

"Underage," Tessa whispered.

"You know it. But it wasn't just that. The penalties by the Council for any injury, damage or wrongdoing to a unicorn was high. They are our most prized treasure. It's why the town was named as it is. Unicorns created this town. It killed John to have to wait until James was sixteen before he could even begin to see if there was even an inkling of a relationship there.

"And yes, James had feelings for John. but at times, I could see doubts. James was 16 and John was 18. When James was 14 he thought John was not just his protector, but his soulmate. But growing up sometimes has a way of messing with that. James seemed to drift away from John when he was 16 and John took that as a sign of rejection, so he started looking elsewhere. John started dating another guy from the football team, Henry, we thought it was going to get serious even though they had only been dating a month. Then one day right on the football field they had a blow out argument. It was nasty and really harsh things were said. It was an ugly breakup that came to blows before the coaches could intervene.

"John told me later on it wasn't the physical part of the breakup that hurt but it was what Henry had said that was so painful. He yelled for the whole team to hear that John was still a virgin at 18 and couldn't make up his mind where he wanted to stick his dick. John almost strangled him. When Henry walked off that field no one ever saw him at that school again. From what I was able to find out, his parents had been contacted and informed of what went on and they figured he was better off at another school."

"What happened to John?"

"He was about to quit but the coaches begged him to stay. He was their star quarterback, after all. John agreed to finish out the season but he felt like he had been shattered.

James found out about it and was at John's side in an instant. It drew them back together and cemented their relationship. A few months after that incident, John and I were hanging out. James was away with his parents and Carol was away with her parents.

"He told me that he and James had made love. It was a very special night for the both of them, both virgins and scared out of their minds. I knew right then that they would be together forever. They were careful to use condoms. They wanted to take things slow. Maybe, someday, they would have kids, John had commented, but not until the path they would take in life was clear.

"When John graduated high school, he went to Twelve Oaks University to take business courses along with the Protector courses. He knew where his future was. His father, Corbin, wasn't well and John knew he wanted him to take over the Lounge and his position as Protector when he could no longer handle the workload. But he wanted John to have a solid business degree and to know all the ropes.

"John took to it like a fish in water. He shared little tricks with his father to help improve business and set up things in ledgers instead of loose sheets of paper everywhere. When John was 22, his father turned the business over to him completely. The upstairs that was empty and used for storage, Corbin turned into a loft for John to move into."

Jack's face grew wistful.

"It wasn't long after that, Corbin had a heart attack. It took him quickly but devastated John and his mother. It might have been four months after he retired that he died, roughly anyway. Corbin Carstairs had always been a strong, healthy man and to be taken out like that. I don't think

Tianna ever got over it. You could see her shrink back into herself day after day. John didn't know what to do. He tried everything he could think of to help, but in the end, everyone knew it was a broken heart that ended her life too, almost a year to the day after Corbin died."

"I don't think I remember reading any Carstairs obits in my research."

"It really wasn't publicly known. Obits like that are kept out of the paper. The Council didn't want the world knowing that Unicorn Valley had lost a Protector, lest hunters got some ideas."

"How?"

"Hunters aren't known for stupidity. Even if you didn't mention in an obit if the person was a Protector or a shifter, there would be ways to find out. Unicorn Valley may be protected, but they can still get in if they work hard enough at it. Though they seem to have given up since we no longer have any unicorns."

"When did James's parents die?"

"Not long after he did. John's parents were lucky they didn't have to bury their son. The Conners lived directly across the street from Greyson House. The agony they must have been feeling, I can only guess as indescribable. I know it was for me. Mrs. Conners just shut down. I cannot begin to imagine what she felt, watching those stretchers and body-bags being brought out and knowing one of them contained her only child.

"I tried to talk to her at the funeral, but she was lost. The light in her eyes was gone, he was the same. She was hospitalized a few times, she wouldn't eat and barely slept. Two years later she quietly passed away. He followed her not long after."

"How?"

"Went to sleep one night and never woke up."

"Oh, I don't need to know anymore."

"No, he didn't commit suicide. His heart gave out, was what the ME reported to me. We all figured it was a broken heart. Just like John's mother. His wife and son were everything to him. The main reason he lived. Without them he was lost and lonely."

"So sad."

"I petitioned the Council to have them buried in the Carstairs family cemetery with their son and family. They granted it. Their bodies would be safe there."

"Grave robbers?' Tessa ventured.

"Yeah. Even dead unicorn parts are still valuable."

"Even as human?"

"Not so much, but if they died in shifted form they would remain that way. Hunters and robbers would have a field day. Being buried as a human their bodies would have no value but robbers would try to dig them up just to see if they hadn't been lied to."

"That's just sick."

"Don't I know it."

"So, John and James eventually moved into Greyson House?"

"Yeah, they sealed off the door going down to the Lounge from the loft and used the back door as an entrance and rented it out. It worked well in a way, because James was always running to his darkroom at Greyson House to develop his film. The basement at his house was not really adequate for a darkroom so John talked his father into making one for him in the basement of Greyson House where there was more than enough room to make a really decent sized one. "

"So, it was James' darkroom originally."

"Yes, he was becoming an amazingly skilled photographer. He showed me quite a bit of his work. It was incredible. That boy had talent. It wasn't long before people were asking him to do grad and prom pics, even weddings.

"That's when John took a huge chance and bought that old abandoned 3 story Victorian out on Kessler Street and turned it into a studio. It had enough rooms in it that he could make different backgrounds. He was able to make the basement into a darkroom and office. It took just about everything John had saved up. All of his inheritance and some of the profit from the Lounge. It worked out in the end, but when James found out how John had paid for it and what it cost, he was furious. The neighbors thought there was a domestic dispute in progress, so they called me.

"They were surprised to see me when I banged on the door.

The yelling was so loud I was surprised they even heard me. When I explained they were disturbing the neighbors they looked at each other and started to laugh. John explained to me the source of the very loud argument, I couldn't help but laugh myself at how it must have sounded to the neighbors. Once the studio took off, though, James was grateful for what John had done. It made the perfect wedding present."

"That would have been the ultimate in wedding gifts."

"Yes, I believe it made the bond between them even stronger, if that was possible. They got married when James was 21. That was one wild weekend, I can tell you that. Back then it was not common for gay couples to blast it to the universe that they were getting married. It was allowed, you were who you were and if you wanted to marry the same sex, then it was fine. For the fun of it, I researched how many gay marriages there have been over the years. There were none until they got married, the following years, maybe, a dozen or so. The last five years, probably, about 20."

Jack shook his head and snorted.

"I called it groundbreaking but it really did wonders for James, he was booked for months in advance. It helped John along too. That's when they thought it was time to try for a baby, knowing that they were financially secure and had the perfect home. They had wanted to wait until they were established and properly able to care for a baby."

Jack's voice hitched and Tessa could tell he was having a hard time controlling his voice. It was starting to shake. Tessa decided to change the subject for a bit.

"How does a male unicorn even birth a baby? Even carry it? I did research but it seems like everyone has a different opinion on how they carry and give birth. The best I could come up with was that he was an omega."

"Yes. An omega. They would go into heat at which time they could get pregnant. Their most fertile time. They would carry for roughly 8 to 10 months. Then give birth just like a female would, only they would birth the baby through....."

Tessa cut him off,

"I read it but I still don't believe it. I seriously hope you're not going to tell me that the baby comes out their...."

"Yep."

"I came out my father's...."

"Yep."

"Oh fuck!" Tessa hung her head.

"Yeah, I've always been secretly grateful that I don't have to deal with that."

"You're not an omega?"

"Nope, an alpha.." Jack shifted his eyes over to Tessa, for a second, then back to the road. "Have you shifted? Or can you?"

"I shifted for the first time when I was 12. I shift to wolf. I didn't know that I was only part wolf. I thought I was some kind of freak, that maybe there was a birth defect at play. They never told me what I actually was."

"They were prevented from telling you a lot by the Council. It was for your own safety. They didn't want it out that you were part unicorn and part wolf."

"I know now because it's listed under their names on my birth records, but for years after I first shifted, I thought I was a freak and rarely did it. If I felt the desire to, I would travel for miles to find a secluded place where no one would see me. But I guess that's why I was placed with wolf shifters. I have traits from both my parents, not just one. My fur is black but not thick like a dog's would be. It's thick but kinda reminds me of a horse's fur when they grow their thick winter coats. It's all black, except on my forehead is what looks like a white star."

"Steven was a wolf shifter so it stands to reason since he was the one doing the impregnating that his genes would be the dominant ones. It was still 50/50, but everyone was leaning towards wolf shifter. And I can guarantee you that, if you moved here, you would be welcomed into the pack. You would be treated with respect. You would not be shunned because of what your wolf self looks like."

"Was Daddy part of the local wolf pack? The Unicorn Falls pack?"

"From what John told me once, the Alpha, Luka, approached James and John about Steven becoming a member of the Pack. Steven was so scared, he didn't know what to do. He and Michael had just moved there, they had nothing to their names and had not yet begun to settle in. Alpha Luka didn't push, he left the offer open. Steven was 16 when he joined the Pack, they readily accepted him.

"They are not a strict Pack. They would only ask you to come to the first few meetings to see what goes on and how the Pack works, then take in a couple of runs. After that, if you joined, then you could donate monthly like a lot of us do, or volunteer for their activities and fundraisers then they would be fine with that. Or you could do both, they would be fine with that too."

"How long has the Pack been here?"

"100 years, give or take. A couple of exiled wolf shifters came here seeking protection and shelter. They were gay and lovers, their Pack didn't approve when they came out. Over time, other wolf shifters came, and they started the Unicorn falls Pack. Pack roster now stands at about 100."

"Are you in the Pack?"

"Yeah. Carol and I are active members. My dad, on the other hand, was an active member for awhile but then he just didn't seem to have any interest anymore, didn't care anymore. Mom never did. But that sometimes happens."

"What do you do for the Pack?"

"I'm Lead Enforcer. Will be until I decide to retire. With me being a cop, it only stood to reason. The other Enforcers respond to calls from the Police Dept. when they are needed, which really isn't all that much."

"I never actively went looking for a pack to join. I felt too much like a freak when I shifted. I didn't want anyone to see me. I usually find a secluded place to run."

"I know for a fact that the Unicorn falls Pack would accept you no matter what you look like when you shift."

Tessa cast her eyes down to her lap. That was something to think about. A pack to call her own that wouldn't pass judgement. It sounded just absolutely heavenly. The packs where she lived were strict, and only accepted full wolf shifters. She didn't have much time for the arrogance that they showed towards half breeds. The Unicorn Falls Pack was perfect. A big plus to move here, provided she accomplished her task in solving her family's murder. But even if she didn't, she would consider moving here anyway. It sounded better and better all the time.

"I wish they had been allowed to tell me earlier who my parents were and why I was given up, but I understand why their hands were tied."

"We only wanted you to be safe."

Jack felt a warmth on his hand and looked down to see Tessa's resting hers on his.

"Tell me more, please."

"John kept all his promises to James. They rented out the loft and moved into Greyson House, and things ran well," Jack repeated. "Then James got pregnant the third time."

"The third time? I thought he just had Edward."

"He did." Jack's voice hitched. "He lost two babies prior to that. The first one at two months and the second one at four months. It was devastating both times for them. They didn't think they were going to be able to have a child. Then James got pregnant with Edward. He was so scared that he would lose him too.

"Thankfully there was a doctor in town who studied the care of unicorns, including male pregnancy, so they weren't completely in the dark. The doctor told him to take it easy, to stop working and try to keep the stress out of his life as much as possible. He wasn't really cranky or anything, he just found it hard to do the things he was used to doing with ease. But the fear grew. I had found it odd that the doctor would tell him to quit working altogether and rest a lot. It seemed like there was something they were not telling me. Something they were hiding, but I didn't pry. If they wanted me to know then they would have told me. But I could always see something behind the happiness, something sad. They did eventually tell me when I questioned what the doctor was telling James."

Tessa smiled, "Do you have any pictures of him while pregnant?"

"Oh, hell, no. He would not allow that in any way, shape or form. If he caught us trying to take pictures he would destroy them. He would get savage. He wanted no pictures at all. That was the only thing of it all that made him really bitchy."

"Can't really say I blame him, I don't think I would want any pictures of myself looking like a beached whale.

Jack had to laugh.

"Yeah, I can totally see that, really I can."

When Jack pulled into the parking lot of the Sunset Grove motel in front of the main office, he looked over at

Tessa then back to the glass double doors. Turning off the car, he hesitated.

"What is it?" Tessa asked.

"I don't know. I just get the feeling that neither of us is going to like the information that we find here."

"Who ever said we would? We are here to find as much of the truth as we can, be it good or bad."

"I know." Jack got out of the car, Tessa followed. He held the door for her as they went into the lobby of the main office. Jack looked around and felt like he was going to puke. The walls were four shades of orange starting with the darkest and moving to the lightest from top to bottom.

Even the sparse furniture was a deep orange. The only thing that wasn't was the front desk, made of a dark wood.

"Holy shit, this is cheesy. Look at her uniform," Tessa whispered in Jack's ear. Jack looked the girl up and down. She wore a burnt orange long sleeved blouse with a black knee length pencil skirt with inch wide orange stripes up the sides.

"That poor thing," Jack whispered back, then plastered a smile on his face as he went up to her.

"Excuse me, Miss. We have a reservation for a double room under the name of Raskins."

The girl smiled politely as she looked down at her computer.

"Of course. Ground floor, around back. Room 12." She handed him a card to fill out, along with two keys. She took the card back as Jack took the keys.

"How long will you be staying?"

Jack looked uncertain,

"I'll say three days for now, with the ability to extend if necessary."

She typed the info into her computer.

"Very good. Enjoy your stay. We have breakfast from 6 to 9 in the dining area, then we have lunch and dinner items after 11."

"Thank you."

They went back outside. Jack drove the car around as Tessa walked. Tessa took the keys and held the door for Jack to bring in their bags. Jack sat the bags on one of the beds then looked around. It looked like an average motel room. Two beds, a dresser, and a nightstand in between the two beds. There was also a desk and chair, with a large screen TV above it.

It was painted in muted blues to match the two pictures above the beds, of sailing ships on the open seas. His eyes focused on the paintings and he shook his head.

"Blinded by orange, now seasick. I really would love to know what their interior decorators were thinking when they came up with this scheme."

"I really don't think I want to know," Tessa replied as she headed to the bathroom and closed the door.

He knew it was way too early to be drinking, but he didn't care. The Itchy Parsnip was always open from noon time on. If he ate, he could drink. He was always willing to do both. After his fifth shot of vodka, Adam Doherty started to feel mellow. He picked up his cell phone and stared hard at it. Laying a few bills on the bar he headed out to his car.

"We need to end this." He dialed a number he hadn't dialed in years as he leaned against the hood.

"What?" The harsh voice asked.

"I've got some information that you may not like."

"What?"

"You've heard about Tessa Carstairs and that damn book of hers?"

"I've heard. You'd have to be living under a rock not to. Those kids should have been killed too."

Adam remained silent for a long moment, then let out a huff.

"It wasn't like that was possible. As soon as they were taken out of the house they went into Council custody. But there may be a chance to shut it down before it gets started again. Jack and Tessa are going to NorthRiver. They located Cody and are planning to ask him questions about that day. And before you even ask, no, I did not say a thing to Jack. I've kept my mouth shut, but he's determined to see it through."

"Could end up getting themselves killed. When?"

"They left this morning."

"I'll take care of it on my end, then you can take care of it on yours." The line disconnected. Adam dropped the phone onto the passenger seat as he got into the car. And wiped his sweaty palms on his pant legs. What could he say to that? This was turning into one hell of a shit show and the bodies were going to start piling up again.

When Tessa came back out, Jack had set their bags against the wall by the desk then lay down on the bed closest to the door. His hands were behind his head and his eyes were closed.

"Uncle Jack?" Tessa whispered.

"Yeah?" His eyes remained closed. "Just resting up a bit. That was a long drive."

"How about you rest and I'll ask at the front desk if there are any good take out places around here within walking distance."

Jack pointed to the desk.

"Take the car keys in case there isn't. And make sure the place has chicken. I don't care what's on it or what it's wrapped in, just chicken."

"Okay." Tessa grabbed the keys on her way out. "You want me to lock the door?"

"No." Tessa closed the door quietly on her way out. She walked around to the main office. The girl smiled as she approached.

"Hi again. You wouldn't happen to know if there are any really good take out places close by?"

"Depends on what you're looking for."

Tessa thought for a moment.

"Pizza."

The girl's smile grew big.

"There's an awesome place about a five minute walk from here and they deliver. They'll bring it right to your room. A lot of our guests order from them." She disappeared under the desk and came up with a menu. "We like keeping a few menus around. We send guests their way and they send customers our way."

Tessa accepted the menu.

"Thank you." She went back to the room and slipped in. Jack was lightly snoring. She sat on the other bed and looked over the menu. She dialed the number and waited for the shop to pick up.

"Hello, I would like to place an order. To be delivered to Sunrise Motel, room 12. I would like a personal sized pepperoni pizza and could you add anchovies to that?... You can?.... Thank you. I would also like a personal sized barbecue chicken pizza with extra chicken. And a medium size spicy chicken wings. And two bottles of pop.... a Cola and whatever clear kind you have. And that's all. Okay..... We'll be here. Thank you." She hit disconnect on her phone and looked over at Jack. There was a small smirk on his lips.

"You got something to say?"

"You are your father's child, that's all I'm going to say."

"You are not going to let that go, are you?"

"Nope." Jack opened his eyes to look at her.

Tessa got up and went over to his bed, leaned over and hugged him. He hugged her back.

"I love you, Uncle Jack."

"I love you, too, Tessa."

"Do you want to go over to Cody's apartment after we eat?" she asked.

"Yeah. The sooner we get this done, the better."

Tessa nodded.

"Do you think he will tell us the truth, or tell us anything for that matter?"

"I don't know. He's under no obligation to tell us anything, let alone the truth. And he should know the Council Law regarding unicorns. If he had any part in it, he'll be just as guilty as those who pulled the trigger."

"He'll be subjected to the same punishment as they would be?"

"Yes."

"I wonder, in his mind, if it was worth it all in the end.

What did he get out of it, what was he promised if he was part of it?"

"I don't know. Money, most likely. That seems to be the key factor in a lot of crimes."

At that moment there was a knock at the door. Tessa flew off the bed. "Food!" She opened the door. "Come in." The delivery boy came in and unloaded his delivery bag on the desk.

"I got it, Tessa." Jack asked the boy what the total was. He gave Jack an order slip. Jack looked at it then dug a few bills out of his pocket. He handed the money to the boy with a smile, "Keep the change."

"Thank you." The boy grinned as he left, closing the door behind him.

"Oh, that smells heavenly." They unpacked the meal and ate in silence.

When they had finished eating they both stretched out on their beds.

"That was the best pizza I have had in a long time."

"Me too," Tessa moaned.

They laid there for a few more minutes before Jack sat up.

"You ready?"

"It's now or never."

They got up, locked their door and got in the car. It might have been mid afternoon, but after a feast like that, Jack had no energy. At that moment he truly felt his age.

CHAPTER 11

"SO, IT'S BEEN bugging me. Why is everything so restrictive, if that's the proper word? When it comes to the Carstairs'?" Tessa asked.

"The Carstairs' were the oldest family in Unicorn Valley. They were the first Protectors. They were old blood, nomads, if you want to look at it like that. They were one of three groups that came here with the unicorns. The unicorns met up with them. The three groups were working together to survive. The unicorns told them they were going to a safe place to live far away from hunters. The groups decided to go with them, they protected the unicorns, especially the black breeding males and, in some cases, were able to bond with them. They only took surnames when they finally settled in Unicorn Falls. Of the three groups—the Wheelers, the Archers, and the Carstairs', the Carstairs' are the only ones left. There are other Protectors, offshoots of the original three, but they are not as strong or as powerful. John was the last of the original three groups."

"Were they unicorns as well?"

"No. They were humans."

"Did they come with the unicorns from where they were originally from?" Tessa wanted to know.

"Yes. The herd that founded Unicorn Valley was a very old herd. The origins of where they originally came from have been lost in time. As far as I know. Though if you really were desperate enough to know, you could probably petition the Council to look through their records hall to find out. But from what I heard about that, their records hall is so vast you'd need to leave bread crumbs to find your way back out again. Their origins were not really put into the local history books. But from what I have heard, when they settled by the falls, they were a herd of around one hundred, significantly lower than when they started to move. They were a herd of a thousand but as they moved and time marched on they separated and went their own ways.

"But I do know that they were predominantly white unicorns. The black omega unicorns were rare, and that is why they had Protectors assigned to them. It's like here in the animal kingdom, I guess would be a better way to say. Take deer for example; they are all brown but every now and then you see a white one. Even if both parents are brown, there is some kind of genetic mutation that turns the fur white but does not affect any other part of their bodies. It's illegal to shoot them and some are put in sanctuaries to protect them. Same with the unicorns only in reverse. There were white omegas but the rare black omegas always had a huge price on their heads.

"The human Protectors had the ability to protect their charges. They could weave or cast spells that could shield or repel attackers, they even bonded with their charges so that they could communicate telepathically. I don't know exactly when or how the Protectors came about, but, most likely, it would be in the Council files somewhere.

"Then you had your hunters who, I guess, are everywhere. They hunted unicorns for their hair, horn and parts but went after the black omegas before anything else. They would capture them and force-breed them until they died of exhaustion. The white ones were just used for parts for rituals. Unicorn Falls turned out to be safe as they made their home there. Though all the original unicorns are gone and the ones that came to the Valley for protection are now gone too."

"So, in the beginning, it was a unicorns only town?"

"Yes, in the beginning. Unicorn Valley was, and still is, a self-governing town with very strict rules about outsiders. At first it was only unicorn shifters who were being hunted. Then they allowed other shifters who were being hunted. Very few full humans were allowed unless they were mated to a shifter or a provider that knew. The Protectors set up wards, spells and watchtowers to keep the valley safe and it does work."

"Most of the time?" Tessa blinked questioningly.

"Most of the time. But there have been a lot of advances and new training for the Protectors in the towers. Technology has been incorporated as well and it's very rare now that someone with evil intent can get in. The Protectors in the watchtowers are trained to use wards and spells that blind evil intent so that all they can see is a forest. Not the town. Plus, the Protectors in the towers have sensors around the town perimeters that can feel the heat of anyone coming near. There is a difference in body temperature. The only way to get past that is to be brought in at the two gates. One on either end of the town. But even then a request has to be put in to the Council and thoroughly and rigorously checked before permission is granted, especially if you are human. So, you can see why we're not exactly on the top ten tourist attractions.

"Unless you are a registered card holder such as police or fire department, then you can come and go with that. When you requested to come here, even though you used to live here, I contacted the Council and they looked up my info which shows that I am employed by them, and they assume that I am responsible for you while you are here. They give two weeks then you leave, unless you decide to move here. Or request a work permit. If you find a job here while visiting or it's the reason for your visit, they grant a month at a time until you have a proper chance to decide if the job is right for you. If it is, then you move here. If you cause any trouble while on a visiting permit then I can be held responsible. Depending on the severity of what you did, I could lose my job or be imprisoned. You would have a spell placed on you so that you would never be able to find Unicorn Valley again.

"Years ago, all you had to do was call the police department, give the reason as to why you were there and they brought you in. The town was more open then. It had slacked off on some of its restrictions. Now access is considerably more restrictive."

"But what about deliveries and mail and things like that? You said they were approved by the council." Tessa asked.

"All are prearranged and approved by the Council. If

there is a change in the driver, the Council has to know about it in advance and then they are escorted in and back out. The companies we deal with are trusted and secure."

"It's too bad it wasn't this tight 30 years ago."

"If it was, it never would've happened, but good comes out of bad even if it isn't fair," Jack muttered with pain in his voice.

CHAPTER 12

CODY'S APARTMENT BUILDING looked like it had seen better days. The beige brick front looked faded. It was surrounded by a broken down metal fence. The gate was open and hanging by one hinge. The walkway was paved to the front stoop but grass and dandelions grew through the cracks.

"Are you sure this is the right address, Uncle Jack?" Tessa asked.

"That's what the intel said. Might be outdated and this place is abandoned. Only one way to find out."

Jack pulled open the glass door that probably hadn't seen glass cleaner in a very long time and let Tessa go ahead of him. The lobby looked a little cleaner with a row of mailboxes on the left and stairs leading up on the right side.

The bottom half of the wall was painted a light beige and the top half a light brown which had faded and was peeling. Jack headed for the stairs with Tessa following.

"How many floors?"

"Just two."

"Thank goodness. I don't trust these steps."

Jack chuckled as he stomped hard up the next few steps. "Nope. Sturdy."

"Probably about the only thing."

They reached the second floor and started down the hallway. The walls were painted the same as the lobby except the floor had dull brown carpeting instead of tile.

"I guess being a cook doesn't pay very well," Tessa mused.

"Not in that two bit dive he's working at. From the little background check I did for fun, that place has been closed down three times in the last six months for health code violations."

"Guess I won't be eating there."

"Not if you don't want to spend the night in the hospital having your stomach pumped." Jack chuckled.

"Gross. So, what is this guy anyway? Full human, shifter or what?"

"According to the intel Tara managed to get for me, he's a coyote shifter. He has no pack. His family refused to belong to one. His mother is Thea Mitchell. More money than she knows what to do with. Husband is dead, apparent mugging. Cody moved out on his own when he was 18 but stayed in close contact with his family. Though he liked to be a loner, I guess he did like to be with his family."

Jack pointed down the hall.

"It's 203."

They stood in front of the dark brown door to Cody's apartment. Jack knocked. When he received no answer he knocked louder. The door across the hall from them opened, they turned quickly.

"You looking for Cody?' The gray haired elderly lady asked.

"Yes," Jack smiled cordially, "Do you know if he's home?"

"No, dear, he's not. He's at work. He was supposed to have today off but he picked up a shift because they were short staffed. They gave him tomorrow off."

Jack dipped his head at her.

"Thank you very much, ma'am. We'll try and catch him there."

"Is he in some kind of trouble? He is such a good boy. Brings me leftovers when he can."

"No, ma'am," Jack assured her. "Just wanted to ask him some questions about something that recently popped up."

"Okay. I'm sure you'll find him there."

"Thank you, ma'am," Tessa murmured as they left the building.

Jack pulled the car into the diner parking lot.

"You weren't kidding. This place looks like an ad for food poisoning."

Jack snorted. The outside looked like it had stepped out of the fifties and been left to rot. The main door was in the middle with five windows on each side. The roof was a faded red and looked like an upside down rectangular plate. The rest of the building was painted white and looked dirty.

The parking lot was butted right up in front so they didn't have to walk far, but what little space was between the two only held dead weeds.

"Not much of a landscaper," Tessa snarked. Jack could only snort. They got out of the car and went inside. The smell of grease was the first thing that hit them.

"Gross," Tessa whispered in his ear. "That grease smells like it hasn't been changed in years."

"Probably hasn't."

They looked around as they made their way to the counter. There was a row of eight seats in front of the counter and about a dozen tables in the dining area. The kitchen was in back behind the counter. It seemed quite busy for mid-morning. They took seats and waited for the waitress to come over.

She was a petite blond who looked like she would rather be anywhere but there.

"What can I get you folks?" she asked sweetly.

"Do you have a Cody Mitchell working here? We were told he was a cook."

"Yeah, he's working today."

"Could you tell him we'd like to see him. We have a few questions we'd like to ask him."

"Sure. May I ask names?"

"Jack Raskins and Tessa Carstairs."

She moved away and went through a door leading to the kitchen.

Cody Miltchell leaned over the grill, pushing the patties lightly with a spatula. He was 5'7 with a thin build. He used to enjoy going to the gym to keep himself decently fit but since it had suddenly gone out of business, he didn't bother trying to find a new one. Right now the only thing he cared about was making enough to be able to afford that flea infested dump he called an apartment. He really wished he had been able to stay in

Unicorn Valley. He could have found a lot of better paying jobs but that was just not an option. When he had come to NorthRiver he thought he could live high on the hog for a while, and pick and choose what job he wanted. But it seemed that working at The Lizard's Lounge came with a black mark. With John Carstairs dead there was no one to give him a reference, no one to call about his job performance and not enough years experience.

People here were not willing to give him the chance that John had. He took what he could get until he ended up at this greasy spoon and this was where he had stayed.

He looked up as the waitress came back into the kitchen.

"What's wrong? Something get screwed up?" But when he saw her empty hands, he looked perplexed.

"No, nothing. The orders are fine but there are a couple of people that want to talk to you."

Cody's heart skipped a beat.

"Who?"

"An older man and a young woman. Jack Raskins and Tessa Carstairs."

Cody's face paled.

"Fuck!"

She took a step closer.

"Are you okay?"

"Yeah, just my past is coming back to haunt me and kick my ass. Tell them I'll talk to them on my break in about 10 minutes."

"All right." She left the kitchen.

Cody watched to make sure she was gone then went to the back office. He knew the manager always left the office door open for them if they needed to use the phone. Cody slipped in and closed the door. He picked up the phone and dialed a number he hadn't used in years. It was picked up on the third ring.

"What?"

"Shit is about to be stirred up again."

"How?"

"Raskins is here wanting to talk to me. The Carstairs woman is with him."

"Yeah, I know. Adam already called to let me know they were on their way to you. Those fuckers move fast, either that, or Adam delayed in telling me. Doesn't matter, you know now. Just tell them what they need to hear, fill them full of shit. Make it up if you have to, but leave our details out of it."

"But I thought you wanted the Carstairs baby? You always claimed it was valuable."

"It was valuable 30 years ago."

"Why isn't it valuable now?" Cody felt like an idiot for asking.

"Because now that she's surfaced and put herself out there I've had a spy watching her the last couple of months, especially during the full moon, to see if she would shift. She can't shift or was never taught to. If she could or had been taught she would have within those two months but never did. Not that my spies ever saw. If she could shift into a unicorn, yeah, she would still be valuable. If she could shift into a wolf and had unicorn markings, yeah, she would still be valuable but from what my sources found out she can't do either. It was one of the reasons we delayed. If we could have gotten ahold of that child, depending on what she could have shifted into she could have made me millions. But if she is unable to shift into anything then she's useless, nitwit." The line went dead.

Cody hung up and left the office suddenly full of doubt. Was that a smart move? Should he really have just done that? There was no statute of limitations on murder and while he had not actually fired a gun, he had been there. He was an accessory, that was just as bad. In the eyes of the Unicorn Valley Council, he might as well have pulled the trigger. Going back to Unicorn Valley would be an automatic death sentence.

CHAPTER 13

After a few minutes the waitress came back out. "He'll be going on his break in about ten minutes. Can you wait till then? We're busy and short staffed. He'll have someone to take over for him then."

"No problem. I'll have a black coffee and a..."

"Whatever clear pop you have," Tessa supplied.

Jack's heart jumped and slammed into his chest. She sounded so much like James when he was a kid. Michael had been the same. Anytime they went to restaurants, when asked what he wanted to drink he would get clear pop. The only time he was really allowed to have it.

The waitress smiled and left. When she came back she set a cup of coffee in front of Jack and a glass of iced pop in front of Tessa. Jack gave her a couple of bills and she left to wait on other customers at the other end of the counter.

They had finished their drinks when Cody came out of the kitchen, wiping his hands on his apron.

"You wanted to see me?"

"Yes. Any place we can talk privately?"

"Sure." He motioned them to follow him outside to the alley where a few beat up chairs and a table sat. "We take breaks out here when it's warm to get away from the noise."

They all took seats.

"What do you need from me?"

"I'll assume she told you our names?"

"Yes."

"Do I look familiar to you?"

Cody studied Jack carefully.

"Yeah, I guess. You were sheriff."

"30 Years ago. I'm Chief of Police now but 30 years ago I was sheriff."

Cody swallowed hard at the mention of 30 years ago.

"What do you want?" He pulled a pack of cigarettes out of his pocket, taking one out with shaky hands, he lit it up.

"You worked at the Lizard's Lounge? As assistant manager?"

"Yeah." Cody took a deep drag off the cigarette. "I was hired as bartender but when Michael Carstairs decided he wasn't coming in anymore and spent all his time in the studio with James Carstairs it left John short a person with a brain. Not that we didn't see it coming.

"John told me there was a good chance the position would become permanent, because once Michael had his kid, John figured that he would divide his time between being a stay at home parent and possibly staying at the studio with James since they loved it so much. The only reason Michael stayed at the Lounge instead of being at the Studio was that John seriously needed someone that was excellent with numbers and Michael was more than perfect, but it didn't take a genius to see that his heart wasn't in it. Michael told John on numerous occasions that he wanted to be at the Studio but wouldn't leave John short handed. Some even turned into arguments. John felt like he was being deserted by his family. It ticked him off in a way, too."

"How so?" Jack looked curious.

"They had been looking at plots of land to buy if they could get a loan. They wanted to get a distillery going and make their own version of those flavored vodkas. Raspe` they were going to call it. Raspberry flavored. Sounded sick to me."

"It fell through?" Tessa asked.

"Yeah, they never went ahead with it. Too much on their plates. John talked a lot when he got a few drinks in him over the course of a day. And when he would get some booze into him he would talk. That's also when some of the arguments between him and Michael got loud."

"You heard their arguments?" Tessa asked.

"Who didn't? There were times John would storm out to the bar for a drink and Michael would be right behind him."

"I didn't think John drank. I mean, I knew he drank beer but nothing stronger," Jack mused.

"He was a closet drinker of the hard stuff to you all but, yeah, he was an alcoholic. Wouldn't be uncommon for him to go to the back room, grab a 40oz and see it magically appear in the trash a few days later. The more he drank some days, the yappier he got. Usually he'd hang out at the bar and we'd get an earful."

"You fed his habit to get info out of him?" Tessa couldn't believe what she was hearing.

"Hell, no, he did that all on his own. We'd try to cut him off but he'd just go out back and grab a bottle."

"I can't believe John was a drinker." Jack had a shocked look on his face.

"Believe it. If Yadira was alive, she'd tell you the same thing when she would tend bar. You couldn't reason with him, either, so we just let it be. He was never like that until he found out Michael was pregnant. Why that mattered I do not know. But in all honesty, John had too much on his plate and his parents being gone was hard on him. John's parents would not get to see the baby. But there was something else, something in his past that he seemed to remember, but just when you think he would tell you he'd clam up good and tight."

Jack and Tessa looked at each other.

"Their parents," they said in unison.

"I can just bet, the pain of the deaths of Steven's and Michael's parents came back when he found out Michael was pregnant. They would never get to see their grandchild. And he started once again blaming himself for their deaths," Jack remarked.

Cody nodded his head thoughtfully.

"Seems to me, I think I heard a snippet of an argument where the word 'grandchild' was used."

"How much of Michael did you see after you were hired?" Jack asked.

"Never saw him much before or after I was hired. Only when the arguments came out into the bar. Heard a lot from behind the closed office door though. I usually worked late afternoons to evenings or till closing. He would usually leave at 5. Though there were times he did stay late and would get something to eat from the kitchen. I don't know why he stayed late those nights but you didn't dare talk to him lest you wanted an earful of curse words explaining how it was none of your business."

"Of all the employees that were hired at the Lounge and Studio, you were the only one who left town after the murders. Did it affect you that badly?"

"No."

"How did you get the money to move here? I know what John paid his workers well and for that short amount of time you were there..."

Cody sighed and cut him off.

"I guess it doesn't matter now. I was paid to leave."

"Paid to leave? Why? And by who?"

Cody turned to look Jack square in the face.

"Bennett Raskins. Your father."

Jack's face went red.

"Are you fucking lying to me? Dad would never do that! He wasn't dirty or on the take or anything." But even as the words left Jack's mouth, he knew there was truth there.

"Bennett was as dirty as they come. Him and that other cop that worked with him. The hunters paid them a shitload to set it all up. He paid me to keep an eye on Michael and James to see what their routines were. Then Bennett paid me a small fortune to keep my mouth shut and leave town.

"They wanted pure unicorn parts and James and Michael were it. The money was more than I had seen in my entire life. And since you figured me out, then you know who my parents are. So, yeah, I know what you're thinking since I came from a rich family. The only thing I got from my parents was shit when I refused to follow in their footsteps. Do the family business." Cody let tears streak his face.

Tessa flew to her feet.

"You had my family slaughtered for money!!" She practically screamed at him.

"The plan had been to capture James and Michael, give them drugs that would force them to shift and...." Cody let his voice trail off. He swallowed hard. "The baby would have been an extra bonus once he had it..." He swallowed hard again before taking an exceedingly long pull off his cigarette. "I made the mistake of asking what plans they had for the others. I put my foot in it. They knew they were unicorns and omegas. But what they didn't really know was that James was black furred and could be used for breeding more using another unicorn or horse shifter. They hadn't done their homework and I started babbling with the hopes of scraping more money out of them. The only reason I knew was some well placed questions to my coworkers. Fuck I was so stupid and they all died because of me."

"Okay." Jack scrubbed his hands over his face. Tessa was seething and rightfully so. "Let's start at the beginning. When did these hunters contact you, and why you?"

"I don't know why they contacted me but I'm pretty sure I was the only one because no alarms were raised. No alerts put out. The Protectors should have been notified immediately if they were asking more than just me. John never got any notification as far as I knew. Back then it was easy to get into town and spin a story. I had a hard time finding work because I had just arrived in town. I had put in a request to the police station. Told them I was a coyote shifter on my own for the first time and scared. That I was looking for a safe place and a job. I had a hard time finding work since I was new in town. I wasn't that long out of high school so I didn't have any experience of any kind at anything. I puttered around at different things when someone would give me a chance but I really wanted to work at the Lounge because I had heard from employees how great the tips were and a month's pay would cover rent and food."

Jack nodded thoughtfully. "John was a good man, all you had to do was explain your situation to him and he would do what he could to help."

"Entry level pay was decent. It paid rent and gave me food money. I was allowed to take home leftovers at the end of the night and it was within walking distance, though sometimes someone would give me a lift if they had an empty seat."

"You said you started out as a bartender then went to assistant manager. How did you do that so fast? And then to betray him like that," Tessa growled out as she glared at Cody.

"I didn't start out to betray him or anyone," Cody hissed but let his voice go back to normal. "John said I was a whiz at remembering things. I was sharp with numbers. I did the tills at shift change and he noticed how fast and accurately I could do them. I was quick to catch mistakes. He even called me in a couple of times to help with accounting. When Michael got to the point that he couldn't handle working at the Lounge anymore, he quit to go work with James at the Studio."

Tessa interrupted.

"So, how would working at the Studio be easier than at the Lounge when he was pregnant?"

"Because he liked it so much better. He loved the work, he hated sitting and dealing with numbers all day and crap like that. He only started at the Lounge because John's accountant left him high and dry. So he asked Michael to help out till he could find someone else, but that someone else was never hired because John liked the way Michael worked. As I said, there were more than a few arguments on the subject, a lot dealing with that exact question. But it left John short-handed, he had hoped that John would have found someone by the time he left. But John put off things and had no one. It was a week later when John saw me balancing the tills and asked me to help with accounting. Next thing I knew he hired me as assistant manager. Better hours and better pay.

"When I was contacted by the hunters I had been in that position for a couple of months, though I had been working at the Lounge as a bartender for almost a year. The pay raise as assistant manager had been nice, but I was a greedy bastard, I was not going to turn down the money they offered. I know it's not an excuse but I really did not know what they were planning to do at first. I was just told what to do on a need to know basis. I think they may have had someone inside keeping an eye on employees who came and went, so they would know who was really loyal. They might have targeted me as I was always trying to get extra money any way I could and they figured they could buy me. All they wanted me to do at first was to track them."

"Track them?" Tessa asked.

"Yeah, see where James and Michael spent most of their time and when they were alone. I was given a number to call and the person on the other end took my info. I assumed it was the other cop that was in on it. Day and night. When Michael got close to delivering, he holed up inside Greyson House. They thought that was perfect. Thing was they really had no use for Steven or John."

"But Eddie was a unicorn baby, why didn't they consider him?" Jack asked.

"Because Edward was not a pure blood unicorn. He couldn't shift. That drops the value to practically nothing because if he couldn't shift they couldn't get what they wanted, so he was useless. John was a Protector, nothing about them are valuable. They are essentially humans with a particular brand of magic. Steven was a wolf, he was valuable but the only thing they could have gotten money out of him was his pelt but not the big bucks they were after. They figured if I watched long enough then they could get Michael and James alone long enough to take them. I think, in a way, I knew what was going to happen but I really didn't want to believe it."

"What were their plans for the baby?"

"I don't know. They never really said. I assumed they would take the child and raise it or just leave it behind, I don't know. It would have been part unicorn and part wolf. I thought….fuck that…I didn't know what I thought. I was insane with greed. I've lived with that guilt for 30 years. It's eaten me raw."

"Were you there?" Tessa snarled.

Cody buried his face in his hands, his breathing heaved like he was about to vomit.

"I went there to make sure that James and Michael were at the house alone. I had no idea that Michael had gone into labor, and that John, Steven and Edward were there; Edward having just gotten home from school. Michael, I assumed, had called John, because he had come home. Steven was already home, there was no getting him out of the house. I never saw Edward or the baby. I found out later they had been hidden away. Where, I didn't know and I wasn't going to ask, but Bennett was already there so I assumed he told them to hide them."

"Was the birthing doctor there? One was supposed to be called the minute labor was detected."

"Yes, she was there, for a while."

"Who?" Tessa wanted to know.

"There were no records of anyone leaving the hospital or of an ambulance being put on standby in case of a delivery emergency. It's hospital policy to sign in and out and record if an ambulance may be needed," Jack pointed out.

"I knew who she was. Her name was Dani Haley. Why there are no hospital records I have no clue. I only knew her because she came around the Lounge a lot on the weekends, came alone but generally left with someone, even me a time or two.

"She was Dr. Shea's assistant. She was letting her mouth run one night more than she usually did and told me that if Dr. Shea was unavailable to deliver Michael's baby then she was okayed to go."

"Why did Dr. Shea think she might not be able to assist when Michael went into labor?" Tessa asked.

"Dr. Shea was skilled in more fields than just dealing with unicorn home births and knew that Michael was very close to delivering when she went over to check on him a few days prior. That's when she discussed having Dani as her stand in. She had three c-sections scheduled that week. As long as there was someone there who was qualified and approved by the patient it wouldn't be anything to get the Council's knickers in a knot."

"What happened to her?"

"Probably dead. They didn't want any leaks.. She left that day but I can bet she never saw the sun set."

Tessa let out a screech and dug her hands into her head. Jack's throat, suddenly, went dry.

"Who else was there other than Dad? When did you get there?"

Cody lifted his head to look at Jack.

"I was there before him, watching the house. I saw Dani get there and I saw Edward get off the bus. Then I saw Chief Raskins arrive and I wondered what the hell he was doing so I followed him in. I didn't know what I thought I was going to do. I stayed just out of sight at the top of the stairs."

Tessa's face was pale.

"What was Chief Raskins doing?"

"He was telling Dani to get the hell out of there if she wanted to live. She tore out of there as fast as she could. There was someone else in the car with Bennett, most likely the other rat. I stayed out of his sight as well. I couldn't really make out who it was but I have my suspicions that it was his right hand man. He probably saw her come out and nabbed her. I didn't see any sign of Edward and the baby so I assumed that he had just gotten them hidden."

"Dad knew what was going down?"

"Yes, Jack, I'm sorry, he was in on it but he had a change of heart when he saw that baby. But it was too late. They got Edward and the baby snuggled away safely just in time.

"Bennett asked John to get his gun. John got his Glock 17 out of the gun case that was in the darkroom. The basement door upstairs swung out so I hid behind it when I heard the dirty rat coming, he made it down partway but got shot for his efforts. He tore out of there as fast as he could. But it didn't do any good, it was too late. They were coming down the stairs. I had to know what they had planned so I followed them down. It wouldn't have done John any good anyway even if he tried aiming for them, as soon as they were off the last step they shot him and Steven first."

Cody quickly got up and ran for a dumpster, sticking his head in, he vomited violently. When he came back, he caught his breath and lit another cigarette, hoping to calm himself. After a couple of shaky drags, he looked sideways at Jack knowing what the reaction would be when the next words came out of his mouth.

"They had syringes in their hands and started to move toward Michael and James.

I didn't know what was in the syringes, sedatives or force shift drugs or both, I don't know. Jack, your father shot and killed James and Michael, then covered it up. He let the hunters go."

"Why?" Jack bellowed in a strangled voice, "Why the fucking hell did he kill them and not the hunters?"

"He let them go so our bodies wouldn't end up in the pile on the basement floor. There were two of them and even if Bennett managed to kill one, the other would have killed him and me before Bennett ever managed to squeeze off another shot."

Tessa shook her head, clearly frustrated and in tears.

"So, why didn't they shoot Bennett for killing James and Michael and robbing them of their prizes. And if John was a Protector why didn't he send out a mental alert to the other Protectors?"

"He did. I saw his eyes when he did it. They saw it too

and knew it. Have you ever seen a Protector send out a mental alert? I had read about it but never actually saw it until that day."

Tessa shook her head, "no."

"Their eyes flash from lavender to black then back to lavender. Once they saw that, they knew their escape window would start closing fast. They needed Bennett alive to get them out of Unicorn Valley in one piece and they didn't have time to waste.

"Jack, I'm sorry, I hate saying this to you because John talked about you often. He showed me, one time, the picture of you as a kid in a singing contest you won. Said you had the best set of pipes his dad had ever heard but said you loved and respected your father so much that you shut down that part of your life to be a cop. His father was so disappointed because he believed you would have made it big time. That you have even sold a couple of the songs you wrote. He was on one of his reminiscing streaks that night.

"But your dad enjoyed living the easy life, and the money they gave him for letting them into Unicorn Valley was more than he would ever need in a lifetime. You may have seen your dad as a good and honorable man, but he was as black as they came. I saw every ounce of evil he exuded when he put bullets in those men."

"Though if you want to flip the coin over, he told me that he did it to save them from being brutally tortured before being killed anyway. We got out of that house as fast as we all could when we heard the sirens from your truck. Didn't you ever wonder how he got there so fast?"

Jack didn't know what to say, he was shaky and cold. He felt numb. He felt like any minute he would have to make a visit to the dumpster as well.

"You do realize that we'll have to take you back with us?" Jack finally managed to choke out.

"I guess I kinda knew that. I knew that the past had come back to haunt me when Camry came back and said you wanted to ask me some questions.

"If you knew, why didn't you run?"

"What would have been the point now? After 30 years?"

"Why didn't you come back and tell the truth? Set the record straight."

"I never would have made it into town limits, your Dad would have killed me. If I wanted to stay alive I had to leave. Your father paid me a crap load to shut up and get out of town. I got what I was due from the hunters and left. I was warned that if I ever came back to Unicorn Valley it would be a death sentence one way or another. I gladly took it all, left town and never looked back.

"Though I had thought about it, but as long as your Dad was alive I didn't dare. I would have been planted in the woods somewhere and the truth would still never have been known. I thought about it again when I found out your father died. Then I got a note under my door a few days later, saying that if I went back I would never live to get on the bus. So I had to let it die."

Tessa suddenly looked nervous.

"Do you think they are still watching you?"

"I don't know. Unless they somehow found out that you were coming here, I doubt it. You didn't tell anyone in town that you were coming here, did you?" His eyes flitted back and forth like he was holding something back, not quite telling the truth.

"When I did my interview I suggested that I was going back to Unicorn Valley but nothing about coming here. This is totally off the record. I didn't even know about you until yesterday."

"But it still puts it out there that there is interest again, which could draw attention. The only ones that know in the department are Dale and Adam," Jack murmured.

"Adam? That wouldn't, by any chance, be Adam Doherty?" Cody questioned.

"Yeah, why?"

"Because, by telling him, you just screwed the pooch. He was, or should I say, is your dirty rat."

"What the hell do you mean by that?"

"Adam was Bennett's right hand man. He paid off all of Adam's debt and bookies and, in return, Adam did whatever Bennett told him. So, if you told him, and I go back to the Valley with you, we could all find ourselves planted in the woods somewhere."

"I knew it!" Jack practically screamed. "I fucking knew it! I knew my gut wasn't lying to me. And don't ask me to explain it. I thought it was wrong for me to start suspecting my friends and fellow officers but when I saw those reports missing and the last one up there had been Adam...."

"Wouldn't surprise me a bit. I thought I was a greedy bastard. He'd find a way to suck his own dick if it meant netting him a cool million or more."

"Was he in on the killings?"

"Yeah, more than likely. Though I never saw him much. He was probably in the background helping Bennett set things up. He did call me a couple of times to set up meetings for me and Bennett, but nothing more. And I assume he was the one I reported to while I was doing my spying."

Jack shook his head.

"I just can't fucking believe it."

Cody glanced down at his watch.

"I seriously have to get back to work. I'm off tomorrow, come by my apartment around 9. We can discuss more then. And, no, I have no intentions of running. I'm tired of it and I'm done. I often wondered if this day would ever come. I think in a lot of ways I'm glad it has come."

"Just a couple more questions?" Cody looked at Jack with a slight trace of paranoia in his eyes.

"Do you know the names of the hunters who contacted you? Who paid you?"

Cody hesitated for a few seconds.

"No, they never told me. The dealings were all done with numbers."

"And why did they send you to Barbados? And did you know that they got you in a few of their pictures?"

"I was sent there to observe."

"Why?" Tessa looked at him with a confused expression.

"I had told Bennett that I had asked John for a few days off and that I wouldn't be around to do his spying. I think even back then I was having a change of heart, but not so much that I was giving up the cash flow. So he said that if I wanted a few days off he'd send me down to Barbados. I could have some fun in the sun while watching them."

"But I still don't see why he wanted them watched."

"If I knew the answer to that, honey, I would tell you. And I figured I got into a few of their pictures, I got too close. I know they never noticed me. I got out of the photographic line of fire as fast as I could. Told Bennett there was a chance I was in a few of the pictures. He said he'd find a way to find out but I guess it never did happen."

CHAPTER 14

CODY GOT UP and went back inside, leaving Jack and Tessa alone. Once Cody was out of sight, Jack looked at her. Tessa got up and started towards the car.

"But what I can't seem to understand is that if they took that trip when Michael was five months, why wait so long to develop the film? Why was it never developed?"

"I don't know. Time might have gotten away from him, I guess. Only thing I know for sure was that it was not in the crime scene photos, yet you found it on the table. Deep in my gut there is something at work that wants this finished."

Jack and Tessa sat in the car for a few minutes, lost in their own thoughts. He started the car and pulled out of the parking lot into traffic, which seemed to be light for the time of day. After a few minutes, Jack gave Tessa a side glance before looking back to the road. She was looking at him intently, wondering if he would say anything and what it would be when or if he did.

"I still remember the day that Steven and Michael came to live with James and John. They were 10 and 12 and scared to death. Michael's mom had been hired to work as a waitress at the Lounge. Steven's dad worked at the Studio. If I remember right, Michael's dad wanted to get hired on at a firm in the Valley. But I think they have long since gone out of business.

"They had been with the Studio and Lounge for about a month coming and going on a workers card with John and James as sponsors since they were working for them, when they decided to move to Unicorn Valley, I think. They had an appointment to meet with the Council to finalize their request to move to Unicorn Valley permanently. They had houses picked out, and everything was good to go, but they all had to be there. The boys had school that day, otherwise they would have been in the car as well.

"What they hadn't planned on was the asshole drunk driver that ran the red light trying to escape us. He slammed into the side of their car so fast and hard that he drove both vehicles through the guard rail and over the embankment out by Shell Creek. They all died including that fucker. I wish he had lived, then I could've personally killed him myself. I called James and John from the accident scene to let them know. I knew they had kids but had never met them.

"I felt so bad for John. He had serious guilt. He blamed himself as if he had killed them. He had told them to go that way, it was a short cut. It was quick and would save a little time. The boys were put into an orphanage until the next of kin could be notified and arrangements made for whoever wanted to adopt them.

"I never told James or John, but after I talked to Dad, he

went to the Council. As it turned out, most of the relatives were elderly and didn't want to raise any more kids. I remember John got so guilt ridden he called their lawyer, and with the Council's help, they got the kids adopted. The Council and the lawyer made all the proper connections and made sure all the proper agencies were contacted.

"And since John was a certified Protector in the Council's employ, things were expedited, so the children didn't have to spend any more time in the orphanage than they already had. Especially since Michael was a unicorn foal and Steven was a wolf pup. They were wide open there.

"Once the Council took care of all the paperwork and contacts, and the lawyer took care of the legal stuff, I took them to Greyson House. Michael was skittish as a cat, I thought he would bolt. Steven was fascinated when he saw James on the couch feeding Eddie, who might've been a week old. Steven looked over at them, then up at me, and I said to go ahead. James smiled at him and told him to come over. Steven went over and looked at Eddie. Eddie, whose eyes never roved away from James while he was feeding, shifted then to look at Steven. Steven's face lit up. 'What beautiful eyes. He's looking at me.'

"John spoke up from the kitchen, 'That's the traditional eye color of a Protector.'

"'Do you want to hold him when he's done?' James had asked. 'Yes, please.' Stephen sat down beside him and Eddie never took his eyes off him. I guess that made Michael relax, as he came over to look, too. John got them some hot chocolate and cookies, which they munched while they watched Eddie take his bottle. I took John aside, his eyes were so haunted. I told him it was not his fault, but it took a long time for that to sink in. But those boys couldn't have been in better hands.

"Once all the paperwork was settled, wills and funerals dealt with, Greyson House was the boys' new home. Steven loved taking care of Eddie and once Michael found out that James was a photographer, they bonded instantly. It was incredible how fast they became a tight knit family. And you know, those boys knew that I had been chasing that asshole and that I had been at the accident scene. I didn't want to tell them that when I had to tell them that their folks were dead, but it just spilled out. But they never held any malice towards me.

"They grieved and they cried but never laid any blame that I wasn't able to save their parents. Those boys were very special young men. I became their Uncle Jack, they came to love me as much as they did James and John. I was sort of like their godfather. And I think a lot of it was that they knew I had children of my own but they were distant from me."

"Distant?" Tessa looked at Jack curiously.

A small grin crossed Jack's lips.

"Who tells all their friends that their old man is a cop when they're smuggling porn magazines back and forth or trying weed for the first time. Tucker and Haley were just a couple years older than Stephen and Michael, but they acted like they were a lot older than that."

When they arrived back at their motel room, Tessa ordered more pizza and chicken wings. Jack was not about to complain. They ate in relative silence until she looked up from her pizza. She felt tired, upset and furious.

"He's lying."

Jack paused in mid swig of his pop. He lowered the bottle.

"What do you mean?"

"How could Cody have walked out of there knowing what he knew, after seeing what he did? Even though he was in on it, he didn't have to go into the house, but he did. If you were a murderer and saw me watching you kill people, what would be the odds that you would let me live?"

"Slim to none. I would kill you and add your body to the pile."

"So, why didn't they? I can understand letting your father live, he was their ticket out of there, out of the Valley. It smells."

Tessa put her paper plate down on the desk and flopped back onto her bed. Jack took a long pull off his bottle.

"And the birthing nurse; Bennett told her to get out if she wanted to live. If they were close behind Bennett, did they kill her there or somewhere else and bury her body? Or was he lying about that, too?"

"I don't know. Somehow I don't think so." Jack's face twitched like he was trying to recall a memory that was eluding him. Something just out of reach. Taking another drink, his hand tightened on the bottle so tight Tessa was afraid it would break in his hand.

"She's dead."

"I think that has been established."

Jack shook his head as he set down the bottle.

"If Dad was there before them and gave her a way out, they would let her go rather than risk shooting her in the front yard, assuming that's the way she left and the way they came in, but there would be no place she could hide. They must have tracked her, knocked her out and hid her until they were ready to dispose of her, because as far as I know she never made a report to the police. And if they had no face coverings they would know she could describe them. There might have been a missing persons report that went out, but I can't remember."

Jack got up and walked to the window by the door and looked out.

"I think it might have been about 5 years ago, maybe 7. I'm not sure now, but a couple of teenagers were down by Shell Creek Pool. Shell Creek runs shallow until it turns into a deep spot. It literally looks like a pool. Kids dammed it up so they could have a place to swim. Been like that since I was a kid. Anyway, the ground must have eroded away enough there to expose a skeleton. We logged it as a missing person/ cold case.

"When I got the ME report, he concluded that it was a woman and she had been murdered. No clothes, wallet, purse or anything. Her neck had been broken so no bullets had been found. Her teeth, hands and feet had been removed, so no identification could be made. At first we thought it might have been animals that had a snack with the hands and feet but the ME stated that the hands and feet had been sawed off and the teeth pulled."

"Were the teeth found anywhere around?"

"No, so dental records could not be used. Very thorough. Wanted to make sure no identification could be made if the body was found before decomposition was complete."

"Oh God, I hope it was after they killed her. How can anyone be so evil?"

Jack frowned.

"I'm betting my pension it was Dani Haley."

"Fuck!"

Jack scrubbed his hands over his face and heaved a heavy sigh.

"This is really hard for you, isn't it?" Tessa asked.

"The memories that are being stirred up are quite painful, still feel fresh."

Tessa put her hand on Jack's arm.

"I'm sorry."

Jack shook his head, his mind going off on another painful tangent.

"I can't believe that Dad would be involved. Dad was not that kind of person." Jack paced the length of the motel room. "He was a firm believer in upholding the law. He instilled those values in me. Why? If he didn't hold his standards up so high then why did he make me hold them so high?"

Tessa sat on the desk chair, reaching out to grab his hand to stop his pacing.

"I know it's a horrible thing, Uncle Jack, but people do evil things for money and hide behind perfect masks."

"I know, but.... My Dad."

"Uncle Jack." She gripped his hand and pulled him down so he knelt in front of her. "We have to look at this from all angles, including this one. I know it's going to add more pain to what you're already feeling, but we cannot overlook it. We can't afford to overlook anything."

"Hopefully Cody will give us a little more information. There is more that he's not telling us, I'm sure of it. Like, how did he know Dad was in on it? Why is he saying that? I think he is in on it more than he's letting on."

"That's what we need to find out and hopefully he'll tell us everything we need to know. Something is screwy, there's got to be more. And he seems willing to come back with us. I think if it was me and I'd had threats not to come back I think I wouldn't necessarily be so ready to agree to come back."

"Me neither. Just because there has been silence since the last note doesn't mean that they aren't still watching."

Jack got up and laid back down on his bed raking his hands through his hair. "This is provided they are all still alive."

"I can't see why they wouldn't be. But I can't see them being vigilant anymore. 30 years have passed, why would anyone be interested anymore, the case was considered closed but unsolved. All interest should have died."

"Yeah, but there is no statute of limitations on murder. If they are still alive then they need to be brought to justice. And Unicorn Valley justice for murdering unicorns has only one conclusion; execution. It's just going to be a matter of time."

"But what if we don't find them?" Tessa whispered.

"We have to. We have to this time round. We can't fail."

Cody had just come back from dropping off leftovers to Mrs. Gleason when he heard a knock on the door. He had been late getting in, but he was glad that she had stayed up waiting for him. That way he could give her the leftovers, knowing there would be something in the house for her to snack on when she didn't feel like cooking. He stared at the door for a long minute as he draped his jacket over the back of the couch. He felt ice form in the pit of his stomach. He knew who was on the other side of that door without even looking.

Swallowing hard, he walked over to the door and yanked

it open. An older woman stood there with a younger man at her side.

"We need to talk, you disobedient brat."

"Then get your fucking asses in here before the neighbors see you," Cody snapped with a bravado he did not feel.

They walked past him and into the apartment.

"Is that any way to talk to your mother?"

Cody shut the door quickly behind them.

"What the hell do you want?"

"What did you tell the cop?" the man snapped.

"Nothing that's going to implicate mom, douchebag. I told them there were two hunters, not one. I'm not that stupid. It's my neck on the line. I never gave descriptions and just made a passing remark about incompetence and pinned most of it on Bennett. Rather convenient that he isn't alive anymore to defend himself. And even when they take me back I still won't tell them anything. Though I did rat out Adam."

"That's all it better be, you little shit." Thea suddenly snapped her head to an angle to stare at him hard. "Wait, you did what? Why in the hell did you do that? We may still need him, you idiot."

Cody just shrugged his shoulders.

"Better him than you, isn't it?"

The fist that connected with Cody's jaw was fast and hard.

"You are so fucking dead, big brother."

His mother reached out and lightly laid her hand on the man's shoulder.

"Easy, Milo. Now, what was that you said about going back?"

"They want me to go back. I told them I would, I'll feed them more shit and then come back here. No biggie."

"What about the stuff?"

"No way anyone's going to get their hands on it now."

"What do you mean?" His mother snarled at him.

"I kept it in my gym locker with all my crap. Who would think of looking for it there? The place went out of business a couple years ago without advance warning, so no one had a chance to get their stuff. I imagine it's all still there unless someone is willing to break in. It's not going anywhere."

"How can you be so sure of that?" Milo shoved Cody backwards.

"Because, little bro, I have been keeping an ear out. I have a scanner in the bedroom tuned into the police department. No one has tried to break in there and even if they did I can't see them wasting any time breaking open lockers and going through them hoping to find valuables." Cody pushed back.

His mother's hand lashed out, striking hard and fast across Cody's cheek.

"Don't get smart, you little bastard. There is no way in hell that I'm going down after all these years. You're going under the bus first."

Jack forced the truck as fast as he dared. He had jumped for joy when John had called him to tell him that Michael had gone into labor. He was still quite a distance away when he pulled over to call John, to see how things were progressing. John told him that Michael was doing good, the pain was tolerable but he was uncomfortable.

"*Is the baby close to coming?*" Jack had asked.

"*Soon,*" John had replied. "*He's eager to make his appearance.*"

"*Fuck! I'm back on the road and should be there soon.*"

Jack huffed out a breath as he put the truck into gear and peeled her back onto the road. He knew it would be his luck to get there just after. Of all the days he had chosen to go backpacking. He was about 10 minutes out when the screams came over his radio.

"*Jack! Shots fired at Greyson House!*"

Jack hit the toggle to reply.

"*What the fuck are you talking about, Connie?*"

"*Neighbors are phoning in that shots have been fired at Greyson House! Get your ass over there!*"

If it had been any other time, Jack would have chastised Connie for her lack of protocol, but right now he didn't care.

"*Get back up over there right now!*"

"*I'm broadcasting this on all open channels. Everyone should be receiving this. Jack, you're the closest.*"

Sweat broke out on Jack's forehead as he gunned the engine. What the fuck was going on? He pulled up in front of Greyson house and sprinted up the walk to the front door. It stood open. Jack drew his gun.

"*John! James!*" He went in cautiously. The house was still and quiet. He gave the first floor a cursory glance. The patio doors were open as well. Jack took a quick glance out. The back gate was open. Turning, he headed for the basement stairs. The upper door was open. He slowly crept down the stairs, keeping his gun at arm's length ahead of him. Something wasn't right, it was too quiet for someone who was giving birth.

The bottom door was closed. He took a breath and pushed it open. A scream emanated from his throat and his stomach *churned. He turned on his heels and tore back upstairs. He flung himself over the toilet, his gun clattering into the tub as he violently threw up. His body wracked with heaving. He couldn't stop the shaking as he pulled himself up to take the glass from the sink to swish water around in his mouth before spitting it into the sink. He just faintly registered a sound behind him as he flushed the toilet. A strong hand came to rest on his shoulder. He turned to see his father standing behind him, holding his gun out to him. His face was pale and eyes were haunted.*

Jack took his gun and put it in its holster. He tried to speak but Bennett cut him off.

"We're searching the house and grounds. We got here just minutes after you did."

All Jack could do was nod his head. He knew he had put himself in danger by coming in alone and then again by allowing himself to be open and vulnerable when he ran up the stairs to puke. Jack straightened himself up and went with his father back down to the basement. It hadn't changed from the first time he had gone down. His stomach flopped again and he ground his teeth and swallowed hard to keep from vomiting again. Tears welled up in his eyes and he stared at the corner of the basement where Michael had piled blankets to make a nest to give birth. He had wanted to be home rather than at the hospital. Michael lay in the middle of the blankets, completely naked, his chest stained red from two bullet holes. The same was repeated for John, James and Steven.

"Where's Eddie and the baby?" Jack's voice was harsh.

Jack's father touched the toggle on his radio.

"Attention all units. Search the grounds and surrounding area for a 15 year old boy and a newborn infant girl."

After a few minutes the calls came back negative. No trace at all. No trace of anyone. Jack racked his brain.

"Keep searching," Bennett hollered into his radio.

"They have to be here somewhere." Jack's eyes slowly scanned the basement. His mind racing. He needed to do something to keep his eyes from going back to the carnage at his feet.

"Wait...." He went over to the wall that housed the stairs. "Where did he leave it?" He started tipping the pictures on the support wall of the stairs from side to side.

"Jack, you're disturbing a crime scene. You know better than that."

"I know, Dad, but I haven't got much choice. The key is not in its usual spot on top of this picture frame." Jack pointed to a small framed picture of John and his parents. Jack turned his head, the workbench under the window held plant pots and small bags of potting soil. Something silver glinted in the sunlight. He went over and picked up a silver key.

"They were in such a hurry they didn't put it in its usual place but just chucked it on the bench, thinking they would be able to come back or the killers had their back to the bench and never noticed it."

Jack went back to the wall and slid it in an almost invisible lock.

"Dad, get the paramedic down here."

Bennett spoke into his radio as Jack turned the key, the lock clicked and opened slightly. He turned his head as the paramedic came down the stairs. Jack watched him turn green before averting his eyes. He pulled the door open.

"Uncle Jack?"

Jack could see a terrified 15 year old at the back of the

room holding a tightly wrapped little baby. She looked like she was asleep.

"Yes, Eddie, come here sweetheart."

Eddie came over.

"Stay there and let me take the baby."

"It's a girl."

"It sure is." Jack took the baby from him. Bennett came up behind him and Jack handed the infant off to him. Bennett gave her to the paramedic.

"Get her to the pediatric hospital immediately."

"Yes sir." The man hurried off with his small charge in his arms.

"Eddie, close your eyes." Jack reached in to pull Eddie out but before he could put his hands over Eddie's eyes, Eddie's line of sight landed on the horror in front of him. He screamed and tried to scramble out of the secret room. Jack grabbed Eddie up only to be greeted by a savage growl and glassy black eyes. He felt Eddie pounding his back and kicking at his legs. Another snarl emanated from his throat. Jack got him out of the house as quickly as he could. Eddie collapsed in his arms.

"Da…" was the last thing Jack heard him say.

Jack woke with a start, but he kept himself from crying out. He didn't want to wake Tessa up. His heart felt like it was about to explode in his chest. He sat up and raked his hands through his hair. He was sweating, though the room had a coolness to it.

Tessa lifted her head and looked over at him with bleary eyes. He knew that she understood the pain and the memories he was reliving were agonizing.

"Uncle Jack?"

"I'm fine. You can go back to sleep."

"No." She got up and went to sit beside him on his bed, "You're not okay. It was a nightmare, wasn't it?"

She glanced over at the clock, it read a little past one. They had both gone to bed around nine, their tired minds wanting to escape all that they had processed that day. She had fallen asleep right away, but he had taken longer.

He nodded his head.

"Yeah, since we started this up again, they are coming back, and quite frequently, too." He looked over at her. His eyes red rimmed. "I'll be okay. It's just hard dragging all this back out into the light."

Tessa shifted her eyes away.

"I'm sorry, I didn't know this was going to be so painful for you. Maybe I should have just left well enough alone, but I had to know. I had to know why my family died."

Jack touched her arm.

"You have every right to know. It doesn't matter what I feel. I knew it would be hard. But if I didn't want this solved so badly I never would have allowed you to come. I almost didn't let you come but, deep down, I knew I couldn't tell you no. And, deep down, I knew, even though I was sitting there yelling at the TV for you not to stir shit up again, it had to be done. Now we need to end it."

Tessa smirked.

"You were yelling at the TV?"

"Yeah, I'm old. Old fools do that."

Tessa put a hand on Jack's chest and gently pushed him to lay down. Once she had him back down she got under the covers with him and laid her head on his shoulder.

"It's going to be solved, Uncle Jack. We'll do it. We'll get through it. Everything will work itself out."

She moved to kiss him on the cheek and she could feel him smile. "You knew them since you were kids, and had a lot of good times together. You deserve to see their killers brought to justice." Jack wrapped her in a warm embrace. "I know hunters exist and I know what they do, but it doesn't feel right. Were they inexperienced or did they have more in mind than what they told Cody?"

"I wish I knew. It smells, Tessa, it really does and to know that my father was in on it… Do you know how bad that hurts? How badly I don't want to believe it? But Cody was right about one thing; if Dad left from the station, there was no way he could have gotten there as fast as he did. Minutes after I did. It would've taken him at least 15 minutes at top speed to get to Greyson House. I might have been inside for about five minutes when he got there. The others arrived shortly after."

"How did your Dad die?"

"He was killed in a botched bank robbery. It was his day off. He had some deposits to make, I guess. He had no vest nor his gun. Just in plain clothes. These two teenagers walked in with guns, high on booze and dope. The parents were the kind that didn't believe in locking things up so the kids had a great time and how they ever got to the bank in a straight line, I'll never know. They started to demand money from a teller but when they saw the manager press the silent alarm, they opened fire.

"The teller, Dad, and three others were killed. Three more wounded. It was a nightmare by the time I got down there. The elderly couple that were behind Dad when he was shot caught him and eased him to the floor but they said it was too late. The paramedics said it. He was dead before he hit the floor. Right in the chest. Coroner said silver bullets to the heart. Most people in the Valley use only silver bullets in their guns, even us.

"The Council forgave my actions that day. When the mother came down to the station, demanding to know why her kids had been arrested and jailed, I told her. She wanted to know what the fine would be and she paid it. Normal story for those kids. I went over my desk and grabbed her by the throat. Adam and Dale had to pull me off her. The kids were put in a juvenile detention center for shifters till they were 18 then moved to an adult facility. It was almost ten years later when the mother called to apologize, for what good it did. Her eldest was not repentant, kept screaming at her he did it and didn't care. He'll be there for life, I'm pretty sure. The other one, cleaned up and took courses to be a minister, got out and has his own church and flock. I thought he did well but it had to take my dad dying to set him straight."

"Only good thing was; he didn't suffer."

"No, I was always grateful for that. But, I know, if he was alive today he would have a lot of questions to answer."

When Jack opened his eyes again, Tessa had gone back to her bed and was sleeping soundly. Light was filtering through the sides of the black out curtains. He must have been in deep enough sleep that he didn't hear her wake up and move. He quietly got up, grabbed some clean clothes and went to have a shower. The warm water masked his tears. He didn't understand where they were all coming from. Hadn't he cried enough? Why wasn't he dry yet? He shook off the depression that had started to sink in, and got out. He dried quickly and got dressed.

He glanced over to Tessa's bed, but it was empty. She was sitting at the desk on the landline that was sitting there. She was still in her night dress with a robe on over it. His stomach growled as he listened quietly. The pizza and chicken wings they had for supper last night didn't seem to stay with him. He felt like he was starving.

She turned and smiled at him as she hung up.

"Took you long enough, is there any hot water left for me?"

"Ha ha, funny little girl, yes there is some hot water left. Though there might not be much," he snickered.

"I ordered breakfast. I'm going to jump into that nice hot shower before it goes cold. It shouldn't take them too long to bring it around."

"I'll take care of it." Jack watched her grab up some clothes and go into the bathroom.

She was right, it didn't take them long to arrive with breakfast. When he heard the knock at the door, he pulled it open. A young man in a hotel uniform stood there with a trolley.

"Come in. I knew they served breakfast but I didn't think we could get it delivered."

"Of course. Some like to eat in their rooms."

"Very good." He handed the boy a tip and closed the door behind him.

Jack sat staring at the food. He poured himself a cup of coffee and waited for Tessa to get out of the shower. He would be so glad when this was all over, if it ever was. He wasn't going to let it go this time, he wasn't going to drown himself in a bottle and leave it be. He was going to continue once and for all.

He jumped slightly when Tessa came up behind him.

"Oh, that smells good. I'm starved."

"Me too. Let's dig in."

They ate in silence. Each lost in their own thoughts.

Adam sat at his desk staring at his computer monitor. His hands rested in front of the keyboard. He had no interest or concentration to fill in his morning reports. He jumped in his chair when his cell phone rang. He stared at it as if it was going to bite him.

"Hang on," he answered, as he got up and closed his office door. "Go ahead."

"The Cody problem has been taken care of. Now, I want you to get me a visitation pass, get me through the gates. I plan to leave a message for those two to leave things alone. Back off or they'll be next."

"That isn't going to be easy. You haven't been in the Valley since...since then. It's not that easy anymore to fake a pass. I'm going to need legit info. The Council approves all requests now instead of the liaison."

"I'm not giving you anything."

"I'll come and get the problem," Adam found himself saying. "I'll meet you at the old Sanchez place at midnight."

"Fine by me." Adam hung up and pinched the bridge of his nose, trying to stave off the impending headache.

Why did that brat have to start nosing around? He had managed to keep off the radar the first time. He'd hoped to stay off it now but it was going to be hard. Tessa should never have been allowed access to her birth records. He had gone absolutely pale when he had seen her on TV promoting her book. He knew she had been spared, her and Edward. But he had never been able to find out where either of them had been taken.

Being careful not to leave a trail back to the phones at the station or his house phone, he had gone to numerous pay phones, calling institutions in the neighboring cities. He had hoped that a nurse would slip and give him even a tiny hint of info as to where Edward was being kept and they could have eliminated that problem. One less thing to worry about. But since he could not use his real name, or even the fact that he was a cop, the phone calls had yielded no leads. He knew Tessa had to have been in the care of one of the female Council members once she had been checked out of the hospital. Adam knew there was no way he was going to find out where they had put her either.

He had thought they would have given her to Jack, but that would have been way too obvious. There was no way he would have been able to keep that secret, especially when he had two teenage pups to tend to.

So she would have to have been placed in the care of people who were able to provide for her and keep her hidden. They most likely would have sent her to Twelve Oaks from the time she was five to the time she graduated. No public school for her, Adam assumed, all paid for by the Council. He had taken the police courses there and had put himself in debt. Only one of the reasons he accepted Bennett's offer.

Adam scrubbed his hands over his face. Where had he gone so wrong? Why had he chosen to be a part of it? But he knew very well why. The damn money. It was the root of all evil, all right. A young cop fresh out of school with debts and with barely a penny to his name, taking risky chances, hoping for that lucky break to make rent, and maybe food money, too.

More nights than not were spent living on instant noodles and box pasta. Walking to work because he couldn't afford a car. When Bennett came up to him one day, so long ago, overhearing him pleading with his landlord for a few more days to gather rent money, he was all ears to hear what Bennett had to say.

Adam slammed the phone down, raking his hands through his hair.

"Fuck!"

"Something wrong, Adam?" Adam looked up from staring at his desk to see Bennett standing in front of him. At 6'2, roughly 185 pounds, salt and pepper hair with dark brown eyes, Bennett Raskins was an impressive man, especially in uniform.

Adam was still new to the force so he did not have an office to hide in to vent his frustrations.

"My landlord won't give me an extension on my rent. I can't pay it this month."

"I can lend..."

"No, sir, please," Adam cut him off. "I wouldn't feel right because I have no way of knowing when I would be able to pay you back."

"Come to my office, Adam."

Adam swallowed hard as he got up and followed Bennett down the hallway. When he went in, Bennett closed the door behind him and motioned for him to sit in the chair in front of the desk. Bennett sat on the corner of his desk.

"If you won't take it as a loan then would you consider it as an incentive?"

"For what, sir?"

"For your help and your silence. I am taking a very big risk right now by even talking to you about it."

Adam looked Bennett straight in the eyes.

"What is said in this room, stays in this room."

"It had better, because honestly, you may not like the outcome anymore than I would."

Adam tightened his knuckles on the chair arms as he silently nodded.

"I have an arrangement with shifter hunters. And, before you say anything, I am a wolf shifter, just like you. I just really don't happen to care. The pack in this town is pathetic but I have no desire to take it over.

"Alpha Larc came to my parents when we moved here. He was fairly new at being Alpha since taking over for his father who wanted to retire, I guess. He wanted to introduce himself and my parents joined the pack, I didn't have much choice. It wasn't a strong pack then, still isn't now. Since the crime rate isn't extremely high, the pack doesn't serve much purpose in defense but they have a good size number.

"The only benefit that pack is to me is that Larc is so laid back that if a member goes missing once in awhile they don't bother to investigate, usually a loner."

"Are you saying what I think you're saying?"

"For a nice price I access pack records and town registry and

they get a nice, shall we say, souvenir of their visit here. The price is even better when I get them back out. And, if I find other non pack shifters, then the payout gets a little fatter."

Adam's face went pale.

"Doesn't the Council have to approve who you bring in, especially if it's the same people each time? Wouldn't they get suspicious if you brought them in too many times?"

"The liaison does that. And I space it out. Sometimes months go by, even a year. I've been at this quite awhile. I know how to stay under the radar."

"So, these missing persons, if they are reported, like if they don't show up for work or whatnot, are cold cases up in the file room?"

"And will stay cold cases."

"And, as I said, if anything leaves this room, you'll become a cold case box yourself."

Adam swallowed hard. He didn't like what Bennett was proposing, but it wasn't like he had much of a choice. He was inches away from being homeless, and possibly dead, if he didn't get his gambling and "get rich quick" debts paid off and fast. Not to mention his student loans.

"What do you want me to do?"

Adam crossed his arms and put them on his desk, then laid his forehead on them. Bennett's offer had been too fat to resist. He had been watching Adam and noticed how slick he was at doing reports and processing permit requests to pass along to the Council when Bennett didn't have time. He listened intently while Bennett explained in detail what they did and why he needed extra help on occasion. It made him feel like he wanted to puke. But when Bennett took him to meet Thea, the advance she gave him to seal his silence soothed his jangled nerves.

But, now, no amount of money in the world was going to soothe his jangled anything. He felt like the last man standing. The end was coming, one way or another, and he knew it.

Jack and Tessa arrived at Cody's apartment shortly after nine. Jack knocked hard but on the second rap, the door swung open.

"Fuck, what now?"

"He better not have taken off on us."

Jack pushed the door open all the way cautiously. The main room was trashed and there was no sign of Cody.

"Double fuck!" he hissed.

They cautiously looked around the trashed apartment. Cody was gone. Tessa touched Jack's arm and let her head fall on his shoulder.

"This can't be happening. Where did he go? Did he go willingly or were they really still watching him? Are we responsible for this?"

"No, don't think like that. He brought this on himself 30 years ago. I think it's come around full circle to bite him in the ass, unfortunately right when we need him the most."

"But if we hadn't come here and questioned him, he might have still been flying under their radar. They would've still left him alone."

Jack ground his teeth together.

"But where is he? If they killed him, where is the body? And why trash the place? What were they looking for?"

"I'm going across the hall to the lady next door, see if she heard or saw anything."

"Go."

Tessa went across the hall and knocked on the door of the elderly lady she had talked with the day before. She opened the door cautiously, then opened it wider when she saw who it was.

"Oh, good morning, miss. What a nice surprise to see you again."

"I'm sorry to bother you...."

"Mrs. Gleason," she supplied.

"Mrs. Gleason, do you know where Cody went this morning? He was supposed to meet us at nine."

"No, I don't. Today was his day off. I do know that."

"Do you know if he had any visitors this morning or even last night?"

"Yes, I do believe he did have visitors last night, it was after he dropped some leftovers off to me. I think it was around 10:30 or so. I was getting ready for bed and came out to make sure the door was locked. I could hear someone knocking at his door. I peeked out and saw it was an older woman and a middle aged man. Cody opened the door and I could see his face go pale. I always try to keep an eye on the boy since he's been so good to me."

"Have you seen the man and woman that came to see Cody before?" Tessa asked.

"No, I haven't. But the woman looked to be in her late 80s. And the other roughly in his early 30s maybe."

"What did Cody do?"

"He let them in and closed the door. I had no idea

what time they left as I went to bed right after. I get tired easily now."

"That's all right, very understandable. Thank you, Mrs. Gleason."

Mrs. Gleason stepped back into her apartment and closed the door as Tessa went back across the hallway and into Cody's apartment. Jack was in the middle of the living room, looking through the mess.

"What did she have to say?"

"A man and woman came to see Cody sometime after 10:30 last night. He had dropped off some food for her, so she was still awake to hear them knocking."

"Did Cody let them in?"

"Yes, she peeked out and Cody opened the door to them but she said he went pale. They went in and the door closed."

"Could she tell how old they were?"

"She figured the woman to be in her 80s and the man in his 30s."

"Fuck. How much do you want to bet they were still watching him even after all this time?"

"I bet his life they were still watching him," Tessa whispered. "But why trash the place? Were they looking for something that they thought he was going to give to us?"

"They must've thought he had something?"

"But what? And did they find it?"

"Only one way to find out."

They searched the apartment but found nothing.

"This is pointless. What are we looking for?" Tessa wiped her forehead with the back

of her hand. "I swear we've gone over this place twice."

Jack walked over to the living room windows and looked out.

"Maybe we're looking for a non-existent needle in a haystack."

"You're probably right. I don't even know what we should be looking for to begin with... Wait." Tessa turned on her heels and went back over to Mrs. Gleason's apartment. Mrs. Gleason opened up after a quick knock.

"Yes?"

"Mrs. Gleason, I'm sorry to bother you again, but did Cody leave you anything? Ask you to hold onto anything for him for safekeeping?"

"Why do you ask?" Mrs. Gleason looked at Tessa suspiciously for a long moment. "I'm not sure I should tell you."

"Please, Cody's gone missing and his apartment has been trashed. Those people who came to see him last night are most likely involved and were looking for something. We're not here to hurt Cody but to help him and save his life."

Mrs. Gleason looked uncertain for a moment, like she was warring with herself about what to do. Finally she went over to her china hutch and took out a small cat shaped teapot. She took the top off and shook the contents out in her hand, replaced the lid and set it back on the shelf. She brought over a key and a small business card.

"When he first moved in I introduced myself. We became fast friends and I loved that he brought me food. He wanted me to hang on to this for him until he asked for it back or something strange occurred, as he put it."

Tessa stretched out her hand and Mrs. Gleason laid a business card and a small key in it.

Tessa picked the card up and looked at it. It was a business card for, she assumed, a local gym. The key, she presumed, was to a locker there. She looked up at Mrs. Gleason,

"He worked out?"

"Used to, but not so much anymore. I think he still keeps his membership just in case he gets more free time but I'm not entirely sure. He came to me about a couple of years ago with this card and key and asked me to hold onto it for him."

"Did he tell you what it unlocked?"

"No, I asked but he didn't tell me. Said it was safer that way. I questioned him but he just said it was probably his paranoid imagination, but I told him I would keep it anyway. I assumed it was his locker key at the gym, otherwise why would he give me their business card with it. He's a strange boy but a sweetheart."

"Thank you very much, Mrs. Gleason."

"Please, bring him home safe. He's a very good boy. I'll miss his food drop offs."

"We'll do our best."

Tessa turned and went back into Cody's apartment. "A gym key."

"To what one?

There could be dozens around here."

"Luck shines. There is a business card."

Jack took the card and looked at it. "Bod Fitness. Men only gym, open evenings." He dialed the gym number, listened, then disconnected. "Phone number no longer in service."

"How far away is it from here?"

"Not sure. I'm not familiar with the area. Let me GPS it. Jack brought up his maps app and punched in the address for the gym. It only took a few seconds to get a result. "About a half an hour away."

"Let's go." They left, closing the door behind them.

A half an hour later they arrived at their destination. Bod Fitness was closed, abandoned. They had gone out of business.

"Shit," Tessa muttered. "If this is a locker key for one in there we haven't got a prayer of getting to it."

Jack rolled down his window and called to a man that had been walking by. The man came over and looked in the window.

"You wouldn't happen to know when that gym closed and went out of business?"

The man turned his head to look then looked back at them.

"About a couple years now. Just right out of the blue they closed their doors. People who had memberships and paid yearly lost a crap load of money. No one got refunds."

"Thank you," Jack replied as the man moved on.

"If Cody paid yearly then he may not have known they closed."

"Can't see it. If they've been closed a couple of years, unless he had it set to auto renew in his bank account, he would have to actually come down here to pay for another year. If they closed suddenly then he most likely didn't get a chance to get whatever was in the locker."

"I wonder if whatever he put in the locker is still there?"

"We need to find out."

"How?"

Jack stared down at the steering wheel.

"I guess we are going to have to find a way in."

Tessa looked at him with wide eyes.

"Do you think it'll be safe?"

Jack chuckled grimly.

"Probably not, but what choice do we have? We need to find out what is so important that he felt he needed to leave this key with Mrs. Gleason in case something happened."

"But how can we be certain that whatever he put in there is still there, that they didn't take the stuff out of the lockers when they closed?"

"I guess it's a chance we are going to have to take."

Back at the motel room, they went through what little stuff they had, looking for anything nondescript. They had dark clothing but nothing black. Tessa came out of the bathroom in a pair of dark grey leggings and a deep blue sweater.

"I guess it pays not to be a bright colored person."

"It'll do."

"So, here's a question. Most likely a dumb one, but why give someone something and not tell them what it's for?"

"To protect them, so they won't get nosy and go have a look to see what it is. Less likely to be discovered with something you shouldn't have and get yourself killed over it."

Jack turned to face her. He had put on a pair of dark blue jeans and a dark green T-shirt. The only black thing he had was a thin jacket.

"We'll park the car a block away and walk over, do a walk by just scope things out and see how many people are floating around. Hopefully no one, then we'll head down the alley and see if there is a side or back door."

"It's most likely to be locked, you planning on busting them down?"

Jack gave her a sly look, then dug into his jacket pocket. He pulled out a small case.

"Something made me bring this. I can't really explain it. The feeling that I needed my pick kit was so strong that there was no way I could ignore it." He put the case back in his pocket. "When I was packing my bag I had the strongest feeling that there was something I was forgetting. I keep my pick kit with my shoulder holster, and when I looked at it I knew that was what I had to take with me. There was no way I could leave it. It was, almost, like someone was screaming in my ear 'take it!' And as soon as I put it in my bag it felt complete."

Tessa's face took on a solemn look.

"Someone or something really wants this to be over."

"And that's not the only strange thing that's happened since we've started digging. When I went to the file room to look at the photos to see if the film was there, I had such a pain in my chest that I thought I was having a heart attack, that's how strong the pain got. But it wasn't the kind of pain that I knew I should be yelling for help. It was the kind of pain that had direction, if that makes any kind of sense."

"Like it was telling you something?"

"Yes. I looked back through the box, took everything out and the closer I got to the bottom the worse it got. Then I realized what was wrong, that something was missing. The bullets and reports were gone. And as soon as I discovered that, the pain was gone."

Tessa put a hand to her chest.

"They were shot twice in the chest."

Jack could only nod, then took a breath.

"I went to the house. It had started out as a drive to clear my head, but ended up there. I was on the pool deck making a promise that I would solve this thing and....I felt certain I felt John's hands on my shoulders. I turned, but nothing was there. I know it was John, Tessa. He used to rub my shoulders sometimes after football practice. I knew it was him." Jack's voice cracked and he wiped at his eyes.

Tessa went over and gave him a light hug. He hugged her back then went into the bathroom to splash cold water on his face. She waited until she could see Jack's composure coming back, then looked out the window.

"Think it's dark enough?"

Jack followed her gaze.

"Yep, let's go."

They parked a block away from the abandoned gym. Walking down the sidewalk, they kept their eyes roaming, looking for everything and anything that might be considered a threat, but things seemed to be quiet. That was good. They walked past the gym and down to the end of the block then turned around. They were alone. The few people walking on the sidewalk across the street paid them no mind.

They came back up and slipped down the alley, finding a side door. Tessa leaned against the wall to hide Jack picking the lock from anyone passing by. No one paid them any mind. The door screeched as Jack pulled it open. Tessa arched her back and shivered.

"Fuck!"

A quick look around yielded no unwanted attention. They turned on the flashlights on their cell phones and slipped in. Jack let the door lightly close behind him, then shone his light around. It looked like a storage room. Nothing seemed touched. He went over to boxes that were sitting on the shelf at eye level. Opening up a small box he picked out a bunch of business cards like the one Tessa had gotten from Mrs. Gleason. He showed them to her before putting them back and moved on to the row of shelves on the side wall that held larger boxes.

Tessa moved up behind him and looked over his shoulder as he opened one of the boxes. It was full of T-shirts. Tessa wrinkled her nose.

"Smells musty."

"Yeah, and I can bet it makes great nests for rodents."

"Shut up. Shut up."

Jack chuckled deep in his throat.

"Come on, I don't want us to be in here any longer than we need to be."

He shone his light around the room, looking for the door into the main part of the building.

"Here," Jack pointed. He opened the door, but he aimed his light at the floor. He knew the heavy blinds had been pulled in the main windows but he didn't want to take any chances that even the slightest bit of light could be seen by a passerby and the police called. He really did not need that hanging over his head. An out of town Chief of Police busting into an abandoned gym.

"Wow." Tessa carefully moved around the main room. "Look at all this equipment, it's got to be worth hundreds of thousands of dollars. Why didn't they sell it? That way they might have had a little money to pay back their debt, provided that's why they closed their doors. I've done quite a bit of urban exploration. Abandoned malls and hotels. A lot of stores just close up and leave all their stuff behind. Some do clean out their stores and sell off what they can, but some don't. Either they just don't have time, or they write it off. It's like abandoned houses where someone dies and it all gets left behind for one reason or another. Makes for great photography. Remind me to show you my albums sometime."

"It would be a logical thing to do. It's what I would've done."

"Uncle Jack." Tessa walked past him to a door next to the storage room. It had a wooden plaque that read "Locker Room" in gold painted letters. Tessa pushed the door open,

"I always wanted to see a men's locker room."

"Ha ha." Jack followed her in. "If it's anything like most locker rooms you are bound to be disappointed."

It was not a big locker room, two of the walls had rows of small lockers while another wall had hooks for coats and a mat that was on the floor for boots. The fourth wall had an opening that led to showers and washrooms. There were three long benches in the middle. Jack shone his light over the lockers, they all had numbers but no names. Some were open and some were closed.

"Is there a number on the key?"

Tessa took the key out of her pocket and shone her light on it. "Yes." She held the key close to her light to see better. "35."

Jack shone his light over the lockers "Here."

Tessa came over and slipped the key into the locker. It turned, surprisingly easy. She took a hold of the latch and pulled it open. Jack shone his light inside. In it there were a pair of sneakers, shorts and a shirt. Jack pulled them out. At the back of the locker sat a small box. He took it and went over to sit on one of the benches. Tessa came over and sat beside him. He took the top off and they both looked in it.

"Bank books?" Tessa asked.

"Yep." Jack picked up one and skimmed through it. "30-year-old bank books. And bank statements. Look at the size of the deposits. And I believe these are his phone statements with circled numbers."

Tessa reached in and picked up a cassette tape.

"I wonder what's on this? I have no way of playing it. I don't own a cassette player."

"I do, back at the house."

"What's this?" Tessa picked up a small square card out of the box and turned it over.

It was Bennett's business card. The number for the station had been scratched out and another number written in its place. Jack flipped the card over and looked on the back. There was another number but no name.

Jack dialed the first number but it had been disconnected.

"No longer in service. I know that second number but I am not going to use my phone to dial it. When we get out of here we're going to find a pay phone and I'm going to call it from there."

"We need to get out of here so we can look at all this in the light before our phones die."

"Agreed."

Jack put the lid back on the box. They quickly made their way back through and out the door. Jack was careful to make sure the door was locked behind them before making their way back to the car. Sitting inside with the doors locked, they both let out the breath they had been holding.

"Why would he do something stupid like that? Why on earth would you hide valuable papers and such like this in a gym locker?" Tessa asked.

Jack shrugged. "Maybe he didn't want to pay bank fees for a box. Maybe it was the first place he thought of. But it still doesn't make sense. This is the one thing that can happen to make you lose access to stuff. He must have known they closed, figured the papers were gone forever."

"Why didn't he say anything to us about it when we were talking to him?"

"I don't know. Let's see if we can find a pay phone and try this number. I know this number and if he answers I just may puke." Jack started up the car.

After a few minutes of driving, Jack was able to find a pay phone. They huddled around it as Jack slipped a quarter into the slot then dialed the number on the back of the card. He turned the receiver so that Tessa could listen as well. It rang five times before Jack could hear the receiver being roughly picked up.

"Detective Adam Doherty." Jack slammed the receiver down.

"Fuck me!" he screamed into the night.

Adam felt cold from the sweat that seemed to pour off his body. He gripped the steering wheel so tight his knuckles were white. It had been 30 years since he had made this journey. Slowing down, he searched for a dirt road. If no one had come here in that length of time it was going to be overgrown, worse than it had been before and hard to spot, especially in the dark.

He slammed on his brakes, it was definitely overgrown. He backed up and slowly pulled in. He crept along, trying to go easy over the potholes and ruts. After ten minutes a huge two story abandoned farmhouse came into view. He was surprised to see it still standing after all this time. Though the years had really taken a toll on the ramshackle building.

He pulled the car to a halt in front of the broken down front porch and looked around. The forest around the house and the one outbuilding, a large barn, was slowly reclaiming the land. He turned the car off and got out. Taking a flashlight out of his pocket, he turned it on and shone it around. Everything seemed so much darker without the beams of his headlights. Even the light of the full moon didn't seem to illuminate much.

The double doors of the barn slid open and Adam pointed his flashlight at it. Two more flashlights came on in response.

"Took you long enough." A male voice came from behind one of the flashlights.

"Yeah, well, that road is not as easy to find as it used to be. Nor as fun to drive, either."

A snort was all he got in return. The female voice that spoke he knew all too well.

"Let's just get this done. I'm not in the mood for pleasantries."

Adam said no more as he walked towards the flashlight beams.

When they turned to head back into the barn, Adam's flashlight briefly caught the man, a sharp intake of breath caught in his throat.

"Bennett..." The name slipped past his lips.

"Fuck you," The man hissed.

The woman turned to face him.

"Not quite."

"The features are so distinct."

"Yes, Milo is Bennett's kid. Sadly, he didn't get his dear old mother's looks. Unlike my firstborn."

"Was it necessary to kill him?"

"He knew I would if he ever opened his mouth. I warned him and he understood."

"Thea...."

"Enough. Let's just get this done. I don't care where you put him as long as the message is loud and clear."

They had parked their car in the barn and the trunk lid was open.

"I should have parked closer," Adam snapped as he leaned over the open trunk, looking at the plastic wrapped body. "So kind of you to gift wrap it."

"Milo, help him. But don't leave just yet, Adam dear, I'll need a favor from you. You will be compensated, of course."

Adam pulled the body from the trunk. Milo took the feet while Adam carried it by the under arms. Together they lugged it to Adam's car, laying his end down he got his keys and popped the trunk. Raising the lid he picked up his end and tossed the body in. He slammed the lid down then went back to Thea.

"What kind of favor do you want?"

"Take Milo with you?"

"How the fuck am I supposed to get him through the gate without a pass? It's not like I have a spare up my ass right now. And what do you want him in town for anyway?"

"I might be premature in this but I want my bases covered. Drop him off at Bennett's old house. I want him to comb over that place to see if that bastard hid any incriminating evidence, and if he did, I want it destroyed."

"Getting uncomfortable with what they are uncovering?"

"You should be too, your ass will be on the line just as much as mine will be. You're in as deep as I am with no way to hide it."

"I'll find a way even if I have to add to the fucking body count to do it."

"Bennett was so proud of you, you turned out to be just as slimy and dark as he was. And all for the love of money," Thea snarked.

"Just shut the fuck up. Get in the damn car, Milo. You can hang out with your brother in the trunk while I get through the gate."

Milo went back into the barn and came out with a rifle and a small shoulder bag.

"Snacks, flashlight and extra ammo. I'm good to go." He jumped in the passenger seat, waiting for Adam to get moving.

Adam got into the driver's seat without another word. It was going to be a very long night.

CHAPTER 15

ADAM WIPED THE sweat from his forehead. He had no idea why he had agreed to do this. He thought he was done with it all. But it was now coming back to bite him in the ass, big time. If he managed to pull this off it would be a miracle. After dropping Milo off at the Raskin's homestead, he parked his car around the corner of Greyson House.

Even though it was midnight, he knew he was taking a huge risk at someone seeing him. The house across the street had been for sale for the better part of a month, so no one would be looking out a window there. But there was always the chance of someone looking out another window of another house, a car going by or a late night walker.

He knew he was a greedy bastard otherwise he never would have agreed to this. He was in too deep to get out, so might as well finish it out. Adam got out of the car. Digging his flashlight out of his pocket, he went around to the back gate. Where the fence ended and the trees began he knew there was less chance of him being seen. But unfortunately, the gate was not that close to the trees. He unlatched it. An ice cold chill wound its way down his spine as he stepped in. Shining his light on the empty pool, he wondered if there was more than just leaves and debris in it. The deck looked like it could use a good scrubbing. Three loungers that had never been collapsed and put away sat haphazardly in the far corner where the wind must have blown them.

Adam walked up the three steps to the patio doors, pulled out his lock pick kit and picked the lock. Sliding it open, he quickly stepped inside. Shining his flashlight around the kitchen and living room, he walked in a little further. The place was immaculate.

"What the hell?" He rubbed his fingers over the top of a small stand by the basement door. Not a trace of any dust. "This place is fucking cleaner than my place."

Going down to the basement he shone his light over Michael's nest of blankets. "Someone is taking care of this place. All the better, someone will find him sooner or later. Be a hell of a lot easier than dumping him on Raskin's doorstep. Less chance of getting caught."

Adam went back to the car and opened the trunk. Looking around quickly, he lifted the plastic wrapped body out of the trunk and heaved it over his shoulder in a fireman's carry. He gave a quick scan of the lining, thankfully no blood. He shut the trunk with his free hand.

Quickly going back inside, he was surprised to see that the door to the basement was closed. He stared at it, he didn't think he had closed it. He tried it and it opened again, the bottom one was closed too. Shaking off the insane fear that he was not wanted there, the feeling that he needed to leave starting to build in the pit of his stomach, he dumped the body on the floor and took off the plastic. Putting the body on the blankets, he bundled the plastic up carefully to avoid getting any blood on himself, not that there was much. By the time he had picked it up, it had bled all it was going to. He straightened up and stared down at the body.

"I know someone has got to be cleaning this place on a regular basis. There's no getting around it, so it shouldn't be too long before someone finds you."

He turned and was halfway up the stairs when a loud bang made him jump. He turned around, the basement door was closed. Adam ground his teeth together, his blood ran cold and he knew he needed to get out of there now. He ran the rest of the steps and was no sooner out the stairwell and turned when the top door slammed shut.

"Fuck!" He got out and relocked the patio doors and the back gate. He jumped into his car throwing the plastic on the passenger side floor. He stared up at the house. Nothing moved. "Fuck! You are losing it, Doherty, get a grip. You are tired and need rest. It's been a long day."

Adam turned on the car and got out of there with the insane feeling that he was being watched.

"I need to go clean." Eddie sat restless on the couch, Carol sat beside him.

"Eddie, you don't need to. Why don't we play a game? Do you want some lunch?"

"No."

"You miss Uncle Jack, don't you?"

"He needs to come home. Why has he been gone so long? He never leaves for this long."

"I know." Carol stroked a stray hair out of his eyes. "And it's understandable. He will be back soon."

"He promised we could go fishing when he got back. I really want to go. But not until he comes back. Want to keep busy."

"No, Eddie, it's fine. I'll read you a story."

"No." Eddie got up and left by the back door.

Carol grabbed her phone and dialed Jack's number. He picked up on the second ring.

"Carol?" His voice sounded concerned. "Is something wrong?"

"When will you be home?"

"Possibly tomorrow, why?"

"I know I really shouldn't say this on an unsecured line, but Eddie is getting really upset and restless. I'm starting to worry."

"What's he doing now?"

"He's going to clean."

"If that boy cleans that house anymore it'll be museum clean."

"It's hospital clean now, I swear. And I don't think it's good for him to be over there right now."

"You should never have let him go over there to clean to begin with. It's going to get shit thrown at us."

"I know. He wants to go fishing. You promised."

"I know I did. But we ran into a snag here and it's taking a little longer than we had planned."

"Can you talk about it?"

"Not over the phone. I'd rather not. But I'll try to get back as soon as I can."

"Please, hurry."

"I will." Carol ended the call. She looked at it. She rarely said goodbye to her husband. She didn't like Jack being away so long herself but she understood why. She could only hope that he found something that would finally put it all to rest.

Eddie walked up the path to the back fence. He unlatched it and opened the door, slipping in. He stared at the empty pool. He'd loved swimming. Da had taught him. Now he played around in the falls behind the cabin when it was warm. As he looked at the pool, his heart ached. Instead of warm sparkling water, there was nothing but dirt and debris. He slipped his key into the lock at the patio doors and went in. Locking the doors behind him he went and laid down on the couch. He couldn't understand why he continued to come here, it hurt so bad. But he needed to keep it clean. Da and Daddy didn't like a dirty house, they were always so neat and tidy. They would be mad if he let it get messy. Tears streaked his face,

"I miss you, Da." He got up and wiped his face.

Walking over to the sink, Eddie reached for the tap then stopped. No water. He should have brought a bucket with him, he couldn't do proper cleaning without it. Reaching under the sink he dug out a rag.

"Guess it's just a dry dust today."

He started up in the attic. James and John had it renovated into a game room when Michael and Steven moved in, to help them settle in. Eddie had enjoyed playing games with them there. Going down to the second floor, he quickly moved through the bedrooms. His had been on the end when he had gotten too big for the nursery. Giving the living room and kitchen a good dusting, he ended up at the basement door. He hesitated, he hated going down there. He tried not to neglect the basement but it was scary down there. The pain in his chest was the strongest there. Taking a flashlight from the table drawer by the door, he flashed it on. It was always good to have a few working flashlights around.

"Got to clean but it will be a fast one today. Me and Aunt Carol will do a better job soon. A job for another day."

Opening the second door, he automatically went to the couple of lanterns he kept down there and turned them on. There was a little light coming in the windows but not enough for him to see clearly in the waning light of the late afternoon. He steeled himself to turn around and take in the basement as a whole. Something was not right. His eyes shifted down to the blankets on the floor, Michael's nest. A body lay there.

Eddie backed up, his brain screaming at him to get out of there. Turning quickly on his heels, he let out a horrific scream and tore up the steps. Not thinking about the way he had come in, he unlocked the front door and tore down the steps.

Around the corner of the house, he briefly turned his head to the road. Hearing an idling car engine he sprinted into the woods to make his way to safety, to Aunt Carol.

Once again, Adam sat in his car across the street facing Greyson House, he had left the engine idling, debating whether he was going to sit there and wait to see if Cody's body was found or go into work and wait for a phone call that the body was found. It swirled around in his head like all the other thoughts he was having, threatening to give him a headache. Why couldn't this just be over, just stayed dead? He was too old for this shit, he didn't want to be tied up in it again.

He could only hope that dumping Cody's body would be the last of it, that they would get the message, but that was just wishful thinking. The body count had been too high the first time, he really didn't want it to start stacking up again. Nor did he want his own body to be at the top of the pile. And the phone call he had gotten last night not long before he had to go get Cody's body, he had written it off, at the time, as a wrong number, but now he knew. He knew it had to have been Jack. Why Jack had called then hung up, he didn't know. But one thing he knew for certain; the reasoning wasn't good.

He turned his head to look at Greyson House, his breath caught in his throat. A man had torn out of the front door. He turned his head listening to the sound of the car engine before disappearing into the woods.

Adam swallowed hard. His throat went dry. The face was older but he was absolutely certain he knew who the man was.

"Holy sweet fuck..."

Carol could feel something was wrong before it actually was. She tensed up, something was seriously wrong. She heard the crying and heard the back door open and slam shut hard. She hurried out of the kitchen to the back hallway in time to see Eddie open the door to the basement and tear down the steps, slamming the door behind him. Carol was startled. What was wrong? It had been a long time since she had seen him that upset. Carol opened the door and went down. Whatever had terrified him so, she was glad he had come here instead of the cabin. It was quite evident that he should not be alone in this state of agitation. Eddie was curled up tight on the bed visibly shaking.

"Baby, what's wrong?"

"He's dead."

"Who is dead, darlin'?"

"The guy in the house."

"Honey, there should be no one in the house."

"But he's there, where Michael was."

"Eddie, what are you saying?"

"There's a dead guy on Michael's nest. He shouldn't be there. He has no right to be there, but he's dead. I don't know what to do."

"You just stay here. Let's get you out of your coat and shoes right now."

Carol got Eddie uncoiled enough to get his jacket and shoes off.

"You stay here, I'll get you something to help you relax then I'll see what's going on."

"Hot chocolate with big marshmallows?"

Carol smiled as she laid a quilt over him and kissed his forehead.

"All right, sweetness."

Carol quickly went upstairs to the kitchen.

As she put a kettle of water on to boil, then called Jack. He picked up on the third ring.

"We have a serious problem, Jack. You need to come home now."

"Why? What's wrong?" His voice was full of concern.

"Eddie was over to the house and says there's a body there... on Michael's nest. I'm on the landline so my end is secure. I know your cell may not be but I don't think it matters right now."

"Have you seen the body?"

"No, but as soon as I get Eddie settled down and hopefully asleep I'll go over. I don't know what to do if there really is a body there."

The kettle boiled and she turned it off. Putting hot chocolate powder in a mug she poured the water over it and stirred. She could hear Jack sigh as she dropped in a couple of large marshmallows.

"Go, look, but touch nothing. Call and let me know if there is one or not. Call me back and I'll let you know how far away we are, then I may get you to call for the Council Liaison."

"Okay."

"But get that boy asleep and make sure he's good and sound asleep before you leave him. Put a little brandy in a drink if you have to. That always puts him out for a few hours."

Carol was silent for a few seconds.

"I've got some hot chocolate for him now. I'll put it in that. Please come home."

"We're on our way and will be there as soon as we can."

She hung up and went to their wet bar. She hated giving Eddie brandy but it was the only thing she knew of that would relax him enough to let him go to sleep after such a shock. She hated giving him drugs. Going back to the kitchen, she poured a little in the cocoa.

"This needs to end," she muttered to herself. "It really needs to end."

Taking up the mug she went back to the basement apartment.

"Here, baby."

Eddie sat up slowly and took the cup in both hands. He licked the marshmallows.

"So yummy." He looked over at her with a disappointed look. "You're not having any."

"No, baby." She smiled sweetly at him. "Not right now."

She put her arm around him and brought him close as he slowly drank. She kissed his temple.

"We will take care of things, don't you worry. Everything will be alright. You just try and relax."

Eddie finished off the drink and Carol took the cup to set on the floor.

"Now you just lay back down and let the cocoa do its job. Everything will be fine."

Eddie laid back down and Carol put the blanket back over him. She turned on a nightlight then turned off the overhead light. She sat back down beside him and watched his eyes flutter. Brandy was like a heavy sedative to Eddie and it worked quickly. She stayed with him until she was absolutely sure that he would stay asleep. Taking the cup, she went back upstairs and shut the door. Steeling herself, she pulled on a jacket, pair of gloves and got the spare house key Jack hid from its place in her jewelry box. Since the locks had never been changed, Jack kept a hold of the two keys that John had made for him. He never told the Council that he had the keys. He honestly didn't think they needed to know. She sighed heavily, this was not what she wanted to be doing.

Taking a deep breath, she went in the front door. The patio doors were shut and locked. She couldn't blame Eddie for not trying to get them back open when he was in such a fright. She had always taught him to go in the patio doors, never the front door. Then she went down to the basement. Eddie hadn't been joking, there really was a body. And she recognized him. Cody Mitchell. The man had aged but she still knew that face. The man from the photographs. The man Jack and Tessa had gone to see. How did he get here? And did he actually get a chance to talk to Jack and Tessa? How far away was Jack? She dug out her cell phone.

"Jack?"

"Yeah?"

"How far out are you?"

"Be about a half an hour roughly before we get there. Is it there?"

"Yeah. There's a body here. Right where he said it would be. Jack, it's Cody Mitchell."

"Fuck! Double fuck!" Jack yelled loud enough to make her pull the phone away from her ear. "Can you tell me how he died without touching him?"

Carol moved close and knelt down.

"Looks like he was shot to death. Two bullets to the chest."

"Dammit," Jack snarled. "They were still watching him even after all this time. "

"Should I call the Council and let them know?"

"Where is Eddie?"

"Still in the basement apartment, the brandy took hold pretty quick."

"I don't want him involved if at all possible. They'll want to know who found the body. I'm too far out to call them. If they get there before I do, they'll want to know how I knew there was a body there without me actually being there when I reported it. You need to call them. As soon as you mention there's a body, it won't take them long to meet to see how they'll proceed and do it quietly.

"They'll send out the liaison, or should, anyway. I really hope I can get back in time and get ahead of any questions. I have no idea how I'm going to explain how the house is being kept in pristine condition, considering its under Council Law not to be touched. That should be real fun. You are not to mention Eddie in any way, shape or form. They cannot know he has been anywhere except the cabin. That boy does not need to be traumatized all over again. It's enough that he saw Cody's body.

"When you call them, tell them you were over there verifying a hunch for me. That Cody claimed Dad had him go to Barbados to spy on them and was in their photographs. I asked you to go and see if there were any photos from their trip and if Cody was actually in them."

"Okay, we'll do it like that. I was checking a hunch for you and went over there and found him. And I'll take the rap for keeping it clean all these years."

"Carol...."

Carol cut him off.

"I'll say I was keeping it that way as a shrine, so to speak. And if one day this is all over, maybe Eddie could learn to live in his childhood home again."

She could hear Jack heave a sigh.

"We've got no other options. I guess we'll just have to wait and see if they swallow it."

CHAPTER 16

TESSA GLANCED OVER from the passenger seat.

"Uncle Jack, what is going on? What is really going on? What are you hiding from me? And don't lie, I'm not deaf. I heard all your side of the conversation and snatches of hers. There is something you're not telling me, refusing to tell me."

Jack laid the phone down on the seat between them. He gripped the steering wheel tighter.

"The Council has kept me in silence all these years about things. I wish in a lot of ways, things still could have been left buried. But I wish it would all end, too. Please don't hate me for saying this, but I wish you had left things alone. I gave you the help you wanted because I thought nothing would come of it. You deceived me when you neglected to tell me you were writing a book, and I sure as hell didn't expect it to take off like that."

"I didn't mean to deceive you." Tessa looked at her hands in her lap.

"I understand you wanting to know what happened to your family but it scares me to think that these assholes are still out there watching. And now we know they're watching because Cody Mitchell is dead. And I know there was so much more he needed to tell us. Like why my father was involved and did what he did. I have a strong feeling I'm going to have to go home and visit with some ghosts."

"But there is still something very important that you are not telling me. I'm right, aren't I?"

"Yes. Though it has not been by my choice. If it was, you would have been told the moment I met you."

"Please, can you tell me now? What difference does it make any more? If we still manage to solve this, nothing will matter anymore anyway."

Jack set his face, a look of stone before collapsing into sadness.

"Eddie didn't commit suicide. He's still alive."

Tessa gasped sharply as her hands flew to her mouth.

"And if you want to get real technical about it, he's not really your uncle. Not by blood, anyway. The Council thought it best to fake his death so he would stay hidden under the radar in case the hunters came looking for him. But the Council must not think that way anymore if they allowed you access to your birth records. I think they thought that after 19 years the risk was gone. Even after 30 years, if there was a risk I bet they would have tried to shut down the publication of your book. I want to believe that, but something just nags at me.

"They moved him from two facilities because questioning phone calls had been received. Random calls were placed to a lot of facilities and hospitals. The caller never identified themself, and when told they would not be able to get any information one way or the other they would hang up. I could not understand. He was only part unicorn. His blood was not pure so there would be no value there, none that I know of anyway, and if he had any powers of a Protector they did not show.

"They figured his life and yours were still in danger. You were secretly adopted out with a cover story that you were born to a single mother who didn't want you. That was all the adoptive family was told, for their safety and yours. I wanted to adopt you but I was too close. They could track my every movement where I was such a public figure. You could have been in constant danger and so could have me and my family.

"Eddie had been traumatized to the point he was a zombie. It was like his mind was gone. The doctors and nurses were able to get him to eat and drink and go to the bathroom on his own again but that's as far as it went. They could get nothing more from him. It might have been different if I had been able to get my hands over his eyes faster so he couldn't see anything, but I wasn't fast enough. He saw it all. The last word he spoke as I got him out of there was 'Da' then he collapsed in my arms. At that moment, the Eddie I knew was gone." Jack's voice hitched and cracked. He took a few minutes to compose himself.

"It was such an honor for me and Carol when we were named his godparents. Now we are his only parents."

Tessa had paled.

"What are you saying?"

"Carol and I have been caring for Eddie all these years. The Council declared all Carstairs land and properties off-limits. Could not be sold or rented, nothing. Trespassing was strictly prohibited and there were strict penalties for doing so. The Carstairs cabin out by Unicorn Falls was fitted to meet his needs. Cleaned and outfitted with appliances and specially designed generators to be practically noiseless. Push start ones, really nice. One would run constantly to power the fridge, small freezer and pump. The other could be turned off at night. They were new and sophisticated and made hardly any noise, and gas sipping so he didn't need to fill them all that often, since the power lines could not be strung out that far. That had been a lot of the reason John and James had built it out there, for roughing it, sort of. They did have a well dug and pump installed so they could have water and indoor plumbing. The Council wanted Eddie to live out there so he would be safe."

"Are you fucking kidding me?" Tessa snapped. "A traumatized 16-year-old boy stuck out in the middle of nowhere to fend for himself?"

"Essentially, that is what they were saying. I was to teach him how to use the generators and care for himself and Carol was entrusted to teach him to cook and clean when he started showing more signs of independence. I thought it was cruel and inhuman, especially since I had to divide my time with work, as I had to keep up appearances."

Tessa wiped tears from her eyes.

"Bastards."

"Yeah, I thought so too, though I used words a lot stronger than that. Carol and I made up our minds that that was just not going to happen. But we had to be sneaky about whatever we were planning to do. If we were caught, the consequences were extreme. You have no chance going up against the Council."

"What did you do?"

"We renovated the basement. I made everything legit, got the proper permits and hired contractors I knew that were reliable and quick. I used the excuse that Mom wasn't well and it might get to the point that she and Dad could not live on their own anymore and rather than being stuck in a home, he could care for her there. Like an apartment. I wasn't really lying. I knew Mom wasn't well but she was elderly. Her and Dad both. The human body can't hold on forever. Mom was by no means on Death's door, but nobody needed to know that. Dad wasn't in any better health but he still acted like a bull moose. I let him believe I was doing it for Mom.

"Dad put her over everything, even his own health. Though they were both adamant that they would stay in their own home until they passed away. I let it drop. All the better. We had the basement done in record time as it was mostly finished anyway. We just needed it sectioned off for a bathroom, bedroom and a kitchenette. Plumbing and whatnot. We were done long before the Council had the generators imported and installed and everything set up.

"We kept him in that basement apartment and we took care of him. Carol taught him to cook and he opened up to her. They played games and she would read to him. I helped him with the man stuff, took him fishing and swimming back at the Falls. He came out of his shell quite a bit and we gradually got him used to being in the cabin on his own and how to run things, and he seemed to be content. But he's just not the same, he's not that happy little boy that pounded the shit out of me at chess. His eyes changed to solid black and are horrible to look at. He can have fits of rage and Carol is the only one, at times, who can calm him down. I know little

Eddie is still in there somewhere but it's next to impossible to draw him out. He's a 45-year-old man with the mentality of a five-year-old."

"What I want to know is how you managed to hide Eddie all that time in your basement apartment right under your father's nose? Especially if he knew you and Carol were to take care of him but out at the cabin. And, with the fact that you told him that the basement apartment was for him and your mother when they both go to the point they could no longer care for themselves?'

"That was the hardest part of all. Really hard going. The Council believed that Dad should have been the one to take care of Eddie once he was out of the institution. Get him situated in the cabin and check in on him. Since Dad was Chief of Police, Eddie would be safer because Dad was not really friends with Eddie's family so the killers would not really be looking in his direction.

"Since Mom was home she could stay at the cabin until Eddie got used to things and Dad would show him how to use the equipment. Once Eddie got settled into the cabin all Dad had to do was check on him once in awhile.

"Dad understandably balked at that. It was the only time I think he ever went up against the Council. He told me years later that he implored them to allow Carol and I to get him used to the cabin. He said that Eddie may be resistive to an almost stranger and that he would be more comfortable with Carol and me because we were around Eddie so much more. I was shocked that the Council agreed and called me to a meeting to tell me.

"But, in all honesty, the real reason Dad wanted us to deal with it was because if Eddie saw him, there was a high possibility that it could trigger a memory and Eddie would remember Dad being there and Dad wouldn't be able to deny it.

"I never told Dad, ever, that we kept Eddie at the house for the first two years after he was released from the hospital when he started showing signs of more cognitive functions, until he was able to be on his own. Dad died not knowing any different, neither did Mom."

"Not even when he came over to visit?" Tessa questioned.

"One thing we definitely had done was soundproof the basement when we had it renovated, though we never told them that part when we told them we were doing it for them if they couldn't live on their own. Mom and Dad gave up shifting to age, though it made Dad more vulnerable. When he was shot, he bled out faster than his body could heal itself. Carol and I don't shift anymore, we want to age though we are still active in pack affairs, we just don't do the monthly runs anymore.

"But, I'm getting off track. The good thing was with them living at the homestead, with the distance it was from our home, was that they didn't visit a lot. Dad worked all day and was tired when he came home, and Mom wanted us to have our privacy as a young couple. When we needed a babysitter, we took the kids there. They loved playing in the woods. We thought it would be Tucker and Haley who would be the insanely hard part. But Carol and I sat them down and decided to include them in the secret. Because there was just no way we could keep Eddie a secret, especially during the holidays.

"When we sat the kids down to talk to them about Eddie coming to stay in the basement apartment and that we needed their complete and total silence regarding it. They were not to discuss it with anyone, not friends, not even their grandparents. Only us. They agreed. It would be good companionship for Eddie, even beneficial. Tucker was 17 and Haley was 16."

"How was he when he was at your place?"

"In the beginning he would sleep a lot. I believe it was the medication his doctors put him on for depression, PTSD and anxiety but we eventually weaned him off them. The kids were kind and left him alone. We would give him an early dinner then put him to bed. He would sleep all evening and night. Even when we got him off the medications, he would sleep a lot."

"Sounds like his mind was trying to heal itself and exhausting the body so he would sleep to refuel."

"Yeah, he was wasted, mentally and physically."

"Did your dad ever suspect?" Tessa asked.

"No, I don't think so. Even the kids kept quiet. I was really surprised at how well they kept their secret. I think it was because it made them feel like we were treating them like adults by including them in something so big. The first Christmas wasn't really as hard as I thought it would be. I don't think Eddie even really cared. We set up a tree and decorated it for him but he just sat and stared at it. We put presents under it, the kids even wanted to get him something and they surprised him with a sock full of treats on Christmas Day but there was no response. The kids understood.

"Though I was surprised when Dad picked up a gift for him, he simply wrote 'from granddad' on the tag. He got him a gift on his birthday as well. I never thought anything about it then, but now, I think it was the sign of a guilty mind.

"The next year was a little better, he liked having his own

tree and getting presents. It was harder to get him settled down for the evening Christmas Day. Christmas Eve we had a big supper for him then Christmas Day we had a big dinner and once all the gifts were open the kids took him down and played video games with him until Mom and Dad came over for supper.

"They told him that they had to go up and visit with their grandparents. They said he looked at them and said he didn't want to go. They told him it was okay and put in a new video game that he could play by himself. When the kids went back down he was sound asleep."

"How did you get through New Year's Eve?"

"Pretty much the same way both years. We let the kids play games with him while we were out. We figured they were adult enough to be responsible on their own for a few hours. I had Dale call every now and then to check on them. Dale never went anywhere on New Year's Eve, he was movies and popcorn, stay at home on the holidays kind of guy, so he didn't mind.

"We left the house around 11. Mom and Dad weren't much for celebrating, so we left it until later in the evening and usually got home about 1:00. The dance hall was not all that far away, anyway. When we got home the kids were in bed sound asleep and so was he. The plates of snacks and glasses all were empty, stacked neatly in the sink and the gaming system was turned off.

"Just little things like that and being with the kids and watching him when he was with them, we knew he was learning. I really think it did him a world of good having the kids around him. He started to function more like a human being than he would have if he was left alone and isolated at the cabin."

"But having to send him away to be by himself at that cabin must have been hard?"

"It was, he had to learn new things and adjust to being alone somewhere other than the house. It was hard on the kids, too, they really missed him. And not being around all of us, I think, made him somewhat bitter. He was being left alone again. So, in the evening I started going up to stay with him, I would take the kids too. Once Tucker went away to college and Haley went back to school, it was just me that would go up. I tapered it back to a few evenings a week, then to one. He adjusted. Though we would take him up a tree at Christmas and presents, we would spend holiday time there and he would at the house too. We did our best to make it work and to be as easy a transition as possible for him. I would take supplies up to him but when he started coming back to the house for them, we didn't stop or correct him.

"I knew, if the Council ever found out what was going on there would be hell to pay, but we didn't care. He was just a kid. He didn't deserve treatment like that. When Dad was killed, Mom decided to move into a seniors complex so she wouldn't be alone, and wouldn't be a burden to us, though we did offer her the basement apartment. She flat out refused. It made things a bit easier, there wasn't the worry there about them showing up and Eddie being there."

"Do Tucker and Haley ever ask about Eddie?"

"Surprisingly, yes, they do. They don't call very often and I can understand that, but they do make a point and ask about him and I tell them. And I know they would love to see him again."

"So sad," Tessa whispered. "I want to meet him."

"The Council gave that right to Eddie. When I went to get the key to Greyson House for you, I had asked if you should meet Eddie. The Council determined that he has the right to initiate contact. Though I'm surprised they even said that. Though these are newer Council members and they know the history. I have asked him a few times if he wants to meet you, and he has refused. I don't know why, he never gives me a reason. I did make the mistake of pointing out my reasoning to him and got a swollen face for my troubles."

"He hit you?"

"Yeah, his backhand's pretty good."

"Now, I know why one side of your face seems to have a faint green tinge."

"Yeah, bruises heal fast but the pretty colors tend to hang around for a while."

Tessa's smile was wan.

"How is he doing overall?"

"I think he would come around if he was put into intensive therapy. It would be a long and painful road, but I think he would function a lot more normally than he does now. What I would give to see those sparkling lavender eyes just one more time."

"Cody said the lavender eyes come from the Protectors?"

"Yeah. John was full blood Protector, their eyes are lavender. The blackness with a Protector is the eye's window to the mind. When their eyes shift from lavender to black to lavender again that's a sure sign they are sending out a mental distress call for help. It reaches all Protectors regardless of the distance away. You generally don't have long after that to make your escape, if you're lucky enough to do so. But with

Eddie I do not know where that blackness comes from. I do know it can be violent and dangerous. I don't like crossing it if I don't have to."

They pulled up alongside the sidewalk in front of Greyson House. They sat looking at it for a long time.

"Why is it called Greyson House if the Carstairs' have always lived there?"

"Carstairs is the name of the first Protectors of Unicorn Valley and Greyson was the name of the first unicorn family that built the house. But that'll have to be a story for another time, let's get this over with."

They got out of the car and started up the driveway. Jack tried the front door, it opened easily.

"Carol?"

Carol got up from the couch.

"I called the Council. Someone is being sent over. They should be·here any time."

"Okay." Jack went over giving Carol a hug and a kiss. "Bring them down when they get here."

Jack and Tessa went down into the basement.

Jack squatted down beside the body. He looked at the two bullet holes in Cody's chest. His mind flashed back to an unwanted place then back again. He had been in this exact same place. Jack shook his head to get rid of the unwanted images.

"They shut him up because they felt that he could still point a finger at them. But there is no blood on the floor."

"He was killed elsewhere and brought here."

"Damn! We are fucked! He was our only link."

"He could've explained those papers."

"I have a good theory on those. But we need bank and

phone records to confirm. The bank statements show the money he got for doing what he was supposed to be doing. May be still traceable if the banks still have the original records. The phone numbers that he circled may be traceable as well unless they were disconnected."

They turned when they heard footsteps coming down the stairs. Carol moved to the side of the man just stepping off the last step. He was dressed in a pale blue business suit with a white shirt but no tie. He was not a young man, though his face held no lines of an older man, and he seemed to be in good shape, Jack would have guessed to be in his 70s. Most of the original Council 30 years ago had been in their 50s and 60s, so most were either retired or passed on. The Council members now looked to be in their 30s and 40s but had been well trained for their positions they were to hold. He must have been an original Council Liaison that had moved on to become a Council member, possibly the last from 30 years ago. Though when Jack had gone to get the key for Greyson House, he did not really remember seeing this man seated with the other members. But he really didn't care at that moment.

"Jack, Tessa, this is Councilman Jarvis. He acts and speaks for the Council outside of Chambers. He is handling this personally instead of the Liaison."

Councilman Jarvis looked Tessa and Jack up and down with a disapproving look.

"Mrs. Raskins explained to me what was going on. I hope your "hunch" will explain why there is a dead man on the floor and what exactly you were looking for on closed property."

"When I was helping Tessa with the information she requested I got looking through albums. They had gone to

Barbados, and I received photographs of that trip. Cody was in two of those pictures. Tessa had left the key with Carol for me to return, which I'm sorry to say I did not do because things started to spiral out of control. I told Carol to take the key and come over here to see if the original negatives were still in Michael's darkroom, to get a date off them.

"I thought I recognized the face from the Lounge and the date would tell me exactly when the picture was taken. When I compared the dates and I looked at the employee list the name clicked. He had been paid to go there to spy on them."

Councilman Jarvis seemed to take that in. He nodded his head slowly but said nothing.

Jack stood up and gave a slight bow, Tessa followed suit when Jack gave her a quick sidelong glance.

"Councilman Jarvis, this was Cody Mitchell. We went to see him over in NorthRiver. He had information that we needed. It could be enough to reopen the Carstairs case and potentially solve it and bring those responsible to justice. We didn't know we would get him killed. He thought they might still be watching him but after this length of time we didn't think so." Jack stated.

"And why are you re-investigating this case?" Councilman Jarvis had an ugly expression on his face.

Tessa swallowed hard.

"When I wrote my book on the murder of my family I really wanted to have it solved. I came here just to see if my book had dug up any new leads. I had no idea this was going to happen. He said if he tried to come back he would never make town limits," Tessa whimpered.

"What sort of evidence?" Councilman Jarvis brought his cell phone out of his jacket pocket and started typing.

"About who did the killings and why. He was mixed up in it all," Jack hesitated, "and apparently..... so was my Dad. He claimed that Dad shot James and Michael after the hunters shot John and Steven."

Jarvis's head snapped up from his phone.

"That is a serious accusation. And this is why you are involved?"

"Yes, I'm trying very hard to believe that Dad would do no such thing. When we went to see Cody at the diner he worked at he told us a lot of stuff. Then he said to come back the next day, his day off, and he would tell us everything we wanted to know. When we got there he was gone and the apartment had been trashed."

"I went next door and the neighbor said she had seen a man and a woman go into the apartment later in the evening but she didn't know when they left. When we got there, he was gone. They must have still been watching him after all," Tessa supplied.

"Mrs. Gleason gave Tessa a key and a business card that Cody had given her for safekeeping. It went to a gym that had gone out of business a couple years ago. But there was a number on the back of the card."

"What number?" Jarvis asked, going back to texting on his phone.

Tessa told him the phone number.

Councilman Jarvis typed it into his phone as he looked up to her.

"Does not ring a bell."

"It did for me," Jack stated. "It is the landline to detective Adam Doherty's house. He was in on it with my dad." His voice barely a whisper.

Jarvis was silent. He took a deep breath before he spoke.

"Did you get whatever was in the locker? Were you able to gain access to the gym?"

"We had to break in, Councilman. There was no other way. We disturbed as little as possible and made sure the place was locked securely again when we left. There was a small box in the locker there. It has bank books and statements in it. If we can get corresponding records from the bank and phone company we might have a traceable lead," Jack replied.

"You believe Cody Mitchell was in contact with these hunters?" Choosing to ignore the fact that they had broken the law in another town to get information.

"Yeah, he admitted that he was, and Dad was too. He was in contact with Adam, too. Something happened and it all went south."

Tessa laid a hand on Jack's shoulder as she spoke.

"Cody felt the need to hide these statements, possibly to either protect himself or use them as blackmail when he got low on funds. Either way, there's a good possibility that one of these phone numbers would be Chief Raskins. And if that is the case, then Chief Raskins could have gone to the bank and the phone company and subpoenaed the original records.

"I didn't want to say it earlier or any time for that matter but if he did get those records, he's either hidden them or destroyed them. He wouldn't voluntarily put his head in a noose by entering them into evidence and exposing himself. He would have to be sneaky about it and what better time than when he sends his grief stricken son to take a week's leave, so no one was really looking over his shoulder all that closely."

"I was camped out at home for a week, too stone cold drunk to move or even care. I was in too much pain. Maybe he had actually planned it that way. It's not like I can ask him now," Jack murmured.

At that point they heard footsteps on the stairs. Two men came in with a bodybag, they were dressed in jeans and sweaters. Jarvis gave them a sidelong glance.

"Discretion, boys." They nodded and went about putting Cody Mitchell's remains in the bag.

"What will you do with him?" Tessa asked.

"If there is a family plot he will be buried there. All paperwork will be closed. All registry information will be deleted."

"Like he didn't exist."

"Unfortunately, my dear, that needs to be the way of it. Even after 30 years there is still a lot of pain in this town regarding the Carstairs murders. Because if he spoke out about his involvement if he was still in town and alive, no doubt he would be killed one way or another. And being dead would only cause a lot of desecration in the cemetery."

"I understand." Tears welled in Tessa's eyes.

It was all getting too much to handle. Jack put his arm around her.

"Why don't I take you back to your hotel room so you can rest?"

She nodded but didn't answer.

"Before you go," Jarvis' voice stopped them. "Can anyone tell me why this house looks like a showroom piece even after 30 years? With no occupants I would've expected it to be full of dust and dirt."

Jack looked to Carol, who looked back at him uneasily. He did not want to tell the truth but he didn't want Carol to take any punishment that the Council would see fit to slap her with. Carol seemed to sense what Jack was feeling. Eddie did not need any more shit than what he was already dealing with.

"It was me, Councilman, I couldn't stand to see such a beautiful house going to ruin. There were a lot of happy times here and it should be preserved. I'm sorry for doing wrong and trespassing all these years to keep it up. But it helped to ease the pain. The original key that John had given Jack still worked in the locks. It was in Jack's safe, I figured he had forgotten it was there so I took it. He didn't know I had taken it or what I was doing. I didn't tell him. Please don't punish him for my wrongdoing. I will take the punishment."

Jarvis looked to Carol for a long minute, considering her words.

"You and Chief Raskins were very close to the Carstairs'. I will overlook it and not mention it to the Council. This is a beautiful house and it would be a sin for it to sit here and fall down. You may continue to do so but I warn that nothing is to be removed from the property. I will not levy punishment on either of you. I am, actually, glad to see it like this. And this conversation does not leave the property. "

"No, Councilman, I have never removed anything nor will I ever. I did wash Michael's blankets, but they were not taken from the property. I did them with buckets of water and scrub brush and put them back exactly where I found them."

Jarvis turned and looked at the blankets,

"That, too, is understandable."

"And we all agree that nothing spoken here leaves here." Jack states and Tessa and Carol nod their heads in agreement.

"I must get back and log in my notes and report back to

the Council. I trust you are able to make sure the house is locked up securely before you leave. And do you have the key the Council gave you?"

Jarvis asks.

"Yes."

"Then it needs to be returned to the Council. I will not say anything to them about the key that was given to you."

"I will call to arrange drop off, Councilman Jarvis, thank you for coming," Jack replied.

"If I need you for anything further I will contact you."

The three watched the Councilman leave before letting out a collective breath and a sigh of relief. That had been much too close for comfort.

"Why didn't he just take the key with him when he left?" Tessa asked.

"The Council is weird that way. I requested it so I have to return it."

Jack hugged Carol.

"How was Eddie when you left?"

Carol looked over tentatively at Tessa.

"I told her. I really don't care what the Council thinks. She needed to know."

"I stayed until he was asleep. It took a bit before he went into a deep sleep. He should still be sleeping. I put a little bit more brandy in his cocoa than I usually do."

"You give him booze to make him sleep?" Tessa questioned.

"I refuse to give him drugs." Carol's retort was sharp. "He has enough issues without getting addicted to that crap. I only give him brandy once in a while when he is in real distress."

Jack touched Carol's arm but she turned and headed upstairs.

Tears streaked Tessa's face as Jack turned back to her.

"She's so protective of Eddie. She's come to think of him as her son. Our children rarely come to see us. They have their own lives and packs now."

"Seriously?"

"We talk over the computer and they call on the holidays. We still write and send pictures but we can't afford to go visit them nor can they afford to come here, especially with the kids. Tucker lives in Portland, Oregon with his wife and four kids and Harper lives in Myrtle Beach, South Carolina with her wife and three kids." Jack started up the stairs. "I love them and would love to see them but it's just not feasible. And to leave Eddie by himself to his own devices is something I do not like to contemplate."

When he and Tessa were outside he made sure all the doors were locked as well as the backyard gate.

"And I know what you're going to say; I'm putting Eddie before my own family, but I'm not. It's their choice and we abide by their wishes. Though some day that may change."

"Win the lotto, huh?" Tessa chuckled as she got in the car.

Jack snorted, getting in the driver seat. "Yep, that's exactly it. I don't think they intended to stay there on their honeymoons but they fell in love with the atmosphere. The local packs welcomed them so they decided to stay. I don't think they were happy here anyway. They wanted their freedom and we gave it to them, tried not to deny them anything."

"Have you physically met any of your grandchildren?" Tessa asked as they pulled onto the road and headed to the Saltwater motel.

"No, but maybe someday."

After dropping Tessa off at the Saltwater, Jack went back home. Carol was in the kitchen.

"What's for supper?" he asked, lightly touching her shoulders as he kissed her neck.

"Homemade chicken soup. Comfort food for Eddie."

"Tessa didn't mean anything by what she said."

"I know, I can't help it if I'm overprotective."

"So am I."

"I just want it to end. I want to be able to take him out shopping, to take him to the beach...."

"I know, I do too but that's not going to happen. Not until this thing is solved."

"It'll never be solved."

"It will be. I believe Tessa and I are close."

"How can you be close with that guy dead? He can't talk to you now. And I'm extremely surprised that Councilman Jarvis didn't string you up by your balls for reopening this case without Council permission."

"Me too. But it isn't over yet. Where's Eddie?"

"He's on the couch, sleeping. He woke up enough to come up from the basement. I made him lay down on the couch to watch some cartoons and he went back to sleep."

"Dad may have been involved."

Carol just stared at him, shaking her head.

"I can't see him being dirty."

"I don't want to believe he was dirty. I even snapped at Tessa. But Cody said he was in on it and that...." he dropped his voice to a bare whisper in her ear, "He shot James and Michael."

Carol's face paled. "No. I can't believe that."

"I'm going down to see if the ballistic reports and bullets were even logged into the master file. They were missing from the box. I might've been stone cold drunk that week, but I know how procedures should go. I can't see Dad shirking his duties."

"Jack, if he shot James and Michael the bullets removed from their bodies would be different from the bullets removed from John and Steven. If your father used his service weapon and not a personal weapon. If he used his service revolver then ballistics would show that, provided the report ever showed up."

"I guess I'm going to be going back to the old homestead, aren't I?"

"Yep. If there's nothing in the evidence box, I guess you are. If he was hiding evidence, that would be the only place it could be. I seriously can't see him logging it into the master file if he was planning to conceal it. Where he hid it, though, I wouldn't begin to have a clue, but you will find it. I have faith in you." Carol turned the burner off. "Go wake up Eddie."

Jack went into the living room, listening to Carol set the table. He knelt down in front of the couch and stroked the hair from Eddie's face.

"Time to wake up, baby."

Eddie's eyes flickered open and he yawned.

"Uncle Jack?"

"Yeah, baby."

"We going fishing now?"

"Not tonight, sweetness. It's getting dark. It's time for supper but I promise you we will go. I have to go to the station in the morning but when I come home for dinner we can make plans for a trip, okay? Then we can spend the whole day by ourselves wherever you want to go, out to the creek or back to the falls. Wherever you want. We don't have to take any sandwiches, we can take all the junk food you want. We'll cook whatever we catch and Aunt Carol will cook it however you want."

Eddie's grin spread across his face. "Yeah!" He wrapped Jack in a big hug, Jack hugged him back, rubbing his hand through his hair.

"Okay, love. Let's go have supper or Aunt Carol is going to string us up."

He helped Eddie to his feet and took him into the kitchen.

"There's my baby." Carol smiled. "You hungry?"

"Yes, Aunt Carol."

Jack made sure Eddie was seated before he took his chair. Carol sat a big bowl of soup in front of him. He smiled brightly at her. She handed him a roll.

"You be careful, it's hot."

Jack watched as Eddie carefully picked up his knife and cut the roll in half and buttered it, then dipped it in his soup. Spooning a little onto the roll, he blew on it then put it in his mouth.

"Love you, Aunt Carol," he mumbled around the mouthful of soup.

Jack laughed and started to eat himself.

"Damn, I'm hungry. It truly has been a long day. I think I'll go to bed early tonight. Do you want to go back to the cabin tonight or do you want to stay here?"

Carol looked sharply at Jack.

"Stay here." Eddie's reply was just above a whisper.

"Okay." Jack reached across the table to lightly touch Eddie's hand.

"Do you think it's a good idea?"

"Carol, if we solve this, and I believe we will, it's over. I'm done, I'm tired of him being alone and isolated up there all by himself. He needs to start being around people. And if we do solve this, then the Council really shouldn't have any more say in the matter. He needs to be a normal young man."

Eddie looked to Carol then to Jack and back to Carol.

"Cartoons?"

CHAPTER 17

JACK STARED AT the statements and bank books in the box. He had put on gloves to handle the items.

He had entered everything into evidence in the box except for the cassette. He wanted to listen to it. He knew that as soon as it became evidence and the Council got a hold of it then he would never get a chance to listen to it. He put the box in his desk drawer with the paperwork, closed and locked it. A few more hours wasn't going to matter.

He picked up the phone to call Tessa.

Tessa sat on the couch in her motel room, thoughtfully munching on a piece of pizza and staring blankly at the TV. It was tuned to a mindless comedy. She wondered if she would get a chance to listen to what was on the cassette they had found. She knew Jack wanted to listen to it too.

She jumped when her cell phone started ringing. She

quickly wiped her fingers off on a paper napkin before picking it up and swiping the screen to answer it.

"Hello?"

"Tessa, my dear, are you busy?"

"Nope. Just munching and watching a lame TV show."

"I decided to postpone putting the cassette into evidence for a while; I think we need to hear what is on this tape. The Council will get the cassette and box after we're done listening to it."

"I agree."

"I'll be over in a few."

Jack walked into the house with Tessa.

"Carol?"

Carol came out of the kitchen.

"What?"

"Where's Eddie?"

"At the cabin. He wanted to be alone to clear his thoughts."

Jack went over to his stereo and turned it on. He pushed the button to open the door on the cassette deck.

"What have you got?" Carol asked.

"Hopefully some answers," Tessa replied. "I just hope it doesn't break."

Jack looked at the cassette, hesitant to put it in the machine. He wanted to know what was on it, but at the same time, he didn't. Tessa put a hand on his shoulder.

"We need to know."

Jack nodded and inserted the tape. Closing the door quickly, he pressed play before he could change his mind.

"It took months to set that up as neat as a pin so how the hell did you manage to screw it up? And where the hell were your silencers? You were only supposed to shoot John to get him out of

the way before he could send out a mental alert. I could have gotten a nice price out of Steven's pelt and you could have had your unicorns. It took forever to set it up and you screwed it up in less than five minutes," Bennett's voice snarled from the tape.

"Just because they have money doesn't mean they have brains," an all too familiar voice chuckled.

Jack stopped the tape and looked to Carol, his eyes full of pain.

"I knew I was right. I tried to deny what my gut was telling me, but in the end, it's him."

"Uncle Jack?" Tessa asked. "Who is it?"

"It's Adam Doherty." Tessa looked at Carol questioningly. "He's lead detective. They've been friends since Twelve Oaks, took the police courses and got on the force at the same time."

Jack bit his bottom lip hard as he turned the tape back on.

"You can't blame me, he went into labor early," Cody's voice snarked. "It's not my fault everyone came home and screwed things up. I was just doing my job." Static crackled out of the speakers then became clear again.

"A handheld recorder in his pocket," Tessa remarked. "Cody's voice is clearer than Bennett's."

"Too many delays, including Milo, but having a part unicorn/part wolf shifter might have brought in a real penny if there had been time to find out where they were stashed. In a way delays worked out, in a way it's just another way of saying it was fucked up."

"That's what happens when you don't use a condom, deary." A female voice snarked.

"I have a feeling this was going to be a blackmail tape at some point in time. Most likely when the money got thin, because if Dad knew he was being recorded, this tape would not exist and Cody would be in a cold case box."

Tessa shivered.

"Someone would find him in the distant future in the woods somewhere."

"Do you know how far out on the line my neck is? You are here on my card on a two day visitation. It's a good thing Adam is a whiz at it inventing shit and making it look believable."

"Why do you think the kid is here?"

"Yeah, the loving family that lost their pack, looking for a new home. Only here for a couple of days to check out homes, jobs, schools. Makes me want to puke, but they bought it."

There was a sound of crunching gravel, heavy footfalls with lighter ones a step off. There was also a sound that made Carol start. Jack looked at her as Tessa turned the tape off.

"What is it?"

"They really brought the baby with them? You can hear him. Can you play that back?"

Tessa did as requested. "There." Tessa hit stop. "Did you hear it?" Tessa and Jack both shook their heads.

"It's a sound I have not heard in years but know it so well. Cooing. Tucker used to do it all the time when he was relaxed and ready for sleep."

"That's how they got past the gate. Even if it was stated on the visitation pass, they would have had to make a good show for after when all the shit went down. The guards really wouldn't do a thorough search of the car when they left two days later. My guess is the gate security wouldn't be looking too closely at a family leaving. They'd be looking more for an individual or two looking all nervous like trying to get away. That was one issue that seriously was addressed. Regardless of the vehicle or who was in it, it was rigorously checked and scanned."

"The infant would be 31 or 32 by now," Carol murmured.

"The man with the older woman that Mrs. Gleason saw going into Cody's apartment."

Tessa turned the tape back on.

"If those damn Protectors got wind of it, it wouldn't be hard to track back to Adam, and to a greater extent, me. You want to pray that John only had time to get the alerts out and not establish a link for others to gather more information other than an emergency and address. But I can assure you, I will feed you to the wolves before we ever put our heads in the noose," Bennett growled.

"We can sing just as well as you can," A new voice snarled.

"Why didn't you stay at the hotel, Keith? I can deal with this on my own."

"Milo's crying for you."

"Come here, my baby." Thea's voice sounded strained.

"We need to leave, Thea," Keith stated.

A baby giggled and a crinkling sound. A grunt came from Bennett. Thea whispered.

"And another hundred thousand for the both of you when you get us out of town."

"He took a bribe," Tessa hissed. Jack looked green as Carol murmured her affirmative.

"Right now, my dear, the gates are shut. No one comes in or gets out. Not me, or Adam. The Protectors are on high alert. If you had been a little swifter on the draw, John would not have had a chance to send out a mental alert. Plus, you want to hope that none of the neighbors saw you coming or going."

"What would make a nice incentive to make any sighting

reports go away or not be definable? And why were you there, Bennett? Weren't you sticking your neck out? You were there before Keith and I, before Adam? You told the nurse to leave, according to Cody. Needless to say that loose end had to be cleared up."

"Unlucky for her she met me on the way out,"

Adam's voice chuckled.

"Shit, Adam. Nothing had to be done with her."

"She had a very good look at all of us."

"I'll ask you again, why were you there?" Thea's voice was sharper.

"I thought if I went to check on him, I could keep them from going to the hospital."

"And what made you think that was going to happen? I thought your son made it perfectly clear that Michael was not going to the hospital under any circumstances when he gave birth unless there was danger."

"Sometimes complications do happen."

"Why does that sound like a lie?"

"You want the truth?"

Bennett's voice was rough. "I was making a friendly call to see how things were going. John was a Protector, a certified one. He could smell danger a mile away. His defenses would have been up, he would have been on high alert. As soon as you hit the top of the stairs he would've sent out a mental alert and had his frigging rifle in his hands blasting away before you ever got to the bottom. He had a gun safe in the darkroom. You never would have stood a chance. I wanted to make sure he didn't get on the defensive. And with something that important his hackles would have been way up. But unfortunately, he had a gun nearby, like he was expecting trouble. Thankfully, Adam only took a shot to the shoulder."

Jack couldn't believe what he was hearing as betrayal ripped through his heart. He had always upheld the law to the best of his abilities, but to hear his father talk like this, Jack thought he was going to be sick.

I saw him send out a mental alert before I even got halfway down the stairs, that's why I blew him away first. Not going to give him the chance to send out another one to make a connection with his location," Keith chuckled.

"I can understand it being an important event for him, but to already be on high alert he had to suspect something was going to go wrong, suspect a threat. Was he given advance notice to be on alert? Bennett, I just don't believe you. Why were you really there? And why did you kill my prizes?" Thea's voice was measured.

"Why did you kill Steven? I could've gotten a nice penny for his pelt. It's not like I don't have the access to force shift drugs," Bennett growled back.

Tessa snapped the tape off when she saw the look on Jack's face. He ran to the bathroom, he just made it to the toilet before throwing up. She couldn't really blame him. She had a hand clamped over her own mouth as she could feel the bile rising in her throat but forced herself to swallow it back down. She could not believe what she was hearing, that people could be so evil. She could hear him flush the toilet and splash water on his face.

Jack came back a few minutes later, pale. He was visibly shaken. She could see by the way he walked that his legs were jelly. They couldn't hold him up, and he fell to the floor on his ass. He went from pale to white as a sheet. He was swallowing hard and Tessa was sure he would vomit again. His mouth moved but no sound came out. Carol knelt down beside him.

"Jack?"

"I can't believe it. Dad sold his soul for money. That my friends were murdered for money. He was always on my ass about upholding the law. That was my job and I took over for him as Chief when he retired. I needed to be the best I could be. I didn't want the job, I wanted to be a singer. But at the time I was the most qualified. We are not a large force, never have been. The few older officers at the time, who were qualified, were getting ready to retire and did not want the position. The younger officers, especially the ones who had just been hired within that year, were definitely not qualified. I really had no choice. Adam and Dale did not want it and they were well within their right to refuse. I took it because I felt I had to, I was his son, after all.

"I often believe if I truly pushed hard enough I would be a singer today and not the Chief of Police. If push came to shove the Council could have hired someone who was willing to come here for an easy position with a nice fat paycheck. But I did my best to prove to him that I could do it. I could be like him. And to find that everything I upheld meant nothing to him, that he murdered my friends for money, makes me feel dead inside."

Carol murmured in his ear.

"He pushed you to take the position so you wouldn't have the free time to go nosing around and stumble onto things you shouldn't. If it was me I would have pushed you to be a singer, then you would have been far enough away that he could have pulled it off with no worries. You wouldn't be spending all your free time digging around and wouldn't eventually find out all he was doing. He closed the case as fast as he could so you wouldn't get the chance to find out just how involved he was. If it was closed, even if it was unsolved, it was still closed unless new information came to light. But at that time there would have been none, so it got buried and basically forgotten."

"And by giving me the week off he could get all the ends tied up and out of sight so I wouldn't bother with it. I was in too much pain to even go near the box to go over it again."

"When you retire, who will be the next Chief?" Tessa asked.

Jack turned his head to look up at her, she laid a hand on his shoulder. He touched it lightly before hauling himself up to sit in the chair by the stereo.

"I don't know. I do know that it will not be either of my kids. I thought it would be nice if Tucker went into law enforcement, but he made it perfectly clear that he has no desire. Neither did Haley for that matter. I will appoint the officer who is the most qualified."

Jack reached over and pushed the play button. As painful as it was, he needed to hear the rest. The silence on the tape was deafening for a few seconds before Bennett's voice could be heard.

"Go back to the hotel and stay put, if you need anything, have the nanny go after it. Adam will make a few discreet inquiries as to how long the lockdown will last and when you can leave without arousing suspicion. I have to go back to the station, I've been up all fucking night dealing with your screwup. Plus I need to check on Jack. I'm tired as hell and really don't need this shit."

A few seconds later the tape snapped off. It came to its

end. Tessa flipped it over to the second side but after a few seconds of silence there was nothing more.

Jack sat in his chair and watched the fire burn brightly in the fireplace. He had taken Tessa back to her motel room in relative silence. Neither of them really knowing what to say to each other. His head was spinning. How did things get so out of control so fast? Carol came in and handed him a cup of coffee.

"Thanks, love." He gave her a slight smile. He couldn't understand how such a beautiful girl fell in love with an idiot like him. And she had been beautiful, turned his dick rock hard every time he saw her, and she still was.

"What is it?" She stretched out on the couch with a mug of her own.

"Did you lace this?" he asked.

"No, did you want me to?"

"Yeah, I think I might need a little something."

Carol got up and went to the bar, grabbed the whiskey bottle and poured a little into his cup.

"Thanks love." He took a sip as she put the bottle back. "Two things that are definitely getting done tomorrow, Carol, I'm going to go back over the interviews and see who's still alive and I'm going to question them. Then I'm going out to the homestead."

Carol hummed and shifted on the couch.

"Carol, if Dad was a dirty cop, and by the looks of all that has suddenly been piled up against him he was, I need to know for sure. Was he all the time or when it suited him or when the money was right? I don't want to believe it but I have to know for sure."

"I understand that, I just hope you don't plan to go over

there by yourself. That place is falling down. I don't know why you don't sell the land to get something out of it. The house won't be worth anything, but the land might."

"Time just seemed to slip away faster than I intended for it to. I kept telling myself, I'll get to it. I never got to it. Maybe after all this is over, if it ever is, I will sell."

"What do you think you'll find?"

"I don't know."

"Please, don't go there alone. Take someone with you. Tessa, or even Eddie, if he feels up to it."

"No, I won't drag Eddie over there. I'll get Tessa to go with me. That way we can bounce things off of each other while we're looking. Two people searching is better than one. Eddie would have no idea what he was looking for and I'm afraid he would get easily scared. Plus, I plan to take her with me to do the interviews."

"Good."

"Where is he, anyway? Did he come back here after I took Tessa to Saltwater?"

"Yeah. He's down in the basement. He doesn't want to be alone anymore. He's scared."

"I can't say I blame him."

Jack eased himself out of his chair, setting his coffee cup on the stand beside his chair. "I'll go look in on him."

Jack went downstairs and crept into the bedroom. Eddie lay sprawled on the bed in just his underwear. He had to smile. James had always said Eddie might go to bed in his underwear but was usually naked by morning. He crept over and brushed the hair off his face, then took the quilt and laid it over him. Eddie was a sound sleeper when he wanted to be. Jack went back up and quietly closed the door behind him.

"How is he?" Carol asked.

"Sound asleep. I wish I could sleep that soundly in the middle of the day."

Carol laughed.

"Don't we all?"

Jack let a smile cross his face before he became serious again.

"There is one thing we need to do?"

"What?"

"We'll talk to him at supper. I know he's going to be mad and pissed off that I am putting off our fishing trip yet again. I don't want to scare him, but he needs to know that there is going to be trouble and I want him as far away from it as possible. I'll stay here until you two are well on your way up there. Make sure he has enough supplies to keep him occupied until I can come and get him to tell him it's safe to come back.

"Please, Carol, stress to him that he is not to leave under any circumstances. I don't know what's going to happen, but I want to be on the safe side with this. I don't want him to be hurt. But I just have this strong feeling that he needs to be there."

"I'll go shopping now. He's been asking for a few new games."

"Get him some new games, movies too, whatever you think will keep him occupied for a few days."

"Jack, this had better end well."

"It needs to."

Carol grabbed her coat and with a quick look to her husband, she left. Jack gave her a grim smile as he watched her close the door.

CHAPTER 18

THE NEXT MORNING, Jack sat at his desk and played with his pen. His mind raced. He felt like they were getting close to solving this. Though he wasn't sure he would allow his mind to go that far yet. They still had a ways to go. He had sent all the contents, including the tape, to the Council. He felt better knowing that Eddie had promised profusely that he would stay at the cabin and had been excited that he had new things to enjoy. Even though he was grumpy at Jack for not going fishing, the lure of new games seemed to replace that anger quickly. Jack had promised that he would come for him as soon as he could, but wasn't sure how long it would be. He had seen the pain and loneliness in Eddie's eyes when Jack kissed him on the forehead and sent him on his way with Carol. It was a pain that he could still feel in his heart.

"Tara?" He tapped his intercom with the end of his pen.

"Yes Chief?" Came the tinny reply.

"Has Dale come in yet?"

"Yes, he's just walking in the door now."

"Send him back, please."

"Yes, Chief."

A few minutes later, a knock came at the door and Dale poked his head in. Jack waved him in. Dale came in, shut the door and plopped himself into the chair.

"You wanted to see me?"

"Yeah. I know you did night patrol last night. Was it all night or partial?"

"It was a partial night. Split it with Duncan. He missed a few days last week when his daughter was sick. He wanted to make up a few hours here and there and give some night guys a chance to go home early if they wanted."

"Yes, he said she was sick. I don't know how he does it being a single parent. That was most likely the only time she was still. She's a rambunctious little thing."

"Keeps him on his toes, I know that. But, I do know he's seeing someone, and Kyla has taking a liking to her, and stays with her at nights when he does patrol and picks her up from daycare when she gets off work."

"Sounds like it's working for them."

"I hope it does."

"Good. Anyway, did you get enough sleep this morning?"

"Yeah, did you need me to go out again tonight?"

"No. I need you to be quiet backup and recon out at my old homestead this afternoon. I'm not sure what time we'll be out there, as I'm going to go over the interviews and follow up on them. Tessa and I are going to look around to see if we can find any proof that can prove or disprove Dad's involvement in setting my friends up to have them killed. And, with the death of Cody, I have a feeling we're being watched."

"I can almost bet on it. Make it look like you disappeared. Lots of woods around there. Great place to hide bodies and dispose of a car. Wait...what...Cody Mitchell is dead? When did that happen?"

"Exactly. And, if there is something there, there is a good chance they'll try to stop me from taking it to the Council and exposing them. So, I need you to keep your eyes and ears open. Close, but not too close, so you won't be detected. And he was killed after we went to see him. Body was dumped where we could easily find it. Message sent."

"Not surprising with the way things are going. I've got your back, Jack, always have and always will." He got up and headed for the door. "We'll get it done. Just text me when you head out."

"Thanks, Dale."

Jack smiled wanly as he watched Dale leave. He finished off his cup of cold coffee, grimaced, then got up. He opened the office door again and peeked out. No one was in the hallway. Making a show of going to the washroom, he came back to his office and deliberately left the door open a crack. Adam had been in his office when he had gone by and was pretty sure that Adam had not heard the latch click as it always did when Jack returned to his office and closed the door. It was routine, Jack never left the door open, even just a crack. He wondered, as he sat down, if Adam would take the bait.

As Adam walked slowly to the washroom he had to know if he had heard right. The door opened and Jack went to the washroom but it never latched on his way back into the office. He turned his head just slightly, yep, the door was open just a tiny bit. Jack was getting slack.

He stopped just outside of Jack's door, he turned his head but could see no one. He flattened himself against the wall, he had to see if he could hear anything.

"Tessa, It's Jack. Do you want to go with me today? I'm going to reinterview witnesses this morning once I go over the statements, then I'm going back to my dad's homestead. It's been a long time since I've been back there and I really don't like going there alone. But if we could find even the slightest clue about Dad, then I'll suck it up and go. With the two of us looking it shouldn't take a long time, hopefully. Two sets of eyes are better than one."

Adam could hear the click of the handset being placed back on its cradle. He slipped past the door and into the washroom. He needed to get a hold of Thea.

"Are you getting poor, Detective?"

"No, consider this a freebie. Jack and Tessa will be at the Raskin's homestead this afternoon. I happened to hear him talking about going over there to look for evidence to try and clear his father."

"Ha! If they find anything it sure as hell won't be clearing him. Milo should still be there. He hasn't contacted me yet to say he found anything or that he has gone into the woods to hide or hang out or whatever it is he does when he hides in woods back here for days. I'll give him a heads up and possibly kill two birds with one stone."

Jack smiled to himself as he listened at the washroom door. He loved how voices echoed in there even at a whisper. Shifter hearing was such a benefit, too bad Adam seemed to have forgotten that. Snap! went the mouse trap.

Jack stood in front of the Council and bowed slightly.

"How may I serve?"

"It has been a year and there has been no improvement in the mental condition of the Carstairs child, Edward. He has been moved to another secure facility to continue to protect him."

"Has anyone come after him?"

"No one has actually broken into the facilities to attack or capture him, but there have been anonymous calls inquiring if a young boy with mental issues was being kept there. When they were given no information they hung up. It was decided he should be moved."

"How can I help?"

"Since all Carstairs properties have been sealed and it is now law that trespassing on these properties is strictly forbidden, we thought it best that he be made at home at the Carstairs cabin by Unicorn Falls."

"Begging the pardon of the Council, but he's a 16-year-old boy that can barely function mentally. How is he going to be able to survive by himself out there? There's no electricity. The generators there are old and finicky, he wouldn't have the strength to pull start them."

"We agree on this and are making preparations to outfit the cabin for his needs with new, easy to start generators and the supplies they require." Councilman Walters stared hard at Jack,

"It will be up to you to help him on his new journey, as his new guardian."

"I understand." Jack bowed again.

"We will notify you when everything is completed."

"Of course." Jack turned and left. Once back in his car, he slammed his hands on the steering wheel. "Just fucking great! Fucking wonderful!"

"The fucking Council is out of their minds, Carol. There are better ways to protect Eddie, if he needs it. But locking a traumatized 16-year-old boy away in a cabin, secluded all by himself is not the way to do it. I don't care what they say. How am I supposed to teach him to run generators, fill and fix them and live on his own when he doesn't even acknowledge my presence. There has got to be a better way."

Carol sat on the couch staring thoughtfully at the fireplace, its blaze bright and warm.

"Come sit by me." Carol patted the couch seat. "Stop pacing, it drives me nuts." Jack sat beside her and brought her into his arms. She laid her head on his shoulder.

"There has got to be something we can do, but I don't have the ability to override the Council. Their say is final."

"Who said anything about overriding the Council?"

Jack turned his head to look down at her. "Carol?" his voice questioning. "What is going on in that pretty head of yours?"

"They put you in charge of Eddie, right? To teach him how to live on his own, right?"

"Yes." Jack was suddenly wary. "Just what are you driving at?"

"What if we finished the basement like we had planned?"

"Ok?"

"What if we make it into a small apartment?"

"Sounds interesting."

Carol rolled her eyes and huffed out a sigh. Jack could be so dense.

She elbowed him in the ribs.

"We make it a furnished apartment with a bathroom and appliances and keep Eddie here until he is ready to be on his own up there. We care for him here since you are his guardian, so to speak. Then when he's ready, you can start taking him up there to show him how to use the generators."

Jack kissed the top of her head.

"You are a genius. It's just going to be hard to do it without anyone getting suspicious. I have to have permits and a lot of the work I can't do myself."

"We will figure it out. How long do you have before they want him in the cabin?"

"I don't know. There's work that needs to be done, new appliances. They have to put in new generators that are going to be easy for him to learn to use since you can't string a power line back that far. It's going to take a little time. And I'm hoping that they give it more time to see if Eddie will respond to me."

"Hopefully the time we need. I don't know how they can justify things, considering you have a job to do. You can't spend all your time there and with him."

"I have a feeling you may be the next one recruited, to help him learn the ways of the kitchen."

"I would enjoy it. The Council won't go back there to check on him, they'll expect you to report to them. We teach him what he needs to know, here, leave him alone as much as we can so he'll get used to being alone and gain independence then we can graduate him to the cabin. What the Council doesn't know won't *hurt them. And if we're lucky he'll come out of his shell enough that he could function somewhat normally."*

"We can only hope."

Jack went up to the file room, pulled the Carstairs box and stared at it.

"We'll solve this, guys, we have to."

Jack went into his office, shutting the door. Setting the box down on his desk, he went for a cup of coffee. He put two heaping spoonfuls of granules into the cup then poured hot water slowly over them.

"The stronger, the better." He stirred the coffee as he sat down at his desk. Taking a small sip, he grimaced.

"That'll do it." He set the cup down and opened the box. Taking out the folder marked interviews, he flipped it open.

"Okay, guys, let's see what we have here." He slumped back in his chair, looking at the files. He knew he was talking to himself, but didn't care, he wanted to believe that he was talking to his friends and that they were listening.

"Okay, so let's see if I can break this down and make long interviews short. Some of the neighbors were home, some were at work. Some have since passed away, so we couldn't interview them now even if we wanted to. Colby Davis, Zole and Miles Stone, Cristal Cummings, and Caleb Holden were all at work. Their alibis held up, and had been checked out thoroughly. Ethan Werner and Kasey Lowery were both home. Both called 911 after hearing the shots. Unfortunately they have both since passed away so we can't talk to them, I'm pretty sure on that.

"Peter Stone and Donna Walters were both home. Peter was in his garage, he thought they were firecrackers but called it in anyway, that he thought they were coming from Grayson House. Cited a noise complaint. Donna thought they were firecrackers as well and ignored it. Didn't know what was going on until the police came to talk to her. Donna, I believe, is at Sunset Oasis and I'm pretty sure Peter is there too. Darren and Aylih Keller were on their way home. They saw me speeding by. They took the plate number and were going to report me until they got home and saw all the emergency vehicles and my truck there as well. They never saw anything of relevance."

Jack picked up his phone and punched the button for Tara's desk.

"Yeah?"

"Your mom used to know Peter Stone and Donna Walters, didn't they?"

"Yeah. They used to go around to each other's houses and play cards."

"Do you know if they are still alive? Donna is in Sunset Oasis, if I recall."

"She was, passed away while she was in there. Heart failure, I think it was. Peter is gone, too. Quite a few years ago, now, I think."

"Damn."

"You're going through the interviews, right?"

"Yeah, not much enlightenment there. Ethan Werner and Kasey Lowery..."

"Dead."

"Geez, don't sound so broken up."

Tara chuckled slightly.

"Sorry, but it's true. 30 years is a long time, Chief."

"I know, and most of those people were old back then or at work."

"Not finding any clues."

"I'm going to re-interview the ones I can. See if they match up or they were changed after their statements were taken."

"You seriously think that..."

"Yes, I do."

"No problem." Tara hung up.

"Okay, now where were we? Okay, Gloria and Chase Holden were just getting home. They did not hear the shots but saw me pull up and go tearing into the house then saw Dad pulling up seconds later. Dottie Delaney was the only one who saw anything of relevance since she was outside in her garden. The side she was working on, despite the trees, she could see the front door. She had the day off, she says she didn't really pay any attention to who was coming or going, but when she saw Dad's cruiser go by not long before the shots were fired she kept her eyes open.

"When she heard the first shot, she looked up and saw someone running out but didn't get a good look at him. She ran into the house and called 911 when she heard more shots. Gina and Dane Connors. Your folks, James. I felt so bad for them. They were so close. Your dad had come home from work early. They heard the first shot but had no idea what it was, then they heard four more. They ran outside when they heard more shots but saw no one. But they could see the front door open. Dane placed a call to 911 and told the operator that shots were fired from Greyson House. I cannot begin to imagine the pain and horror they felt, especially when all the police and ambulances showed up. I can just imagine the worst part for them was knowing you were in there and they didn't know if you were dead or alive. If any of you were dead or alive, for that matter. Then to see the body bags come out and knowing instantly that your only son was dead and his husband and kids, your extended family, was gone in the blink of an eye. I was devastated, James, but I can imagine your parents were even more so."

Jack laid the files down and rubbed his eyes. He took another drink of the coffee and cringed. It had gotten cold in the amount of time it had taken to read over the interviews. He set it back on the desk and closed his eyes. He felt so tired. Mentally and physically exhausted.

He picked up the phone and called Tessa. It went directly to voicemail. He sent a text instead of leaving a message.

Jack: Call me when you can.

Jack had just closed his eyes and felt like he was drifting off when his cell started ringing. He jumped and his eyes flashed open. His heart was racing. He took a couple of deep breaths to slow it down. He picked up.

"Tessa?" His voice sounded out of breath.

"You okay?"

"Yeah, I must've drifted off for a few minutes while I was waiting for you to call back."

"No worries. I was in the bathroom and didn't hear it ringing. I'm tired, too. I think it's more mental than physical."

"Yeah, it is." Jack straightened himself up. "I'm going to go around and do some interviews, you want to come along? I set the trap for Adam. He bought it. I fake called you to set him up. I wasn't sure if you would want to come with me to re-interview witnesses or not."

"Actually, I had been planning to call you to see if I could come down and talk to you about witnesses because I really didn't want to talk over the phone."

"Look, how about I come to you?"

"Sure, I'll be here."

Jack knocked on Tessa's motel room door. It took her a minute to open it. She was in plain jeans and a sweater. With a slice of pizza in one hand, she held the door open with two fingers of the other so as not to get pizza sauce all over it. She moved aside so he could come in. She closed the door as he turned to face her.

"I thought I would have a little lunch before you got here."

She walked over to the pizza box on the table and dropped the crust in the box, then wiped her hands on the paper napkins beside it. "I always ask for extra napkins. I'm such a slob and I hate using the room towels, they stain so easily. "

"Very respectable girl." He kissed her cheek as she picked up a new slice and handed it to him. He took a bite, after the second chew he looked down at it. "Please don't tell me you had them put anchovies on this. Is that all you ever eat?"

"Yeah, I love the things. And, no, I do tend to eat more than just anchovy pizza, but it is my go-to comfort food."

Jack handed it back to her, forcing himself to swallow.

"You are your father's child. Michael loved anchovies on his pizza."

"Did he also love chips and chocolate? I discovered one

day that if you put a piece of a chocolate bar in between two plain chips it is a most pleasurable sensation of sweet and salty."

"Like I said, you are your father's child."

Tessa smiled wistfully. Jack gave her a light hug as she munched thoughtfully. He guided her over to the couch, then sat beside her.

"What did you want to tell me?"

"Before we go to the interviews, I need to tell you something. I don't know if it'll be in her statement or not but when I was at Dottie's Diner getting something to eat, she told me a few things. She told me that she lived across the street. And that she heard the shots and saw someone running out the front door. She said she was sure she saw blood on his shoulder, that he must have been shot. She said she never saw anyone going in because she wasn't paying attention."

"Did she say who she saw coming out?"

"Adam Doherty."

Jack's face went pale.

"She must've been mistaken."

Tessa shrugged.

"I don't know. What does your statement say?"

"It said she saw someone coming out the front door but never stated any names."

"Then she either lied about who she saw or didn't tell the officer who came out. If she did, maybe was deliberately left out of her official statement."

"We're definitely going to find out."

Jack was silent as he led her over to his truck and helped her get in. He was in the driver's seat before he spoke.

"We'll do it this way. I don't want to make it look like a

formal reopening if I take my cruiser. We're just asking a few questions in relation to your book."

Tessa looked at him for a moment.

"Ooohhh. Sneaky."

Jack pulled into the driveway of a two-story house. Tessa could tell it needed minor repairs, including a fresh coat of paint. Though the small yard and gardens looked like they were being well tended. They walked up the steps to the front door and rang the bell. After a few seconds, the door opened and Dottie stood there. Tessa was surprised to see how different she looked when she wasn't in her work clothes. She now wore faded jeans, a black T-shirt and was barefoot.

"Chief?" Dottie looked surprised.

"Hello Dottie. Do you mind if we come in and ask you a few questions?"

"Sure." Dottie opened the door wider and stood aside to let them enter. Closing the door she led them into the living room off to the left. It was sparse for the couple of arm chairs, coffee table and TV stand with a moderately sized TV on it. Dottie motioned to the chairs.

"Please, sit. Can I get you anything?"

"No, we're fine." Jack replied as they all sat down. "I'm actually surprised that we caught you home."

"Contrary to popular belief, I don't live there. I do like my down time. What can I help you with, Chief?"

"Tessa was telling me that you talked to her about the Carstairs murders and that you saw Adam Doherty come running out the front door after the first shot. When you heard four more shots that's when you ran in to your house and called emergency."

"Yes, I did." Dottie's eyes flickered back and forth

between the two of them. "I went and gave a formal statement and signed it."

"I looked up your statement before I came. It makes no mention of you saying that Adam Doherty was the one running out the front door. It just states that you saw someone but did not recognize who it was, you did not see them clearly enough."

A look of shock passed over Dottie's face.

"That is not true. I told your father that I saw Adam Doherty come running out the front door. It looked like his shoulder was all bloody. I wrote it all out and signed it. Your father stood there and watched me."

Jack nodded his head slowly, a grim look on his face.

"Jack.... do you think......" Tessa started.

"Yeah, a good chance it may have been rewritten and your signature forged. And then, whoever typed out the file copies knew no different."

"It would have to have been that. I'm not lying. I have no reason to. I can't begin to tell you how many times I was asked if I was sure it was Adam Doherty I saw and not someone else, if I could have been mistaken. I kept telling them no, that it was Adam I saw."

"Could we get a sample of your handwriting to compare to the signature on the statement."

"Of course." Dottie got up and went down the hall and went into a back room Tessa assumed was a bedroom. She came back a few minutes later with a notepad and pen.

"What would you like me to write?"

"Your name and just a couple of random sentences would be okay."

When she finished, Dottie passed the paper over to Jack, who tucked it into the pocket of his pants.

"Does this mean you're officially reopening the case?"

"Reopening it but not officially. Please do not tell anyone. We really don't want to raise hopes that it will finally be solved. It may not, we may not get any further than my dad did."

"I understand, and I wish you both all the best. It does need to be solved."

With that, Tessa and Jack got up to leave. Once back in the truck, Tessa looked at him.

"So, where to next?"

"I thought we'd pop in on Chase Holden. He lives in the apartment building past Myron's Bakery. He was married at the time, but his wife divorced him a few years ago, and moved. To where, I have no idea. But according to their statement, they both said the same thing. They were separated when their statements were taken but their alibis held up and pretty much said the same thing when their statements were compared. But I want to know just exactly how long it was after I arrived that Dad and everyone else did."

"To see if they saw something that might not have made it into their original statement."

"Now you're catching on."

After a few minutes, they pulled up into the parking lot of a small apartment building.

"Wonder what it costs to live here?" Tessa asked.

"Don't know, honestly. But it looks clean, might be expensive."

They got out and went to the main doors. They scanned

the tags beside each bell. Jack pressed the one labelled 'Chase Holden 204'.

"Yes?"

"Chief Raskins and Tessa Carstairs. We'd like to talk to you about what you saw the day the Carstairs' were killed."

The door latch clicked immediately. "Come up."

Jack and Tessa went up the stairs to the fourth apartment on the second floor. They knocked on the door. A man with thin gray hair opened the door.

"As soon as I saw that book of yours I wondered if you would be around, Miss Carstairs." He motioned them to come in and beckoned them to sit on the couch in the small living room.

"What makes you say that?" Tessa asked.

Chase sat down in the chair opposite them.

"You've opened it back up and want to know what I saw, what Gloria and I saw."

"It's not open officially again, so we'd appreciate your discretion on this."

"Sure. What you want to know?"

"From your statement, you got home about the same time that I got there."

"Yeah, you shot by us like a bat out of hell. I thought you were going to run us off the road. The only reason we knew it was your truck was because of your police plate."

"Police plate?" Tessa asked.

"Personal vehicles that are owned by police officers have an extra letter added and are a slightly different color than civilian plates. It makes our vehicles easier to identify in case someone tries to report us for speeding or needs help. They see the plate, and if we are in the vehicle they will feel safer approaching us."

"Don't you have light bars?"

"Not in our personal vehicles, but we do in our ghost cars."

"Oh." Tessa fell silent in understanding.

"Your wife, Gloria, was with you that day."

"Yes. We both worked the morning shift together so we could have the afternoon and evening together."

"About what time was that? That you got home."

Chase shifted his eyes upward in thought.

"I think it must have been close to 4 o'clock, we were getting home later than we normally would. We had a surprise shipment of supplies, he was supposed to come the next day but came early."

"You also told the police that you saw Chief Raskins arrive not long after I did. How long would you say that had been, roughly?"

"He had to have been in the area because I don't think it was any more than five minutes before he pulled up and went tearing into the house."

Jack nodded his head slowly.

"Thank you." Jack got up and Tessa along with him. "We'll see ourselves out."

"I hope you finally get it solved," Chase called out.

"We do too," Tessa said over her shoulder as they left.

Back in his truck, Jack sat in deep thought. Tessa waited a moment before speaking.

"What is it?"

"If what Chase said was accurate, then there was no way Dad could have been at the station when the call came in, as it takes at least 15 minutes to get to Greyson House from there. Even at top speed I still cannot see him getting there in under that. He had to have been here already. He had to have been close by. He was not at the station like he said he was going to be."

Tessa laid a hand on Jack's arm.

"He was in there when they were killed."

"Yeah, he was, and lied about it. And it never really occurred to me at the time, but by the time I got there and puked in the upstairs bathroom might have been 10 minutes. I felt his hand on my shoulder when I was in the bathroom. I heard no sirens."

"He slipped up. He didn't feel the need to turn them on. He must've been around the corner. He got out of the house through the back gate, waited for you to show up, then pulled around from wherever he had been parked, and came in."

"It sounds evil but it's logical."

After a moment of silence Tessa spoke up.

"So, who's next?"

"Darren and Aylih Keller. They are the last ones. I looked into the ones who were home and still alive. The others in the neighborhood that were at work all have alibis or are dead."

"Oh." Tessa's voice was small.

"Not really a lot of young people on Greyson Drive. Most were middle aged or older at the time. 30 years is a long time and life can be cruel."

Tessa said nothing, how could she? There really wasn't anything she could say to that. Jack was right.

After a few moments of driving, Jack pulled into a parking space of another apartment building.

"Wow, this looks really new."

"It is. They are assisted living seniors apartments. A

friend of Carol's moved in recently and she says she loves it. The price is reasonable for what you get. Utilities are included, don't have to worry about snow removal. There are apartments for couples and singles. Housekeeping services and security."

"Wow."

"Yeah, Unicorn Valley has come up in the world a bit. Carol's talked about living here a few times if a spot opens up, provided...."

Tessa understood what he meant. Provided Eddie could live on his own if this case was ever solved. But she didn't voice that, instead, she said,

"Would you want to live here?"

"I go where Carol goes. It doesn't matter where we live as long as we're together."

Jack got out of the truck with Tessa right behind him.

"Look at the flowers." Tessa pointed to the two small square flower gardens in front of the main doors.

"Carol loves working in her flower gardens. I think those are petunias and snapdragons."

"Yes, the smaller flowers are pansies. They have such precious faces. I love taking pictures of them."

Jack gave her a smile as he pushed the buzzer on the right side of the door.

"Yes?" A male voice answered.

"Chief Raskins and Tessa Carstairs to see Darren and Aylih Keller."

"One moment."

A minute or two passed before there was a click and the door released. They went inside. There was a small lobby painted in bright blue and greens. There was an elevator and in a small alcove to the left sat a small desk. The man sitting there got up.

Jack strode over and shook the man's offered hand.

"This is some place."

"Yes. I was quite surprised when the Council approved something like this."

"How so?" Tessa asked.

"The owners don't live in Unicorn Valley."

Jack's eyebrows arched.

"Well, I guess the Council really has changed and come into the modern world."

"Seems so."

"What is your job here? If you don't mind my sounding rude."

"I alert the tenants to visitors, if they know them I'll let them go up, if not, then I ask them to leave. Also, each apartment is equipped with a medical emergency alarm. I can contact police or an ambulance if they are unable."

"Chief?" a new voice asks.

Tessa and Jack turn around to see an elderly man with a weather beaten face and short white hair standing in front of the elevator door.

"Darren?"

"Yep, come on up."

Darren hit the elevator button and the door slid open again. They all stepped in. After a few seconds they stepped out onto the fifth floor. He motioned with his hand and they followed him down the hallway to the door marked 502. He opened the door and let them in.

"This is really nice,"

Tessa whispered. Darren gave her a small smile.

"It's quaint. And the price was right. Aylih didn't want to live in our house any longer since she developed arthritis and found it hard to get up and down the stairs. Have a seat."

Jack looked around the fair sized living room. The walls were a light blue with matching blue chairs and couch, with a big screen TV in the corner.

"Is Aylih home?" Jack asked.

"She's laying down, her arthritis has been bad today. She took a pain pill and it makes her sleepy. Do I need to wake her?"

"No, that's fine. Please, let her sleep. We just wanted to talk about the day you came home to the Carstairs being killed. Your statement says you were both in the same car but didn't see anything of relevance."

A cloud formed on Darren's face.

"I'll need to wake her. I'll give you what I know then I will get her. She saw something that I didn't and you'll probably want to hear it directly from her. I don't know why it was left out of our official statements?"

"I have a good idea on that but, please, continue."

"We were coming home from taking her mother to a doctor's appointment. We were just going the speed limit when this truck comes roaring up behind us, whips out and passes us like we were standing still. Scared the hell out of us because he was driving so reckless. We had no idea who it was. I told Aylih to get the plate number because as soon as we got home we were reporting him.

"It didn't occur to us that it was you, Chief, we were more concerned about if you were a psycho going to drive us off the road and getting the plate number. It wasn't until we got home that it occurred to us that it was a police plate and saw your truck in front of Greyson House as we drove by. With all the emergency vehicles, we knew then that something was very, very wrong."

"Did you see anything out of the ordinary for that kind of situation? Like, someone just hanging around or not really doing anything, in plain clothes maybe?"

"No, not really. Not that I can remember. We pulled into our driveway and walked back to where we could watch but not get in the way. I guess I was more interested in trying to take it all in."

"I saw something, Chief," Aylih spoke as she slowly came into the living room. Darren turned sharply, went to his wife immediately, and helped her to sit down.

"I was just coming to wake you."

"I heard voices but it was a little hard to get myself awake enough to come out."

"What did you see?" Tessa asked gently.

"When we were walking back I happened to turn my head and saw Chief Raskins and Detective Doherty out by the Chief's car. It was parked out front. It looked like they were arguing. Then Detective Doherty brings his hand up and he has a purse in it. He shoves it at the chief and walks away shaking his head and waving his hands as if to say he was done.

"The chief looked at it then quickly threw it in his trunk, then went back into the house."

Jack and Tessa looked at each other.

"Why would he have a purse when there were only all males in the house?"

"The only female that would have been in there would

have been the birthing nurse, but there was no purse in the evidence box," Jack responded to Tessa's question.

"Then where did it go?"

"Another mystery." Jack directed his next question to Aylih. "Can you describe the purse?"

Aylih was silent for a moment, her eyes shifted down in thought.

"I believe it was small and green. Not a vibrant green but it was noticeable, it was like a clutch purse. There was no handle or strap."

Jack's face grew dark. His father was in it so deep and so was Adam. He forced a smile onto his face.

"Did you tell this to the officer that took your statements?"

"Yes, though I don't remember the officer's name right now. I know he was a young man and he looked so green like he wanted to run and hide or throw up."

Jack nodded his head.

"Anything else, even if it doesn't seem relevant would help."

They both shook their heads.

"No," Darren replied. "I wish we could be of more help."

"No, that's fine. That's been a big help. Thank you." Tessa smiled at them.

"Do you think it'll get solved?" Aylih asked.

Jack hated hearing that question.

"We hope so. If not this time around then, maybe, someday. Thank you for your time. We'll show ourselves out."

Once back out in the truck, Jack slammed his fist down on the dashboard making Tessa jump.

"When I read over their statements, they said they saw nothing of relevance. There was no mention of Aylih seeing Dad and Adam arguing and him putting a purse in his trunk!"

"Well, naturally not, if you were trying to cover shit up and hide the possible death of that nurse would you leave it in a statement for all the world to see?"

"No, I wouldn't. But if that was the birthing nurse's purse, where the fuck is it? It wasn't in the evidence box. So that means either Dad or Adam did something with it or hid it. I just wish we could find out where."

"We will. We need to."

"The homestead is next." Jack pulled out his cell phone. "Just let me text Dale to let him know we're on our way."

Jack: On our way out to the homestead

Dale: I'm on it

He shoved the phone back into his pocket.

"Let's go."

CHAPTER 19

JACK FELT HIS chest tighten as he pulled up in the driveway to his old homestead. The house was a two-story farmhouse that had definitely seen better days. The front lawn was over-run with weeds and tall grass.

"I haven't been back here since Mom went to the assisted living apartment after Dad died."

"It looks like it used to be a beautiful home."

"At one time. I just didn't have the heart to come back here to do anything with it. I know I should have. I think I probably will sell it now. I will never be back here to live. I know the kids want nothing to do with it."

Jack pulled the car into the driveway and turned it off. He sat for a minute and heaved a sigh.

"What are we looking for?" Tessa asked.

"I don't know. Anything. Anything that could prove that he was either there or wasn't. Tessa, I want so badly to believe that my Dad had nothing to do with any of it. I need solid hardcore proof one way or another."

"Hopefully we can find the proof we need."

"We have to." With that, Jack got out of the car, Tessa followed. Standing at the front door, Jack dug into his pocket. Pulling out a key, he slid it into the lock, there was no sound of the lock disengaging. It was already unlocked.

"What the fuck!?" He reached into his jacket and pulled out his gun.

"Why do you have that? What's wrong?" Tessa suddenly looked frightened.

"The door's unlocked. I know for a fact that it was locked when I left here the last time. I made sure all the windows and doors were locked."

He slowly pushed the door open and quietly stepped inside. Tessa was a step behind him. They were in the kitchen. It looked ransacked. Pictures were on the floor, glass broken. Oven and fridge doors had been left open, as well as all the cupboards.

Doing a quick cursory check of the rest of the first floor, which consisted of a living room, dining room and a mud room, he saw all had been trashed in someone's attempt to find something. Jack had no idea what they could have been looking for but he knew the search had been fresh. Dust had not yet begun to resettle. He only prayed that they didn't find what they were looking for. Whatever that was.

"They were here. They were looking for something. The same thing we are, weren't they?"

Jack turned his head slightly, his eyes full of pain and anger.

"Yeah, but we can only pray they didn't find it."

Jack moved further back into the kitchen. It was an

old-fashioned country kitchen painted in muted blues and browns. The table stood in the middle with four chairs around it. Tessa moved slowly around, closing the fridge and oven door.

"What idiot would think something valuable and important would be hidden in an oven or fridge?"

"A stupid one. Wait here." Jack quickly went upstairs. After a cursory look in all the rooms, he came back down. "All clear." He put his gun back in his pocket.

"I bet you had a wonderful childhood in a home like this."

"Yeah, there's a creek down back I would go swimming in and a few deep spots where Dad would take me fishing."

"Sounds like fun."

"It was." Jack's voice held a hint of sorrow.

"Let's get started," Tessa whispered. "Wait, what's this?"

"What?" Jack looked at her. She held what looked to be a fruit bar wrapper in her hand.

"Looks like someone was hungry."

Jack deadpanned as he made his way, again, back up the stairs. Each step creaked under his weight. They always had. It brought a smile to his lips, you could not get away with sneaking out in that house. The stairs would give you away every time.

"I always loved a creaky stair," Tessa said from behind him.

"You wouldn't if you were trying to sneak out at night. Dad was a light sleeper, came with the job I guess. I never made it past the third step before I could hear his voice. 'If you aren't in that bed in five seconds you are going to know about it.'"

"Did you ever defy him?" Tessa asked as she stood beside him at the top of the stairs.

"Only once. I think I was 16 or 17, not really sure now. It didn't matter the day, I was to be in bed at 10. But a couple other guys were sneaking out to smoke some weed then see if we could slip into the new bar down on Rocy Road. It's gone now."

Jack led them down the hallway and opened the second door on the left and went in. Tessa followed.

"This was my room. Mom and Dad were on the right, end door but what hearing he had. Shifter hearing at its finest. I ignored his warning and snuck out. I think it was around 11 and I didn't get back home and up to my room till about 5:30. We had fake IDs and the idiot at the door really wasn't paying much attention. We were shit faced when we left. I think we actually got thrown out.

"We went back in the woods by Old Man Henkins fields and smoked a little more weed. Puked our guts up then passed out. I had one skillfully crafted headache. I had just crawled back in bed when my door burst open."

Jack went behind the door and pointed to a small dent in the wall.

"He deliberately left that there to remind me. The fury in his eyes was incredible and I could tell he had been up all night waiting for me, but Mom was the one doing the worrying. He never gave me a moment's peace all day. He got the water as cold as it would go and held me in the shower until I was shivering. Then breakfast, which came back up five minutes later. Then it was out the door to accompany him on his morning jog. That was a torturous hour. But the thing I think that hurt the most was when he looked at me and told me how disappointed he was in me for disobeying him."

Jack wandered around the room, it was just as he had

left it. Except for the crooked pictures on the wall, and the broken ornaments on the floor. Tessa reached down and picked up the pieces of a horse ornament.

"Oh Jack..."

He turned to look at her, his eyes drifting down to the horse pieces in her hands. He could feel pain squeeze his heart tight.

"James gave that to me as a birthday present one year. He couldn't find a black unicorn ornament so he bought a black horse ornament and made a horn and glued it on. I should've taken it with me when I moved out. I just thought it would be safer here. Mom and Dad preserved my room—I assume for when Carol and I moved back in, then our son would have this room. So I just pretty much left it all as it was."

"You had no idea this would happen."

"I know, but still...." Jack let his voice trail off, there was nothing he could say.

Tessa gently put the pieces on the dresser and dusted her hands off.

"Maybe it could be fixed."

"Doubt it." Jack's voice was rough with feeling.

Tessa let her eyes scan around the room. Family pictures all over the walls, bed under the window with a soft blue bedspread. A chest of drawers on the opposite wall and a closet.

"I never did it again." Jack ran his fingers reverently over a picture of his father holding him when he was just an infant. "I think from that point on I grew up. I smartened up. I needed to prove to Dad that I could be trusted again. I started by getting odd jobs doing just about anything. It was James who discovered I could sing when he, John and I went down to the Lounge for kids song night, aged 8 to 18, one Saturday afternoon. I brought the house down."

He moved to another picture.

"James took this." Tessa came over and looked at it. A 17-year-old Jack stood on a small stage leaning on the speaker holding up a small trophy.

"You won the contest?" she asked.

"Yeah. One Saturday a month they would have a competition and the audience would vote by way of ballots left on the table to fill out, and John's dad would count them. You got a trophy and 20 bucks. To us kids that was the equivalent of winning a Grammy award."

Jack took the picture down.

"James and John thought I should make singing a career, but I was so hell bent on making my dad proud of me I decided that being an officer was the better way to go. I wrote my own songs, even sold a few. My book disappeared, though. I don't remember where I left it. I guess at the time it didn't matter. I know Dad wanted me to be a cop, but in some ways, I think he enjoyed how good a singer I was."

He put the picture back and left the room. Opening another door, his breath hitched.

"Mom and Dad's room."

Tessa went ahead of him.

"It's so cozy feeling."

"Yeah, Mom liked her softness. Hence the frilly bedspread, frilly curtains and frilly stand covers. Dad loved Mom so much that he didn't care. If she wanted it, she got it. He tried to be gruff but he had a heart of gold when it came to her. They were soul mates. When he was killed I think it killed her too. She couldn't bear to be here without him, but she was lonely and died a few years later."

"That's so sad," Tessa murmured with tears in her eyes.

Jack took in a sharp breath and straightened himself up.

"Yeah. Guess it's time to get off memory lane and start looking. For what, I have no idea, but I guess we'll know when we see it."

Tessa stared at the bed a moment longer. It was like she could almost feel them there still. Jack went over and lightly touched the quilt at the foot of the bed. As if he could sense her thoughts. he murmured,

"Grandma Raskins made that quilt for them as a wedding present."

"It should never have been left here to rot."

"I know. It will be one of the things I remove and have restored when I go to sell the place. If I couldn't live here before, I would never be able to now, knowing that Dad was dirty. I'll take the good memories and leave it at that."

"Will you take the pictures? Some of these are beautiful."

"Yes, most likely all of them. These two have always been my favorite."

Tessa came to stand beside Jack in front of two large pictures that look like they had been taken at a hospital.

"I guess I was only a few minutes old. The nurse took it while the doc was taking care of Mom."

"He looks so proud holding you."

"Yeah, I tried my best to always make him proud of me and everything I did. Even becoming an officer, I thought that would be the ultimate achievement after my bar stint."

The second picture was of all three. His mother in her hospital bed, Bennett laying beside her while Jack was tightly bundled and nestled in between the two. Bennett still had on the hospital garb they had put him in when he had been in the delivery room. Both had big smiles.

"Mom said I was about an hour old there."

"You look so tiny."

"Believe me, according to my mother, I was not. I was 8 lbs. 8 oz. Which might not seem bad to most but I was her first child, and only, and I was a big deal."

Tessa laughed and patted his arm.

"Every woman's body is different. Some can handle pain better than others." Then tears glittered in her eyes. "How did my father handle having me? Do you know?"

"The only conversation I had was with John, he said Michael was handling the pains of the contractions but was uncomfortable. The only one that could tell you anything would be Eddie."

"Will he see me?"

"I don't know. I hope he will."

Jack shook himself out of his dark thoughts.

"We should continue looking. I just feel like I'm intruding in a place that was personal."

"Were you never allowed in here as a child?"

"No, not often. If I had a really terrifying nightmare, yes, but other than that, no. When we had bad thunderstorms we would all get up and make a fire in the living room and stay downstairs. Mom would read to me and Dad would sit in his chair with his pipe, watching over us."

Tessa's heart tightened. What she would have given to have that kind of life with her birth family. But some sick monster saw fit to rob her of that. Her voice cracked when she spoke,

"Where do you think he would hide anything so valuable?"

"If I know my dad, it would be a safe and secure place, but still right under our noses."

Jack couldn't help but notice a tremble in her voice and he didn't blame her. The life she should have had, stolen from her without ever having a chance to even get to know it. And knowing that his father had been a part of it must hurt to no end.

"Did your Mom decorate this room?"

"Yeah. Dad wanted nothing to do with that. He just gave her the money she wanted and let her go to town. He trusted her and she did not disappoint. He loved how homey it was; they didn't have a lot of money to make this house into a mansion. A police chief might have made a decent pay, but still."

"Your Mom was a nurse?"

"Yeah. She left when she found out that she was pregnant, then took a year off after. I think it was only a few months later that she took permanent leave to be a stay-at-home mom. She loved being a nurse, but loved me more and didn't mind leaving."

Tessa came back to the two pictures taken the day Jack had been born.

"Did your Mom ever think about going back to nursing when you got older?"

"Yeah. She did when I started school. She didn't want to miss any time with me when I was small. She knew she would never get back those firsts she would have missed. Once I got settled in school she went back. She only took days, and was sure to be home when Dad and I got home."

Tessa lightly fingered the frames of the pictures, she tried to focus on what he was saying, but her mind was elsewhere.

"Tessa?" Jack touched her shoulder and she jumped. "Sorry. You look so deep in thought, I didn't think you heard me come up beside you."

"No, I didn't. These two pictures are larger than any others in this room. It's like he wanted to be sure you knew this was the proudest moment in his life, but why in such a private place? What are you hiding, Bennett?"

Tessa placed her hands tightly on the picture of the three and gently lifted it off its hanger. Turning it over, she looked at the backing.

"Do you see this?"

Jack moved up to squint at the frame.

"Right there, that crack, or line that extends down from the angle cut." He took out his pocket knife, flipped out the blade and carefully inserted it into the crack and pried. A little flap lifted up to reveal a small compartment and a key.

"It must have taken dad forever to chisel that out. These frames have never changed that I have ever noticed."

"And without damaging or breaking the frame. Unless he took it to someone to have it made."

"That could be possible too, he could have done it when Mom or I weren't at home to notice it was gone."

Jack pried the key out and closed the compartment back up. Tessa hung the picture back up and moved to stare at the other one.

"Would he? Seriously?"

Tessa took the picture down and gently laid it on the bed then to stare at the wall. She reached over and took his knife.

"If you don't have perfect skills in hiding then what

better way to cover up than with the picture. Can you see the square?"

Jack looked at her funny, but leaned in to squint at the wall. He watched her push the knife into the wallpaper and slowly start to cut the unsealed lines. Jack had to shake his head, she sure had Michael's eye for detail. Could see a flaw a mile away. She drove the knife in at various places prying out the square. All Jack felt he could do was stare. He was seeing a side of his father he never knew existed. She took the square of sheet rock and put it on the floor. Jack took his phone, turned on the flashlight and shone it into the hole. A hole had been drilled into a crossbeam and a rope had been attached to it. Tessa reached in and started to pull it up.

"This is heavy." She brought up a box and pulled it out.

Jack held it as she cut off the string. Sitting on the bed, Tessa put the key in and unlocked it. Jack lifted the lid, his heart thumping at what he would find.

A small pale green purse, faded from age, lay on top. Tessa reached in to pick it up but Jack stopped her. He dug into his pocket and pulled out a pair of vinyl gloves and handed them to her. She put them on and picked up the purse. Opening it up, she took out a small wallet. A driver's license read Dani Haley.

"Dani Haley?"

"The birthing nurse. She disappeared the night of the murders. Everyone thought she was scared and took off, left town. We kept an eye on her accounts and house but nothing moved. Her accounts were never used. She had a cat, but never came home to feed it or had anyone go to her home to attend to it, so the pet was removed and put in a shelter. She never came back to claim it."

"This is the purse that Aylih said she saw Adam give to your father. I can just bet."

"I agree. She became a missing persons case, it's still open but is pretty much a cold case. But about 15 years ago, a couple of hikers were camping down by Mile Creek and came across the body that the high waters had uncovered over time. Nothing to identify it."

"The body you told me about with no teeth, hands or feet?"

"Yes. Covered all their bases. Dad must have cleared the purse as evidence but never made it to the storage locker."

"The body count just keeps growing. This is horrible. It's sick."

Laying the purse aside, she reached in and pulled out folded sheets of paper, then dropped them as she stared at the Glock 17 that lay underneath them. Tessa's face went pale, as did Jack's.

"John's handgun. I don't know why Dad would have it. John's guns were in the wall safe. I never saw it while we were processing the crime scene."

"He could have taken it and hid it if he was there before you. Do you think John had time to get it and shoot someone?"

"I don't know. There were no gun powder test results in the box."

"What is on the paper?

Tessa carefully unfolded the paper and looked at them.

"Ballistics reports."

Jack dug out another pair of gloves and put them on. Tessa looked at him strangely.

"Always was taught to keep at least three pairs of gloves on me at all times."

She handed the sheets over to him.

"Yep. The bullets taken from John and Steven's bodies were from a 9 mm Beretta, but the bullets taken from James and Michael were from a Glock. Dad's gun was a Glock 17."

"Popular gun."

"At the time, very much so."

He took a small evidence bag that held bullets.

"They are all silver."

"Yes. Not too many people use regular bullets in their guns unless they are target practicing. Silver bullets are too expensive to waste. Everyone on the police force uses silver bullets."

Jack reached in and took out a faded notebook. His brows scrunched together.

"How did this get here? Did Dad take my song book?" He opened it and a little note was tucked inside.

Jack , if you are reading this then you know everything. You should have been a singer, not a cop, then you would have been far away from the horror I created. I know saying I'm sorry a million times will never make up for what I did. I still need to say it, but the damage is done and will never be repaired. Dad.

"I should have listened to them and tried to get a singing career going. But I went the wrong way."

"No, in the end, you didn't. If you were a singer, though most likely retired now, you would not have the access and resources you would have as a cop to try and help me solve this. Fate helped you choose the path you are on for a reason."

"Logic, won't fight it."

"What's this?" Tessa took out an envelope. It was sealed in an envelope with the police seal in the corner but addressed to no one. She looked at Jack.

"Open it."

Tessa opened it and opened the letter. She read silently for a minute then looked up at Jack like she was going to throw up. Her voice was no more than a croak.

"It's from your father. It's his confession letter."

"Read it."

Tessa cleared her throat and began,

My name is Bennett Raskins. I am Chief of Police, currently. Though if this is ever found, I hope that I am dead and as far away from prosecution as I can get. I have done some evil shit in my life, and sadly, have hidden it well. I have no idea why I have done all I did, greed, maybe? More than that. But I want to make amends. I know I could have confessed when I was alive, but the judgment of the Council would have been swift and final, and I was not in the mood to have my life cut short when I was not done with it yet. I wasn't done living my life, but the guilt ate at me, aged me, tormented me. It was so painful at times, I came close to it, but never did.

I am so sorry for all the pain I have caused my son, more than he will ever know. I know Jack will never forgive me and will hate me for the rest of his life. I had always wanted Jack to take James's advice and go into singing. He had a strong, power- ful voice. I was so proud of him, though I never told him that. I guess I should have, then maybe he might have changed his mind about being a cop. But his final decision was to become a cop. But if he was going to follow in my footsteps I would be damned if he was going to find out what I was doing.

What started out as petty stuff mostly, faking pass cards and IDs for shifter hunters who were looking for a new addition to their collection, became so much more. Kidnapping and shipping to private estates where they could have hunting parties, and learning what parts of different shifters were worth. I brought

Adam Doherty on board when I heard he was in serious debt that could have possibly ended his life, made things a little easier for me. The man was incredible at faking shit. It was also Adam's job to keep things under the Council's radar. Looking for those who had no connections, no family or friends to keep asking to keep the case open. I'd labelled them as cold cases and quietly swept them under the rug.

Then I met Thea Mitchell and her husband, Keith. They had more money than they ever knew what to do with. There wasn't too much I wouldn't do when it came to money but when they asked me for our unicorns I was reluctant to cross that line. No one had ever asked us about our unicorns before. In all honesty, I never even considered letting hunters go after them. I knew they were rare and valuable, but it wasn't until they explained what each part was worth and what my cut would be, that I turned into a greedy fuck, literally I caved. Her offer was more than I could ever refuse. Adam helped me plan it, though Thea was not impressed when Adam demanded his own fees. She started to refuse until she saw his talents. He had balls to demand his own fees, but she paid. Had me laughing.

What stopped me laughing was when I found out that quick little romp I had with her behind her husband's back to seal the deal produced a child. How her husband believed it was his I'll never know, considering he was Jack's duplicate and really didn't look like either of them. She also could use the child against me, so there was no backing out, but if I got her what she wanted then I could disassociate from her for good. But, deep down, I knew what I was doing was the most evil thing in the world, and would destroy my son in the process.

I brought her son, Cody, into town under the premise that he wanted to live and work here. I paid him to stake out the house, lounge and studio, with Adam spelling him off. It was gold when he applied and got hired on at the lounge. I told him to try but didn't think it would work. But he had a gift for numbers, which put him in solidly at the lounge. It was fortunate because Michael was pregnant, according to Jack. They were also planning a trip to celebrate, to vacation or something like that. Thea thought that Cody should take a trip as well. So I got the information out of Jack and sent Cody down. Stalking, she called it. I called her nuts. I thought I had chosen the perfect day, using the information Cody and Adam told me about their routines. I had been hoping that it would be a day that James would come home early, but that was sporadic. Extra bonuses all around but didn't happen. Cody called when he saw the nurse arrive, it wouldn't take long for everyone to come home. Jack was backpacking so he was too late, Eddie got home from school in the middle of it. I don't know when it hit me hard, but it was like a sudden punch in the gut when I realized exactly what I had done. I went over there as fast as I could. I was shocked at how fast the labor had gone and I knew when Thea and Keith were going to get there.

When I got to the basement, Little Tessa had just been born, she was only seconds old, being cleaned up by the birthing nurse. They were surprised to see me. I told the nurse to get the hell out if she wanted to live.

I found out later that Adam killed her. I have no idea where the body is. When I saw that little infant, the guilt was so overwhelming I didn't know what to do, but I had to move fast. I told them to get the infant and Eddie hidden somewhere they would not be seen or heard. I told John to get his gun while James got Eddie and the baby into the room under the steps. I saw him send out a mental alert and knew the time was very short. Adam came down and John shot him without thinking. Shoulder wound, nothing serious, but as he took off outside, Thea and Keith came down and the shooting started. They had no silencers so I knew the neighbors would be on the phones.

But when I saw tranq guns in their hands, I panicked. There was no way in hell she was going to take these men and torture them for their parts. I shot James and Michael. Why didn't I shoot Thea and Keith instead? I guess I knew that either one would have killed me before I ever got the chance to kill them both, and James and Michael would still have been their victims. But I realize now that I should have put a gun in my mouth that day and pulled the trigger, but I didn't, and I have lived with the guilt ever since, even if I didn't want to die. Why didn't they kill me that day, I have no idea. I guess because I was their only way out of town. I don't know where I'll end up when I die, but wherever it is I hope I pay for what I have done. Bennett Raskins

By the time Tessa had finished, both of them were pale and didn't look so well. She carefully folded it back into the envelope and dropped it back into the box.

"We need to get out of here and get this case reopened by the Council."

"Agreed." They put everything back in the box and locked it. Jack put the key in his pocket. They took off their gloves, he took Tessa's and automatically tossed them in the trash can. As Tessa grabbed up the box, Jack sent off a quick text, waited a minute, then looked up. Shoving the phone back into his pocket, he led the way to the door.

"Let's go."

As they made their way to the front door, Tessa mused,

"Even empty, this house has such a homey feel."

"That was my mom. She wanted everyone who came in the front door to feel welcome."

He opened the front door and waited for her to come out. A chime sounded from his cell and he yanked it out to read it. His head came up quickly. Jamming the phone in his pocket, he pulled out his gun. He grabbed Tessa's hand and hauled her towards the truck. Tessa got the message and ducked down, heading for the shelter of the truck. Jack knew his gun had limited range and he could not see anything that was actually within range.

A shot rang out and the gun flew out of Jack's hand. Tessa turned to see Jack bring his injured hand down to his chest as another shot sounded and he flew backwards to the ground.

"Jack!" Tessa crawled over to him, blood poured from a wound in his shoulder. She scrambled around him and grabbed his gun. She pulled Jack's phone from his pocket. The open text message simply read, **'pursue this and you both will die'**.

Screaming, Tessa stood and fired all the shots in the chamber before dropping back down to the ground. She put her hand over the wound, Jack moaned. His eyes flickered slightly.

"Text Dale."

Tessa went back to Jack's contacts. She saw a recent message from Dale and tapped on it.

'Haven't seen anything yet.' It read.

'Jack has been shot in the shoulder and hand. Shoulder looks bad. I fired shots but don't see anything', Tessa texted to him. She laid the phone on the ground beside her, waiting for a reply as she used her other hand to apply pressure to the wound.

She closed her eyes and let the tears flow. Where were

they out there? Who was out there? Would they get out of this alive? She looked down at the phone but there still was no reply. It said delivered but not read.

Jack's eyes fluttered open slightly,

"Tessa?" He brought his good hand up and lightly touched her cheek.

"I sent a message but he hasn't seen it yet."

"He will."

"Who sent that first message?"

"I don't know. I don't know how they got my cell number."

He carefully reached to touch her hair. She looked so much like Michael, it was painful. She was stunning with her long, black hair tied in a high ponytail and deep brown eyes that sparkled. When she smiled, her joy was infectious and Steven came through so strong. He just loved her so much. Aside from Eddie, and his memories, Tessa was the only thing left to remind him of the greatest time in his life with friends who were now gone.

She leaned down and he guided her head so he could kiss her lightly on the cheek.

"I'm sorry..." Jack let his eyes close.

"Uncle Jack..." Her voice seemed distant. The pain in his shoulder seemed further away. Everything seemed to be further away, even the sirens. It was then that the darkness engulfed him.

CHAPTER 20

WHEN JACK FELT he could open his eyes again, he was in a hospital room. Tessa was standing, looking out the window, and Carol was in the chair beside the bed.

"Carol?" he managed to croak out. They both turned to look at him. Carol got up and planted a firm kiss on his forehead.

"It's okay. Your hand will be fine and so will your shoulder. The bullet passed clean through." She took his hand and gently squeezed it, careful of the IV needle.

"Where's Eddie?"

"He's still at the cabin. I slipped up last night to see him. He has enough supplies and I bought him a few new games and movies to keep him occupied for a while. I told him to stay there and not to leave until we came and got him. He's getting scared."

"I'll go up and get him as soon as I can. After they spring me and I see what Thea has to say. As long as you saw him last night, he'll be okay for just a bit longer." Jack's mind seemed to slip into a different track. "What happened to the box?"

"Dale has it," Tessa responded.

"Who shot at us?"

Carol looked to Tessa before she looked back at Jack.

"Milo Mitchell."

"Did Adam show up? Was he there?"

"Nope. He didn't take the bait."

"Fucker is smarter than I gave him credit for."

The hospital room door cracked open and Dale Longley poked his head in. He was still in uniform.

"Chief?"

Jack turned his head and smiled,

"Come in, Dale. Tell me the buzz."

Dale came over to stand by the bed. He looked tired and haggard in his rumpled uniform. He looked so much older than his 64 years. He had something under his arm.

"Between what was in the box you found, the letter, and the other stuff you got from the locker, it's pretty damning. The Council has it all now. Thea and Milo are in custody and being held in the shifter proof cells. Though I have a feeling I know what the end result is going to be. It's all formality right now. The Council is aware that you're in the hospital and will contact you as soon as the doctors release you and you're home. Milo is singing like the stool pigeon that he is. Thank goodness he's a lousy shot. He was aiming to kill," Dale replied.

"How did they catch him?"

"Would you believe with help from the Dennisons? Raina and Rory were out for a run. They usually do it a few times a week now that all their kids are in school and they heard the shots. They smelled an unfamiliar scent and followed it. They saw the monkey up a tree with a rifle. They hid until he came down and pinned him."

"He could've shot them."

"He didn't get the chance. He came down the tree facing the trunk with the rifle slung over his back. Rory shifted to human, came up behind him, slammed him into the ground and Raina bit through the strap and dragged the rifle away. Rory sat on him with his arms pinned behind him.

Raina took off in shifted form since she would be a lot faster, and found me. She told me about the guy with the rifle and that Rory was holding him. As soon as Milo saw my police uniform he started singing and I think most likely still is. They've got enough to arrest Thea and search her house and all her properties. Whether they will find anything is a different story but it's still over. Milo flipped on his mother so fast I don't think it's even sunk in yet."

Jack could feel the weight coming off his shoulders.

"When can I get out of here?"

"Probably tomorrow."

"I want to be in the viewing room when they question Thea. I need to hear for myself my father's involvement in it all and why. And why did they kill them."

"Oh, Councilman Jarvis thought that you might like to have this back. It has no value to them in the way of evidence. Though they did keep the letter that was inside." He handed a notebook to Jack.

"My songbook."

"I thought you lost that," Carol stated.

"I forgot it at Greyson House. I was trying out a new song on James and John. I thought if I could sing in my spare time or sell a few more songs it would help with my school fees. But I just got too busy then...." Jack's voice trailed off. He set the book on the stand beside his bed. "I think I'll give it to Eddie. There was a song in there I wrote but never got a chance to sing, called '*Weeping With Grief*'. I wrote it when John lost his dad. I was pretty sure I had lost it and it was gone forever. Thanks Dale."

"Can you tell us anything?" Carol asked.

Dale looked at Jack for a long minute, Jack nodded his head.

"They know practically all I know and it'll come out in the wash anyway."

Dale hesitated.

"I understand, it's just..." He heaved a heavy sigh. "It looks like your father was in it right up to his eyeballs. We traced the phone numbers and account deposits on the statements. The deposits that Cody received came from your father, which, in turn, can be traced back to Thea's account. Apparently he had a separate account that he used to receive and pay out large amounts of cash. The account has not been active for the last 29 years but the money is still there. To the tune of 7 million dollars. It's just been sitting there collecting interest all these years."

"Wait, what??" Jack looked stunned.

"It's a POD account. He put your name on it as the beneficiary and when he died it should have all gone to you but since neither you or your mother knew about it, it just sat there."

"Then why didn't the teller mention anything to Mom when she went in to close Dad's account after he died?"

"Probably because your mom was only aware of their joint account and a personal account that he owned. The teller never mentioned the POD account because it never occurred to her that it belonged to Bennett as well. It was under a slightly different name and not linked to your mother so the teller didn't think to ask about it."

"What name did he use?"

"Raskins, B.J. The info screen showed us the rest."

"Dad's middle name was Jankins. I was named Jack because Dad always said that Jack was a form of Jankin. But seriously, she should have been smart enough to ask. Mom would have just said yes or no. I mean, how many Raskins did she think were in Unicorn Valley, using the only bank there is here?"

"We talked to her. She wasn't thinking. She was new and afraid of screwing up. She only did what your mother asked. Never thought to question about the other account. It was a bad oversight and she couldn't stop apologizing enough about it."

Dale pulled a small book from his inner jacket pocket and handed it to Carol. Jack put his good hand over his face and gripped tightly.

"Fuck me!" came out from between his fingers. "If she had said something, the deposits could have been traced sooner and we would have had some new leads sooner. Might have had closure by now." Jack's voice was sharp. "Damn, my head is aching."

"I can come back later."

"No, Dale, continue."

"The phone calls were made from a private line that was installed in your house. We went out and had a look around. There was a phone line in the spare bedroom and from what we could trace of the line, it was a second number."

"Never crossed our minds that it was a second line. We had phones in most rooms of the house so Dad would be able to get to one quick in case of an emergency, but we never thought of a second number."

"You really wouldn't have reason to think that. The other phone number circled was Thea Mitchell's house number."

"Calling to tell him what to do, or what she wanted. The three of them making plans."

Tessa looked from Dale to Jack.

"What about the number on the back of the gym card that Mrs. Gleason was holding for Cody? That was Adam's land line."

"Yes. And we have a feeling he's in it just as deep. We just need a way to prove it."

Jack let his head fall back onto the pillow as he stared up at the ceiling. His mouth moved like he was talking but no words came out. After a minute he lifted his head and looked at Dale.

"That money should go to Eddie. The most damage was done to him."

"It's yours to do with as you please, but I have a feeling when all is said and done, Eddie will be well off."

"What do you mean?"

"I had a private meeting with Councilman Jarvis, I'll tell you now, that guy is scary as fuck. He's so rigid."

"They all are." Jack smirked.

"But, and this goes no further, James and John left everything to Eddie. Money and properties. Since John was Council employed he made a nice little penny. After John died they did not stop payments. That money has been filtering into John's account for the last 30 years."

"Are you seriously telling me that the Council back

then was that stupid not to close John's account once he was declared dead? Who the hell was that stupid?"

"Councilman Jarvis."

"What the fuck??"

"He left the account open but hid it from the rest of the Council. He allowed the monthly payments to be deposited as if John was still alive. He knew there was the possibility that someday Edward would come back to himself. That's why he told you he would say nothing about the house being cleaned when it was supposed to be sealed off. The Council wronged Edward all these years by neglecting to check on him at the cabin. This was Councilman Jarvis's way of repaying that wrong. Protectors really do make a cool amount."

"I really, seriously, have a headache."

"I'll get you something." Carol got up and left the room.

"I also had to meet with the Council. You were here snoozing so I had to go. Damn, I don't know how you do it, standing there. I thought I was going to shit myself."

Jack smiled.

"First time I was in those chambers, I nearly did." A small smirk quirked Jack's lips.

"The Council informed me that they will be in contact with the shifter police in the places that Milo mentioned. They have already been talking to Chief Maldonado in NorthRiver to inform him about Cody.

"Then they plan to talk to Thea's lawyer. Since there is no one to collect from her will—Cody and Keith being dead and Milo in prison, possibly for the rest of his life if the Council feels that is appropriate, which means he cannot collect—the Council wants to invoke plunder rights."

"What are those?" Tessa asked.

"It's a Council bylaw that came from the Nomads that joined up with the unicorn shifters and protected them. They took what they felt they deserved from the enemies that did them wrong. But it's never been invoked before even though it is written."

"It deserves to be invoked now."

"If it is, I'm pretty sure there'll be no arguments on it. All of Thea's accounts will be seized and the money put into a special fund, then all the properties will be sold and the money from the sales will go into the fund as well. The Council hopes by going over the accounts it might trace back to some of her contacts and get them off the hunts.

"In the meantime, the Council hopes to find out if there are any survivors out there or family of anyone that have gone missing or killed because of her and all the other hunters we can bring down. They will benefit from the fund, including Edward.

"The Council have all agreed that they will take care of anything Edward needs going forward. He will receive monthly pay. Any repairs to any properties will be taken care of and paid for. The same goes for all utilities. He will be well taken care of. He said it was the least they could do to make up for 30 years of neglect. They definitely plan to make up for it."

Dale hesitated as Carol came back into the room with a nurse who injected something into Jack's IV port. She watched him for a few minutes. When he smiled and nodded his head, she left. Tessa waited until the nurse was gone and the door had closed completely.

"Will there be a trial or anything?"

"No. Once the Council has all their ducks in a row it will go straight to a guilty verdict."

"What will happen?"

Dale looked at Jack a long second before shifting his eyes back to Tessa.

"Thea will be executed, Miss."

Jack could only nod his head as he drifted off to sleep again.

CHAPTER 21

JACK ADJUSTED HIMSELF uncomfortably on the stool in the viewing room. Since he had been released from the hospital a couple of days ago, he didn't feel like standing for any length of time and had an officer get him one. He knew he was getting old, things healed but just not as fast as they used to. It had been good timing, by the time the Council had gotten all the evidence together and Milo confessed to shooting him. He could have reviewed the tape but it didn't interest him. The only one he cared to hear was Thea. He wanted to know how his father was tied up in it, and to her.

She was brought into the interview room and sat in the chair facing the mirror. The officer left her in handcuffs. He left and Dale came in. He took the chair opposite her.

"I don't even know where to start so I'll just ask; why?"

"Why what?" Jack wanted to wipe the smug a smirk off her face so bad his fingers twitched.

"Why kill them? The Carstairs'? Cody? Dani?"

"I'll make it clear that I did not kill Dani, who I'm assuming you are referring to as the birthing nurse that was there. And my hand was not the only one that killed the Carstairs'."

"Adam killed the birthing nurse, didn't he?"

"Yeah. He nailed her when she ran out. He had a silencer on his gun so nobody would hear it. I think he went in to tell Bennett when I heard a gunshot and saw him come running back out again, bleeding from his shoulder. I laughed at him as he threw her body in his trunk then pulled out a fresh uniform, bandaged his shoulder, and tore off to pretend like he was just getting there. That's all I'm saying about it."

"You might as well tell us everything. You have nothing to lose."

"The Council has already decided my fate. Though, if I do talk, can I be guaranteed that Milo won't share in it?" She looked at Dale's stone face. It held no emotion, no giveaway. "I can always take my secrets to the grave just to keep the torture going."

"Milo is only being charged for his current crimes. He sang like a bird. It won't take long for the Council to contact the corresponding shifter police. They'll deal out their own punishments. He will most likely spend the rest of his life in a shifter prison."

Thea sank in her chair, crossed her arms over her chest and legs at the ankles.

"I am a hunter, collector, trader and dealer. We started hunting when we were teens, the only time Keith and I took a break was when Cody came along. Cody was such a clueless child. Couldn't do anything right. Refused to learn the trade, left home when he was 18. The only way we let him go was if he kept his trap shut or he would be dead by the sunset the next day. We kept tabs on him and were quite amazed that he actually did.

"Keith and I hunted all manner of shifter or cryptid, provided the price was right. When we heard fellow hunters talking about unicorn shifters, their rarity and what a person could get out of just a few strands of mane, we started putting out feelers. It took a lot of hard work but I found out about the Carstairs'. I approached Bennett. I had heard he was a dirty bastard too, but I didn't know how far I could push him. Came to find out he was a greedy prick. So was that ass he associated with. Loved the finer things in life. We struck up a bargain."

"Who was he associating with?"

"As if you don't know."

"Pretend I don't and tell me."

"Your dear Detective Adam Doherty."

"So how did Detective Doherty get tangled up with you and Bennett Raskins?"

"He got tangled up with Bennett far faster than me. Adam was in it all the way over his head. Between all the gambling he did, legal and otherwise, plus all the scams he bought into that would have made him millions but only brought him death threats. Bennett was not a stupid man, he knew something was going on, and brought him in on his action then into mine. I was reluctant at first, to include another person, but when I saw how valuable he was at getting IDs, faking permits for the gate. He even had the balls to ask his own fees. I agreed to bring him on."

"What was Adam's role?"

"He got us in by faking a two day visitation pass. We were a family who had lost our pack and we were looking for a new home and protection. We brought Milo with us, he was just a month old. Keith never knew it was Bennett's. He thought it was his, which suited me just fine."

"Milo is Bennett's child?"

"Didn't I just say that? Bennett liked sex just as much as he loved money. When we met to discuss what I wanted and what I was willing to pay out, we sealed the deal with a romp in the sack. I usually do the consultations myself so Keith was not there."

"Continue."

"The pass separated us quite nicely from the crime and we were allowed to leave without an issue once the lockdown ended. The guards only gave the car a cursory look, all our ammo and guns were in hidden compartments all over the vehicle."

Jack frowned, if his father enjoyed the finer things in life he kept it well hidden. He indulged his wife in whatever she wanted. Jack had never wanted for anything but he'd never considered themselves rich. To Jack, they were just the basic things, there was always food on the table, if he needed anything he generally got it, within reason, but was never spoiled.

The same went for Adam. He had been to Adam's place a few times, it had definitely been no palace. He turned his attention back to the interview.

"You made good on your promise to kill Cody if he ever opened his mouth. You knew he talked to Chief Raskins and Tessa Carstairs. How?"

"Stupid ass called me. I had honestly thought that after 30 years, especially after Bennett died, that it would stay dead and buried. I even left him a note to remind him. I kept an ear out and he did stay silent. I was actually proud of him, that he had managed to keep it in all these years. Then he called and said that shit was being stirred up again. So did Adam. He squealed like a stuck pig. He wasn't eager for the shit to hit the fan again either."

"Did you know there was a tape recording that Cody made after the killings?"

"Not until after things died down, he told me he'd use it if he needed to."

"Against who and for what?"

"Bennett more than me. If his funds dried up, he tried bilking money out of Bennett. He knew better than to try it on me, he'd be dead before the authorities heard even one word. But Bennett would bleed for him, he thought it a certainty."

Do you know if he ever used it on him?"

"No, if he did he never informed me. Not that he would have anyway."

"Why was Cody in Barbados at the same time the Carstairs were?"

"I was stalking my prey. If I couldn't do it myself, I would have someone else do it for me. I love the thrill of knowing every move my prey makes."

"You and Milo were seen going into Cody's apartment."

"We needed to know exactly what he said, if he truly left names out of it."

"Why trash the place? What are you looking for?"

"Nothing. But it made you ask questions."

"It wouldn't have been a box of phone and bank receipts that would show numbers and deposits that could possibly be traced back to you."

"So what if we were?"

"To keep him from incriminating you, the same reason you killed him for."

"The little shit was going back to tell the Council everything. He made the mistake of saying he would name names. Couldn't let that happen so we just saved the Council the trouble of dealing the punishment."

"Why put the body in Greyson House? Were you trying to send a message?"

"You really are stupid. What do you think? Of course it was a message to back off."

"You took a chance considering the house is sealed. How did you figure that anyone would ever find the body?"

"It was either Raskins' front door or Greyson House. I would've loved to dump the body on Raskins' doorstep but Adam was too afraid of getting caught. Then when he saw someone sneaking out of Greyson House and saw how clean it was, he figured someone was going in there on a regular basis, sealed or not. So, whoever was going in there would eventually find it. If not right away they would eventually smell it. But when I think about it now, I should have made Adam dump it on Raskins' doorstep."

Jack shifted uneasily. Thank goodness for small mercies. If Eddie had seen it there, the shock could have been so much worse with Eddie fearing that they were all in danger. Possibly enough to drive him completely insane. Finding it in Greyson House had been bad enough.

"What kind of deal did you strike with Bennett Raskins?"

"What can I say? The man loved money and sex. When I first contacted him, he was just a plain dirty cop, him and Adam. He had worked out a deal with Adam, keeping everything that would make them money, out of the Council's eyes and ears. They had their hands into everything. I was looking for unicorn shifters. I heard a rumor that there was a good chance there were some left in Unicorn Falls. I contacted Bennett and offered him an impressive amount for information. Adam kept all inquiries out of the Council's ears.

"They were greedy bastards. But I didn't care as long as I got my prizes. Bennett and Adam set it all up. Keith and I were brought in as a family basically looking for sanctuary. It really helped that Milo was just an infant. Adam pretended to do all the leg work but looked the other way."

"How did that work if Milo is Bennett's child?"

"We'll go around this one more time, officer. Bennett was a sex hound. When he met me to discuss details, we went a few rounds."

"Your husband was okay with that?"

"He rarely came with me when I worked out the deals. He was no good at it so he stayed home. I always met with people on neutral ground, away from where I lived, away from where they lived."

"So, it took almost 10 months to a year to plan it all out."

"Yeah, stalking and planning takes time, having a baby takes time too. Getting them separated long enough to get in and out is not as easy as you think it is. By that time, Michael was pregnant. It would have been a bonus to have had a unicorn/wolf hybrid but we didn't have time to hunt for where she had been hidden, once that asshole Bennett shot Michael and James."

"Bennett killed James and Michael?"

"Didn't I just say that? Ruined it all. Had to put bullets in the others, darn Protector. But not my issue, collateral damage. Once he got that damned alert out, our window was closing fast."

"Why did you let Bennett kill them? Why didn't you shoot him before he killed them both?"

"Because, asshole, he was the only way we could get out, the Valley was on lockdown. Once the lockdown was over we needed Bennett to clear us to leave. That way there would be only a cursory look to the car, Milo helped too. Security back then was so lax. I feel like I'm repeating myself."

"Did you contact Bennett again to do more hunting for other shifters or were you just interested in unicorn shifters? When did you stop hunting in the Valley altogether?"

"I have never stopped hunting, even after Keith was killed. I taught Milo the trade. But that was the last time I hunted in Unicorn Valley. Bennett decided he was through, he turned into such a bleeding heart."

"What about Adam?"

"I have no idea. He contacted me to tell me he was through with hunting shifters, but whether he gave up faking passes and ID cards, I don't know."

"What about Cody? Did he decide to leave town or was he forced out?"

"He left, he got what Bennett owed him and took off. We both made sure that he was far enough away from the Valley that he wouldn't be readily found and questioned, and if he ever did open his mouth, it would be the last time. Even after Bennett died I sent a little reminder to keep his mouth shut."

"So, how did Cody get Adam's number?"

"From Bennett."

"When?"

"Not long after Cody left town. Bennett didn't want anything to trace back to him but if Adam was found out, it wasn't Bennett's concern. He was to call Adam if anyone ever came around snooping. Adam would then pass the message along to Bennett."

"Did he contact you before or after Chief Raskins and Tessa Carstairs talked to him?"

"Before. I told him to fill them with a lot of bullshit, put it all on Bennett. Keep us out of it."

"He contacted you, then confessed to them? Did he tell you what he told them but you planned on killing him regardless of what he said to them?"

"No, until I found out what he actually said. Then I would make up my mind. Unfortunately that boy yapped a little too much, even though he left our names out of it. He made the mistake of telling me he was going back to Unicorn Valley with them, then I knew he would name names. Couldn't let that happen."

Jack stood up and stretched, cautiously wincing at his sore places. He walked out of the observation booth and back to his office. Sitting in his chair, he sagged backwards like all the air had left him. He couldn't listen anymore. He had had enough.

Tara knocked before she came in.

"You want some coffee?"

"Not that crap from the staff room."

Tara came in and went to the shelf with his coffee maker.

"Strong?"

"Strong enough to eat the bottom out of the cup."

Tara set to work.

"How'd it go?"

"As far as I know he's still questioning her but I just

couldn't stand to watch any more. Made me feel like I was going to puke."

"I bet it hurts finding out all that shit about your father."

"Yeah. It's like someone drove a knife in my heart and keeps twisting and twisting."

"What's the Council going to do?"

"Once we're done with her, I suspect they'll wrap things up and quietly pass and carry out sentences on her and Milo."

"What will happen to your father's name and reputation?"

"I don't know. I only hope they keep it quiet. It rips my guts out. And I know that if people in this town find out, my life will become a living nightmare. He was a very well respected man and to find out all this filth? I'm too old to move."

"I'm sure they will. Considering their reputation would be on the line for one of their own being on the take."

"It's all in their hands now."

Tara stopped making Jack's coffee and turned to face him.

"Why don't you go home and rest? Forget about it for a few hours, let Carol pamper you."

Jack considered her suggestion. He would love to be pampered by Carol, but the truth of it was that he had just needed a few minutes to sit down and catch his breath before he headed home. He needed to go get Eddie before the boy thought he was being deserted again. It was going to be a long walk back to that cabin.

"Yeah, I think I'll do that. A nap on the couch seems like a really great idea right about now. Call me if anything important comes up."

"Will do."

Jack got up and left. He was so ready to be done with this day, be done with it all.

"Carol?" Jack called as he came into the house. She came out of the kitchen.

"You're home early."

"I just couldn't stay there any longer. Have you gone up to the cabin?"

"No, I thought you should be the one to bring him down if it's safe to do so."

"Yeah, I think it is. Thea and Milo are in prison and I don't think that Adam is too much of a threat in that regard. Though I really would love to see him behind bars."

"So would I. I can't believe the evil."

"Me neither. I never once thought I would be stabbed in the back quite like that. But with Thea's confession, I'm pretty sure the Council will instruct me to lay charges on him as well. He'll most likely be in a shifter prison for the rest of his life, just like I can assume Milo will be."

"Will you bring Eddie down tonight?"

"I'll wait till it gets a little darker, then head up."

"Damn it!" Adam paced back and forth in his sparse living room. He stopped to stand in front of his picture window. He knew everything was going to hell fast. With Thea and Milo both arrested and being questioned, he knew it was only a matter of time before they came after him. It didn't matter that he actually didn't pull the trigger, he had a big hand in setting it up. He really didn't want to die, but to be stuck in a shifter prison for the rest of his life didn't really appeal to him either.

He stalked back to his bedroom. Pack light and travel fast. Grabbing his gun from the nightstand, he looked at it, he knew he would never be able to be a police officer again but it didn't matter anymore. He would go as far away from the Valley as he could, change his name and start over. The best game plan for now.

He looked around his bedroom. He had lived here for a very long time, kept it sparse but still loved it, and he knew he would never see it again. His heart hurt. He would keep his identity long enough to close out his accounts and transfer them to a new bank under a new name, then fade into obscurity. He grabbed his suitcases and duffle bags from the closet and started stuffing them full. Grabbing up his toiletries, he caught a glimpse of himself in the bathroom mirror. He paused to stare hard.

"Damn, you look like shit." Adam sneered at himself.

After throwing all his luggage in his car, it dawned on him that there was a high chance that he was not going to get past the gate. Either one.

"Fuck!" He slammed his hands against the steering wheel. "How? How? How...wait a minute."

With his mind churning, Adam started his car and took off. He pulled up across the street from Greyson House. He glared at it. It remained dark. Had he really expected to see a light after he had chanced seeing the young man running out the front door?

His mind replayed the scene over and over again. Edward Carstairs. He had only caught a glimpse of the man's profile, the black hair and sharp features. It was a long shot, he really couldn't be sure because of the distance but it was the only logical conclusion. Who else would have been in Greyson House? Edward supposedly had killed himself, but....

"They lied. They fucking lied. Very fucking clever of those assholes to hide him right under everyone's nose. And dollars to donuts he was at fucking Greyson House when I dumped Cody's body there, trying to scare me, make me think that damn house was haunted. I was too close and he wanted me out. Fuck!"

Taking off, he pulled up not far from Jack's house. It didn't seem possible that Jack could have been hiding him all these years without someone seeing him. The cabin. That was the only solution. If he could get his hands on Edward Carstairs it would be his ticket out of there. Once he got a decent distance away he would make up his mind what to do with Edward then.

He got out and ran across the street. Slipping around the back, he could take the path to the cabin. Jack had told him once that he, James and John had carved a path back to the cabin when they were kids, to save time from going to Greyson House and going that way. The path had cut off quite a bit of time when they were at Jack's and wanted to head back to the cabin.

He dropped down behind a bush beside the back door-step as he heard the door open.

"Once Adam is put in prison this will definitely all be over. But I honestly don't think that he would willingly come out and kill him. He'll be too concerned about saving his own skin. It wouldn't surprise me if he was long gone by now. But I need to go up and get Eddie, I've left him too long up there by himself as it is."

"Okay, I'll get..." A distant phone ringing cut Carol's voice off.

Adam peeked his head up to see Jack still standing on the steps holding the door open. Carol called from inside the house,

"Jack." Jack went in, closing the door behind him. Adam took that opportunity. He waited a minute or two to make sure that Jack was not coming out, then sprinted across the yard to the woods.

Jack went back into the house, closing the door as he took his phone from Carol. He looked at the screen.

"What's up, Dale?"

"Tara said you left early, you feeling okay?"

Jack turned his head to look out the window.

"Yeah, just a little...." A movement caught his eye. "What the fuck?"

Carol came to stand beside him.

"What is it?" she asked at the same time Dale did.

"I just saw someone cross the backyard heading towards the woods path going up to the cabin. I'm pretty sure I know who it is."

"I'm on my way." Dale disconnected as Jack dropped his phone, ran to the bedroom. He came back tucking his gun into the waistband of his pants. He tore open the door and headed towards the woods with Carol behind him. She touched his arm and he looked down. She held up her cell phone. He nodded his head as they headed into the woods.

Adam's thoughts swirled around and around in his head as he trotted down the path towards the Carstairs cabin. Jack really had a good idea making this path. For as much as he was out there with James and John, it was shorter than going down to the house then taking the path there. This way was simply straight across. No one was allowed to go back there, and there were probably many who didn't even know the cabin existed.

Adam drew close to the door, crouched down and listened. He could hear movement inside. Crawling over to the window on the right side of the door, he lifted his head just enough to peek in. The young man standing at the counter was pouring chips into a bowl. Adam could not believe how much Edward looked like James. His thick black hair and sharp facial features made him a very handsome young man. He had a firm build that, Adam knew, would make him a powerful opponent.

His head came up and looked towards the window. Adam quickly dropped out of sight. He held his breath at the sudden silence. If that was Edward in the house, he was moving like a ghost, Adam's wolf hearing wasn't picking up anything. Only when he heard movement again did he poke his head back up and look in the window. No one was there, the bowl of chips and chip bag sat on the counter untouched. He moved to the other side of the window, he could see the living room. No one was there.

Adam turned to move again to the other window, when the cabin door jerked open and he came face-to-face with a rifle. A Colt Lightning, John Carstairs' prized long gun. Along with a Glock 17, Jack had told him once that John had loved to keep both guns in perfect condition. He had never seen them but knew them by the way Jack had described them.

"Why are you here? Did Uncle Jack tell you to come here?"

"I can't believe they lied all these years. You been here all this time?"

"Why does that matter?"

"You're supposed to be dead. The Council said you committed suicide when you were 16."

"Nope, don't think so." Eddie brought the gun up level to Adam's face. "So, I ask you again; what does it matter?"

"It matters a lot. You know what went on that day."

"I won't go back there. Uncle Jack can't make me and neither can you."

"You don't need to. You don't need to do anything. Just put the rifle down and we can talk."

Eddie's black eyes bored into Adam's.

"What do you want?"

Adam's hand slowly inched his hand up his side towards his gun.

"I want you to come with me. I…"

"No." Eddie cut him off.

"Don't make me get nasty. You need to come with me."

"No."

"Edward, you have to understand. People need to know you are alive."

"I'm here for a reason, Uncle Jack says so I won't die."

Hearing a twig snap behind him, Adam turned sharply. Jack and Carol stood there.

"Why Adam?" Jack asked, the heartbreak of a long-term friendship destroyed evident in his voice.

"You were there. I remember you. I'm not as dumb and

stupid as you think I am. I heard you coming, like I can hear when Uncle Jack comes. I could smell you. Your smell is not very nice. You had the same smell back then. It's evil. Da had an incredible sense of smell and hearing. I must've got them from him. Unfortunately, I'll never know that for sure, will I? I knew you were going to interrupt my chips and movies. My brain told me to go get my gun, Daddy's gun. You had such an evil look back then and that smell. Did you really enjoy being a part of my family's murder? When Uncle Jack took me out, I saw you, smelt you. You smelt like gun powder and blood but none was on you. But I smelt it."

"I don't know what you're thinking. I never killed them."

"He wants me to go with him, Uncle Jack."

"I just bet he does. He helped my father set things up to kill your family," Jack ground out.

Carol brought up her phone, Adam knew she was going to record everything he said and it would go straight to the Council. His life was over and he knew it.

"Jack." Adam tried to look hurt. "How can you say that? I did not shoot them."

"No, but setting them up is just as bad. Why? I thought you were my friend," Jack growled, taking a few steps closer.

"Yes, why did you betray Uncle Jack? Make him so sad. Take my life from me. Why?"

Adam swallowed hard. He knew that no matter what he said now, he would either go to a shifter prison for life or die as decreed by the Council.

"I knew what Thea did, hunted shifters for sport. I helped Bennett arrange for shifters to be taken, sent to an enclosure where she would track them down and shoot them. Fish in a barrel, we all got what we wanted. Greed is a powerful mistress. I should have known better but I didn't. I should never have turned off the reasoning in my head that told me what I was doing was wrong, especially to my own kind. I really didn't think the Carstairs' would have been killed. That was not my impression. Where they were unicorn shifters and could bring in millions for just bits of mane or tail, even blood. And where they were omegas, James and Michael could have been bred. I was stupid and naïve, I thought that when she collected all she could and made all the money she could get......"

"You had to know they would still die, tortured for profit then killed. There was no way she would let them live, with all that they would have seen," Carol screamed at him.

"What about Daddy and Steven?" Eddie's voice was dark and guttural.

"Collateral damage. John was of no value but Steven could have been forced to shift and we could've got quite a bit for his pelt. Bennett wanted that little extra but Thea didn't see it that way. She didn't want John sending out a mental alert but it had been too late for that. I knew John had sent one out, there was no denying it, before or after he shot me I don't know. But she didn't need to shoot Steven. I should've stopped her but I didn't. After John had shot me I tore off to my cruiser to quickly clean up, dress the wound and put on a fresh shirt. Bullet passed clean through, probably still in the wall. I was an idiot."

Eddie's eyes shifted over to Jack but flicked back before Adam ever had a chance to go for his gun. He shrank back, the sight of those black eyes made his skin crawl.

"Don't even think about it," Eddie hissed. "This is a gun you don't want to mess with. Uncle Jack taught me how to use this. I think I'm pretty damn good. You'll find out if you push me. But, right now, I'm pretty sure Uncle Jack would love to know how his dad was involved."

"Bennett set it up. He set it all up, I just faked the forms and passes. He had Cody and me stake the house out. He came up with excuses for Cody to talk to James about working at the Studio, or talk to Michael about how he could become better help to John at the Lounge to earn extra money. He used a lot of excuses to go over or he and I would just park down the street and watch the comings and goings."

"You said you faked the forms, what did you mean?" Jack snarled. "Tell me."

"I worked the permits and paperwork. The Council files were not as secure then as they are now. Didn't take much to hack in, delete this, rearrange that then add in other things. The liaison, back then, was an idiot. I could easily get just about anything past him. I don't know why I did what I did. Money does nasty things to people, to me it did the unspeakable."

"Did Dad send Cody to Barbados?"

"Yes. Thea wanted him to."

"Why?"

"I don't think you'll believe me even if I tell you."

"Why?" Eddie ground out.

"Bennett found out from overhearing Jack and mentioned it to Thea. She told Bennett to send Cody down there as well, to keep an eye on them."

"That doesn't make any sense," Eddie snarked. "What would be the point? We were having fun, what was he looking for? What did she think was going to happen?"

"I don't know. As she put it, she was stalking. Her and

Keith always liked to stalk their prey. She didn't make any sense then, still doesn't make any sense now. I never claimed to understand her, and Keith just went along for the ride. I just accepted her deposits."

"Why?" Eddie shrieked.

"I was desperate for money. It took all I had to go to Twelve Oaks. I barely made ends meet. I had loans, debts and no way to pay them off. I was a dead man walking. Bennett heard me pleading with my landlord for more time. He took me to his office and told me what he was doing. I readily agreed and everything was paid off just like that. But the threat that hung over my head was that if I did not do what they wanted, or could not do it then I would be killed and it would not be pleasant."

"By who?" Jack asked.

"At first by Bennett, he was taking a chance on bringing me in. Then, by Thea and Keith, she might've liked what I could do but secrecy was more important. But I have done nothing in the years since, since before your dad died. I've tried to pay penance with all the charity work I do. I regret it all. I have for years. Thought about retiring but I kept going. I figure if I stay a cop until I drop dead or someone took me out then that would be my punishment. I have spent the last 30 years regretting what I did. But at the time, Edward, greed had a hold of my heart and Thea and Bennett had my balls. The prices they would have brought in would have set us all up for life and I couldn't pass that up. I should have but I couldn't walk away, I was stupid."

"That's not the word I would use," Jack snarled. "We've been through a lot and I'm repaid by being stabbed in the back. That money was more important to you than my friends, his family, our friendship?"

"Unfortunately, I've had to live with it eating my heart all these years, praying that you would never find out. But that brat had to go and write that book, stir things up again."

"If she had found us, would we have been killed too?" Eddie snarled.

"Where your powers never showed and never shifted, you would've been useless and killed. Tessa, on the other hand, would have been taken and raised until her value could be determined then depending which form she shifted, she would have been sold to the highest bidder. Then what happened after that I have no idea."

Eddie's finger tightened on the trigger.

"Eddie, sweetie, don't," Carol called.

Adam, suddenly, grabbed his gun from its holster, pointing it at Eddie. Eddie's reaction time was faster, he pulled the trigger. The blast hit Adam full in the chest. Adam pulled the trigger reflexively. He knew it was the last thing he would ever do.

Eddie jerked to the side but the bullet pierced his bicep, passing clean through. He screamed and fell backwards to the porch.

"Eddie!" Jack ran to him. Eddie pushed himself up slightly with his good arm.

"Good thing you kept Daddy's promise."

"Yeah." Jack put a hand gently around Eddie's waist and pulled him close, being careful of his injured arm.

"Good thing."

Eddie could just faintly hear Carol calling for a paramedic and Dale's out of breath voice calling for Jack.

Eddie laid his head on Jack's chest, he felt so tired, all he wanted to do was sleep, despite the pain radiating in his shoulder, the vibration of Jack's voice.

"It passed clean through, Dale, he'll need stitches but I think but he'll be okay. I can't say the same for Adam, though."

"Fuck." was the last thing Eddie heard.

Jack stayed close to Eddie as they bowed before the Council as the members filed in. When they had all sat down, Jack and Eddie straightened up. He could feel the tension and fear radiating off Eddie. He really couldn't blame him, this was not his favorite thing in the world. But, for Eddie, it had to be especially terrifying, since he had only been released from the hospital that morning. A day after he had killed Adam.

"Edward Carstairs, do you understand why you are here?"

Jack watched Eddie closely. He was wound so tight, Jack was afraid he would snap at any moment. Eddie shifted his eyes downward.

"Yes, Councilman, Sir. Chief Raskins explained to me what I was to do and what you wanted to see me about."

"Good. Would you please tell us what happened between you and Detective Doherty."

Jack reached out and touched Eddie's back as a sign of reassurance.

"It's okay, Eddie, tell them."

"I was at the cabin. Something wasn't right, I knew

someone was there. I could hear movement. Smell him. It was so wrong. I went to get Daddy's gun. I keep Daddy's gun with me. Uncle Jack said I was not to take anything from the house but I feel safer with it close. I opened the door and he was there. He was trying to spy on me. No one ever came to the cabin except Uncle Jack. He scared me. I wanted to know what he wanted.

"He wanted me to go with him. I didn't want to. Uncle Jack and Aunt Carol came, and he told them everything. Aunt Carol taped it."

"Yes, Edward, we viewed the video that Mrs. Raskins recorded."

"Am I going to jail? Chief Raskins said it was not my fault."

"As we have seen in the video it is not your fault and it was not intentional, more self defense. You will not be charged, you will not be sent to jail."

Jack looked over and could see tears streaking Eddie's face. He took Eddie's hand and gave it a gentle squeeze.

"Edward Carstairs, the Council has been neglectful in its duty to make sure you were comfortable yet safe. You should not have been locked away in that cabin for as long as you were. Previous members should have been checking on you and to see if the threat was still out there. We cannot begin to express our apologies for the neglect that had been forced upon you.

"Since the threat no longer exists, you are no longer confined to the cabin. You are free to come and go as you wish. I am sure that Chief Raskins will be pleased to help you create a new life for yourself. The only thing we insist on is a strong recommendation to have weekly counseling to help you acclimate to society again."

"Yes, Councilman Mata. I will make sure things go as they should."

"Also, now that your death certificate is in the process of being destroyed and your status being updated, all Carstairs properties and accounts will now be unlocked. Everything will be reinstated in your name as they rightfully belong. There will be a messenger sent with the paperwork for you to look over and sign. I'm sure Chief Raskins will help you understand what you are signing and inheriting."

"What about Tessa?" Eddie's voice was small.

"Michael and Steven had accounts and the money from those will go to her, but according to their wills, they had no property at the time."

"No, they didn't," Jack added. "They moved into the room above the Lounge when they were able to but spent a lot of time at Greyson House. James and John loved having them there. I think they had planned on buying a house but never got that far."

"Can I stay with Uncle Jack?"

Councilwoman Chavez got up, came down from the dais and stood in front of Eddie. He let his head hang lower. She reached up and lifted his head up.

"Yes, Edward. You are free to stay wherever you feel comfortable. We are, once again, very sorry for allowing you to fall through the cracks and hope that we will be able to right it. I hope you can find peace. Please, don't ever hesitate to contact us if you need anything at all." She gave him a light kiss on the cheek. "Welcome back to society and enjoy life again."

She gave him a quick smile and walked away as the rest of the Council got up and left.

"Come on, Eddie, Let's go home."

"Eddie." Jack came to sit beside Eddie on the bed of the basement apartment. They had come back to Jack's house after the Council meeting and Jack had left Eddie to rest.

"I didn't think I was ever going to be allowed to come back here. Aunt Carol said I had to stay at the cabin until you came and got me. I didn't think you would ever come."

"I'm sorry it took me so long. I didn't plan on getting shot let alone have to stay in the hospital but this old body doesn't exactly heal as fast as it used to. Plus, I had a few things to tie up at the station to make sure it was safe for you to come back."

Eddie looked at Jack, Jack could tell he had been crying. The loneliness had been getting to him along with the confrontation with Adam.

"I...I.."

"It's over, Eddie, you don't have to live there anymore. You can stay here, you can go back to Greyson House, whatever you want."

Eddie sniffled.

"I don't know what I want. I want to live here but it doesn't feel right."

"Because you're so used to hiding, being in the cabin, being alone. But you don't have to anymore. Your family can finally rest in peace. It's all over. You can do whatever you want."

"Can we go fishing now?"

"Yes." Jack smiled. "We can go fishing. We can take the whole day, do whatever you want."

Eddie stared off into space.

"Do I have to meet Tessa?"

"As I say, it's entirely up to you."

"Will she like me?"

"Yes, she will, and she wants to meet you. She wants to meet the little boy who kept her safe."

"Okay, maybe after fishing."

"Deal."

"Yeah!" Eddie went to give Jack a hug but winced.

"Eddie?"

"Still hurts a little."

"It will for awhile. Want a pain pill? It'll help you sleep."

"Okay."

Jack got up and went to the bathroom, he poured a glass of water and got a pill from the bottle sitting on the sink. He came back and handed them to Eddie. Eddie took them and Jack returned the glass to the bathroom then came back and tousled Eddie's hair.

"I'll help you get ready for bed so your arm doesn't hurt."

Once Jack had Eddie in bed, snuggled down and sleeping, he went back upstairs closing the door behind him. He sat beside Carol on the couch. She handed him a mug that had been sitting on the coffee table as she took a sip from her own.

"How is he?" she asked.

"He's asleep. Got him to take a pain pill. Settled on his good side but if he moves the wrong way, hopefully the pill is strong enough that any pain he feels won't wake him up. We're going fishing tomorrow. He's a smart boy, he didn't forget that I promised him."

Jack hesitated but Carol caught it.

"What?"

"He's agreed to meet Tessa."

"When?"

"After we come home from fishing tomorrow."

"Then I'll plan a special meal. You two had better catch a lot of fish."

"I had planned on that anyway. You should know by now how much we catch on our trips. And fresh fish is perfect."

Carol chuckled.

"Then you should be getting a good night's sleep too, old man. You've got a busy day ahead of you."

"Don't I know it." Jack set his empty cup back on the coffee table. "You coming too, old woman?"

Carol set her cup down, got up and reached for her husband's hand. He took it and led her to the bedroom. Once ready and in bed, Carol laid her head on Jack's shoulder.

"I'm hoping this all goes right."

Jack gave Carol a light squeeze, then yawned.

"Me too."

When Jack opened his eyes again, it was starting to become daylight. He looked over at the clock. It read 6:30, he groaned. He could hear movement but couldn't figure out where it was coming from until he realized he was alone in bed. He could hear faint voices as he got up and dressed. He came out to the kitchen to see a flurry of activity. Eddie was sitting at the kitchen table eating a breakfast of eggs, bacon, toast and orange juice while Carol set about packing a cooler with sandwiches, snacks and drinks.

Eddie paused in his eating to look up at Jack.

"You didn't forget, did you?"

"No, baby. I would never forget, but I am an old man. I don't move as fast as I used to."

"You move really good, Uncle Jack." Eddie smiled brightly.

Jack came over and kissed the top of his head. He sat down at the table across from Eddie. Carol put a plate of the same in front of him with a cup of coffee.

"As soon as I get all this down we'll get on the road," Jack said as he started eating.

Carol looked at him pointedly. He caught her gaze and grabbed his phone from his back pocket.

Jack: Sorry if this wakes you but I thought it would be better than a phone call. Do you want to come over for dinner tonight? Eddie is ready to meet you. We're going fishing, will text when we get back.

Tessa started at the chime her phone made. Who was texting her this early in the morning? She rolled over and picked it up. Seeing Jack's name her heart skipped a beat. She swiped to unlock then read the text. She smiled.

Tessa: Have a great trip. You both deserve it. Text me when you want me there. I'll be waiting.

She laid the phone back down and quickly drifted off back to sleep.

When Tessa finally opened her eyes, sunlight streamed in. The clock read 8:30. She most definitely had been tired. Her mind drifted back to the text she had received from Jack. Was it real or something she had been dreaming? She vaguely remembered responding. Part in and part out of reality. She sat up and grabbed the phone off the nightstand. Unlocking it, she opened the text from Jack and read it over and over again. It was reality, she had even responded to it.

Eddie finally wanted to meet her. The day couldn't get any better. She was finally going to meet the man who kept her safe. Her stomach filled with butterflies. Getting up, she headed for the shower. What would she say to him? Ask him? What would he ask her? What was she going to wear?

Stepping out of the shower, she could hear her cell ringing. She grabbed it up and looked at the number. Jack? Didn't they go fishing?

"Uncle Jack?"

"No sweetie," came Carol's voice from the other end.

"Carol?"

"Yes. Jack took Eddie fishing today. They left early this morning but Jack left his cell behind because they would have no service where they were going."

"Yeah, he texted me before they left. I responded that he should have a good time."

"Did he invite you to dinner? Eddie has made the decision to meet you. That's why I called."

"Yes, he did. He never mentioned a time just that he would text when he got back."

"That man." Tessa could hear the laughter in Carol's voice. "I'll say around 7. By the time they get back and cleaned up and I get the fish cleaned and on the BBQ, that should be a good time. You do like fish, don't you?"

"Yes. There's a place around the corner from my apartment that has great fish and chips. I'm there so much they know me by name."

Carol chuckled.

"That's great. I'll see you at 7?"

Before Carol could hang up, Tessa jumped in.

"Carol," she said quickly. "I'm nervous."

"Don't be, child. All will go well. I think he'll be more nervous. But everything will be okay."

"I hope so."

"I know so." Carol chuckled again. "I'll see you at 7." She hung up.

Jack finished putting bait on Eddie's hook and watched him cast his line into the deep pool of Shell Creek. Jack liked it here. It was so quiet. There wasn't much wind, the air had a little coolness to it but it was not cold. He heaved a sigh of contentment as he baited his hook and cast his own line in. He looked over at Eddie who sat on a rock at the edge of the bank.

"Any nibbles yet, baby?"

"No." Eddie turned to look at him, a strange look on his face.

"Eddie? You okay?"

"I don't know. My head feels strange."

"How do you mean?" Jack felt his stomach come into his throat when he felt certain he saw a flicker of lavender in Eddie's black eyes.

"I don't know. My brain is trying to tell me stuff but I just don't understand what it is."

"Are you remembering things?"

"No, I don't think so. I don't see the pictures in my mind like when I remember things. This feels different. Like... like..I feel...peaceful?"

"How long has your head been feeling strange, Eddie?"

"Since last night, but I didn't want to say anything. I thought it was because my shoulder hurt. I didn't want you to say we couldn't go today. I didn't think anything was really wrong. I just feel...strange."

Jack pulled his line out of the water and went to sit beside Eddie, who pulled his line out and buried his head in Jack's chest. Jack hugged him close.

"Talk to me, Eddie. Let it go, let it all out. Tell me what's going on in your head."

Eddie couldn't hold it any longer. He started to cry, hard wracking sobs. They shook his whole body. He tried to speak but it was impossible. Jack just made soothing noises and rubbed his back.

"It's okay, baby. Let it all out. You've been hanging onto this for 30 years. It's time to let it all go."

"They died, Uncle Jack. I saw them there. They were dead. I couldn't get to them. I couldn't do anything to help them. Everything was taken from me. Those bad people stole everything from me, they took my whole life. Why? Why, Uncle Jack?"

"Greed, son. I think it is the single worst evil in the world and it makes people do hateful, nasty things to obtain what they want in life. They don't seem to care that what they do hurts other people. But it's over, Eddie, they will never hurt anyone again. And you will never have to live in that cabin ever again. You can find peace now."

"But I killed a man. How can I have peace? I took his life."

"Eddie, you did it in self defense. The Council understood that, they viewed the tape. They are not going to change their minds. Adam was a bad man and the Council knows this, and now, knows your side. He helped to kill your family. If you hadn't have killed him he would have spent the rest of his life in a shifter prison or he would have been handed the same fate as Thea was dealt.

"In a way, I think it's better that he is dead. Being in a shifter prison, with it known he was a former cop who helped to kill unicorn shifters, would not have been easy, he probably would have eventually been killed by the other inmates.

"Just know that if you hadn't killed him, I know I would have. He was going to kill you and there was no way in hell I was going to let that happen. Adam and I were close and he betrayed me in the worst possible way imaginable that a friend could."

"Will I get Daddy's gun back? His Glock was gone. It wasn't in the safe but I took the Lightning."

"I'm pretty sure I can get them back for you. But how did you get it in the first place? It was locked in the gun safe. I taught you to shoot with my rifle and gun."

"I knew where the key was. I watched Daddy clean and care for them. He promised that when I turned 16 he would teach me to fire them. That never happened. Daddy said we have strong Protector blood. He wanted us to be safe and the best way besides practicing mental spells and alerts and physical defense was to be able to fire a gun and shoot a perfect target."

"John was a good father to you but, fuck, I didn't think he was that vicious.

He hid that well."

"He also wanted me to learn to shoot because he couldn't understand why I hadn't come into my powers or why I couldn't shift. He said I was past the late bloomer stage, thought that Da spoiled me too much as a baby, wanted me to stay a baby. That's why I couldn't learn like everyone else. Da didn't want to see his baby grow up."

"Ouch." Jack cringed.

Eddie wiped tears from his eyes.

"I heard the arguments. They got loud. It hurt because they were fighting about me, that I was a stupid kid that would never grow up right. Da was scared. He thought I wouldn't live because of the other babies. I didn't understand but was always too scared to ask."

"You know what a miscarriage is, Eddie?"

"Yeah, I've read about it in some of the textbooks Aunt Carol brought me so I could learn stuff because I wasn't able to go to school anymore."

"Well, Da had two before he became pregnant with you and was scared he would not have you. He was scared right up until you were born."

Jack lightly touched Eddie's cheek then brought him into a hug. He could feel Eddie nestle his head on his shoulder then hug back.

"Eddie, Da spoiled you because he loved you so much. Daddy loved you too but all parents fight about their kids at some point. Carol and I used to get into it all the time because our kids didn't want to spend time with me as much as they did with their mother. That she was spoiling them too much while I was too strict with them.

"It's not your fault that your powers were dormant and probably needed something to wake them or that you were not able to shift. But no matter the issue, they loved you. I could see it every time they talked about you. I can just bet they are looking down on you and thinking how handsome and perfect a man their little boy grew up to be."

Eddie started to cry again. It became harsh. Jack held him tight once again and kissed the top of his head. Eddie screamed until his voice was hoarse, then cried again. He kicked and pounded the ground. His breathing became rapid and he vomited. Jack held him tight. He didn't try to stop it, he knew Eddie needed this. When Eddie started to settle down, Jack whispered in his ear.

"Just think, Eddie, they can all rest in peace now knowing that their killers have been brought to justice and you are now free."

"I think I need to sleep. I feel so tired."

Eddie's sobs seemed to slow. The hitching in his chest became lighter. When he looked up to Jack, Jack's breath caught in his throat and he thought he was about to have a heart attack. Staring back at him was the lavender eyed young man he longed to see but thought he never would. His lavender eyed little godson had come back to him.

Carol came out of the kitchen when she heard the front door open. Jack and Eddie came through the door. Jack held Eddie tightly to him. Eddie's head was down.

"Eddie?" Carol rushed over and took him from Jack and got him seated on the couch. She got his boots off and laid him down. "What happened, Jack?"

Before responding, Jack went out and brought the cooler in and took it to the kitchen.

"Very hard day. Got a lot of fish. Got our godson back."

Carol stared hard at Jack then leaned in to smell his breath.

"You been drinking?"

"No. He's asleep?"

"Yeah. I think he was before I even got him to the couch. What the hell happened? Why are Eddie's hands all bruised and scraped up?

"He came back to us, Carol. We have our godson back. I don't understand what happened. He just broke down. And I mean really broke down. He let it all out. I just held him and let him let it all out.

"The pent up pain, rage, anger and what have you of the last 30 years. It all came pouring out. The sobs were so hard he vomited. I was scared to death he was going to choke himself. He was pounding the ground and tearing at the grass. I had to let him be so he would get it out, he needed to get it out."

He whispered when he saw her angry look. She went back to the living room and knelt down in front of Eddie and stroked his hair out of his eyes. She lightly kissed his forehead.

"But then when he looked up at me, the blackness in his eyes was gone and the lavender was back. It exhausted him. He napped against a tree, then when he woke up it was like an awakening, for lack of a better word."

"You mean..?" Carol's face was streaked with tears as she looked up at him.

"I don't know what else to call it. We fished and we talked, talked and fished."

"Let's let him rest a few minutes." She went to the kitchen while Jack took his boots and coat off. Carol took the lid off the cooler and looked in.

"Leave any in the brook?"

Jack snorted.

"Yeah, a few. You said you wanted us to catch a lot, so we did."

"How is he?"

Jack chuckled as he went to a closet and dug out some newspapers. He laid them out on the counter and started to put the fish on them.

"He asked me so many questions. No wonder he's tired out. He asked about that day, about Cody and Dad. I was amazed at how his mind retained things.

"Though there are a lot of things he doesn't remember. I won't force him to, either. Then he started on the life questions."

"Life questions?" Carol looked at him strangely as she started cleaning the fish. "I'm going to have to freeze some of these."

"Yeah, or I guess you could say, embarrassing questions. Questions James and John should have been answering and not me." Jack's voice cracked.

Carol looked sad.

"Oh, those questions." She patted Jack's arm. "Was it easier with him than with Tucker?"

"No, Tucker was easier by far. I'll go get Eddie up and ready. I forgot to tell Tessa what time to come over."

"I called her and told her about 7. And yes, before you even go there, I asked her if she likes fish and she does. Now go."

"Yes ma'am."

CHAPTER 22

EDDIE SAT ON the bed in the downstairs apartment. He was nervous. He had showered and Jack helped him pick out a nice pair of jeans and a loose pullover. Comfortable but not looking raggedy. Jack sat beside him. Eddie turned his head slightly to look at him, Jack could not get over how much he had missed seeing those beautiful lavender eyes.

"Does she really want to see me?" he asked.

Jack put his arm around Eddie's shoulder and pulled him close for a one armed hug.

"Of course she does. She's asked me a few times. It broke her heart when she thought you were dead, and it killed me not being able to tell her any different."

"She was just a little baby. It was my job to hold her and keep her safe and quiet in the room."

"And you did an excellent job. You saved her life."

"When will she be here?"

"Should be any time now."

Tessa stood at the front door for a long moment before she rang the bell, the butterflies growing in her stomach by the minute. Carol opened the door with a big smile.

Jack stared at the door. Was that just some friendly advice, a threat, or one hell of an admission without actually coming out and saying it? He knew that, eventually, he would find out one way or another.

"Come in. What a lovely dress."

Tessa looked down at herself then back up to smile at Carol. She didn't know why she had brought that particular dress but was glad she did. It was a spaghetti strap sundress in a rainbow glitter design. She had piled her hair into a messy bun on the top of her head and wore sandals. She stepped into the house shyly.

"Thank you. Am I early?"

"You're right on time, dear. I'm just getting things set out on the table and Jack went to see if Eddie is ready to come up."

"I am so nervous," Tessa whispered.

"Don't be, dear. There is nothing to be nervous about. I think Eddie is just as nervous. Come in and sit down. Want a glass of wine to help settle your nerves?"

"Sure."

"Sit." Carol pointed to the couch then went into the kitchen. She came back with two glasses of white wine. She handed one to Tessa then sat in the chair across from her. Carol took a small sip.

"Eddie came back to himself today. If that makes any

sense to you. Jack said he broke down and finally let out 30 years worth of agony. His eyes have come back to their lavender color. He's back to himself to a degree. I haven't had a chance to really talk to him or see him. He was so exhausted when they got home, he slept for a little while until Jack took him down to get cleaned up."

Jack kept his hand lightly resting on Eddie's back as he came up the stairs behind him. Eddie opened the door and stepped out into the hallway.

"It's okay, Eddie. Go ahead." Jack gave Eddie a gentle press to his back. Eddie went into the dining room.

Tessa and Carol turned to look. Tessa set her wine glass down and stood up.

"Eddie?"

Eddie nodded his head with a slight blush.

"I held you when I was in the secret room to keep you safe. I was scared but I needed to keep you from crying. You were so beautiful."

Tessa dipped her head slightly.

"Thank you." She stared hard at him. She could not believe how handsome he was even at 15 years her senior. Her heart fluttered. This was the boy, now a man, who had held her in secret while their family was slaughtered.

"I don't know what to say." And she really didn't. What could she say?

Jack led Eddie over to the couch. He sat down and Tessa

sat back down beside him. He had his head down. She could tell he was just as nervous as she was and most likely didn't know what to say any more than she did. Who really knew what to say at all?

She had questions, but didn't know whether she should ask them or not, if it would upset him or if he would even answer her. Finally she decided to dive right in.

"What were my dads like?"

Eddie lifted his head to look at her. She could hear Jack swallow wondering how Eddie would react.

"They were the best adoptive brothers I could ever have asked for. They included me in everything they did. When I was big enough they took me with them to the beach. When I started school they made sure I was okay, and Uncle Jack helped too. Da and Daddy always made sure that we were happy and well taken care of. I miss it."

"You saw me being born?"

Eddie hesitated, his breath hitched before he spoke.

"Yeah. I held Michael's hand, he wanted me there to be a part of it. I watched you being born. It was incredible. You were so tiny and I held you. You cried when you came out but were very quiet in the room. I told Michael when he told us he was going to have a baby that I hoped to have one too someday."

Tessa could feel her heart swell. So much had been taken from him; from her as well, and all because of greed and money.

Carol sat down her glass and got up. All eyes turned to her.

"No, stay. Chat. I'm going to put the fish on the barbecue. It won't take long to cook. Everything else is either in the warming oven or fridge." She smiled and walked out of the room.

"Eddie," Jack said. Eddie looked over to him. "Tessa likes to take photographs."

"Michael and Da loved it. They made a lot of money taking pictures. They loved working at the Studio. Not allowed to go there anymore."

"The Council has taken the restrictions off, baby. It's up to you what happens to it now. The same with the Lounge. Now that there is no longer a need to hide you to keep you safe, the entire estate reverts to you. You can decide what you want to do with the Studio and Lounge."

Eddie looked over to Tessa.

"I don't know what to do."

Tessa hesitated, not sure if she should say what had just popped into her head but decided to take a chance.

"Maybe we could figure it out together." She reached out her hand, it was a long second before he reached out and took it.

"Okay."

Jack came up to stand beside Carol at the barbecue.

"Almost done?" he asked.

"Yep. How's it going in there?"

"A rocky start. I got up and excused myself and went to the kitchen and sort of eavesdropped. All of a sudden they started talking like two little magpies."

Carol put the fish on a platter and turned off the barbecue. Jack followed her and got the table set up and the rest of the meal out of the fridge and oven. When it was all set up and ready, Jack called out.

"Dinner's ready!"

Tessa came in with Eddie a few steps behind her.

"Uncle Jack, can you ask for a visitor's extension?"

One Week Later

Jack laid his cell phone on the counter and turned on the speaker so that Carol could hear as well. It was picked up on the third ring.

"Hello?" came an uncertain male voice.

"Tucker? It's Dad."

"Dad? Is everything okay?"

"Yes, son. Everything is fine now. A lot of things I want to tell you and your sister but it would take too long over the phone. I'm going to call her next. And I have a big surprise as well, it ties in with all I'm going to tell you. I want you to see what free time you, your sister and your families can get off and coordinate. I'll be springing for plane tickets for everyone to come here to visit us."

Jack could almost hear the stunned silence on the other end of the phone.

"Dad?...how?...how can you afford that? You win the lotto or something?"

"Not the lotto, but, let's just say it's one last gift from your grandfather."

EPILOGUE

Three years later

"COME ON, OLD woman. What is keeping you?" Jack stood impatiently by the front door, looking towards the kitchen.

"You just shut up." Carol came out of the kitchen, putting on a jacket. She came to stand by her husband and hugged him. "It's nice having my husband home all the time."

"I'm glad I retired. I didn't think I ever would, that I would just drop dead on the job. I felt like I had to keep watch, to be there for when it finally got solved."

"And it did. Thanks to you and Tessa. Feels good, doesn't it? You two should be proud of yourselves knowing they can finally rest in peace knowing that their killers met their makers as well."

"Yep. And it's nice knowing how things worked out. It felt like such a weight off my shoulders when the Council declared the case closed and solved. I knew then it was time to hang up my badge."

Jack kissed his wife's forehead then led her to the car and helped her in. He went around and got in the driver's side. He couldn't help but smile. "It's weird how things did manage to work out, a sad ending becomes a happy one."

"I suppose." Carol watched the road as they headed towards Greyson House. "I just wish there never had to be a sad part to begin with."

Jack reached over and laid a hand on her leg.

"I know."

They parked out front of Greyson House. The house seemed to have its life back. It had been painted, the lawn perfectly manicured.

"It's so nice to see it full of life again."

"Sure is."

They went up to the front door and Jack playfully banged on it. He could hear a voice drawing close full of fake sarcasm,

"Alright already. Don't break it down."

The door was yanked open and they were greeted by Eddie's smiling face. He stood aside to let them in. Once they were inside, Jack squatted while Eddie closed the door and took Carol's jacket.

"Where's my little rodent?"

Eddie laughed as a flutter of paper went up from near the TV and a two-year-old boy came running across the living room into Jack's arms.

"Unka Jack!"

Jack hugged him close, standing up.

"Look at your face, Jonathan James, you've been eating cheese balls again."

"I believe more than his fair share today," a voice came from the kitchen. Tessa came into view. Carol came over and hugged her gently.

"How are you doing?"

"Not so bad, this time around. Doctor says everything is fine and I'm right where I should be. Taking a little more time off now, though. But when I get further along I'll just go on leave and rent out the two studio rooms that I have been using. I just hope this one is easier to birth. I didn't think John would ever come out."

"It was the pain, wasn't it?"

Tessa pushed out a huff.

"Yeah. That cheese ball eating brat had a huge head."

"Do you know if it's a boy or a girl?"

"Don't want to know, it's going to be a surprise."

"Have you decided on names?" Jack asked.

"Yes," Eddie replied, "If it's a boy, then we'll do Michael Steven. If it's a girl; Stephanie Michelle."

"Oh, such a wonderful idea."

Jack put Jonathan James down who quickly ran back to the TV. They could hear quiet munching.

"Did you give him more cheese balls?" Tessa asked Eddie sternly.

"Nope. He takes his time eating them. The little rodent is like me, savors everything." Then his voice became somber. "I guess we should go." Eddie looked to Carol. "We shouldn't be long."

Carol went over, put her hands on his cheeks and kissed his nose.

"Take all the time you need. I love spending time with my godson."

Eddie nodded as he helped Tessa into her coat and put his own on. He opened the door and let Tessa and Jack go ahead of him then quietly closed the door behind him.

Once they were all down the steps, Eddie turned and squatted in front of a small white rose bush on the right side of the steps. He had planted a small bush at the base of the front steps and was surprised at how it had thrived. He cupped a couple of blossoms and inhaled deeply. He then broke off four blossoms, being careful not to prick his fingers on the thorns. He stood up and forced a smile as he stood beside Tessa, who looped her arm around him.

It was a half hour walk to the Carstairs Family Cemetery in the woods behind Greyson House. Tessa released Eddie's arm as they came to stand in front of two headstones. The walk had been quiet and peaceful. Eddie was grateful, he needed to collect his thoughts.

Eddie placed two white roses at the base of each headstone.

"I love this place," Tessa whispered. "It's so peaceful."

"Yeah." Jack looked around. "I'm glad they're here on Carstairs land, it's where they belong. Not the Valley cemetery."

"I don't remember if I was at the funeral or not. I still can't remember a lot."

Jack laid a hand on his shoulder.

"No, you weren't. The Council refused to let you go for your safety. You barely moved from your hospital bed the first month or so. The doctors didn't think you would be able to handle it. That it would make you worse than what you were."

Eddie heaved out a sigh.

"The psychiatrist thought it would be good for me to come out here often. To make my brain understand that even though they are here, what I know of them is here." He touched his heart. "I need to understand that to make it easier to deal with, but I have not yet been able to do it until now.

"She also has a theory or an explanation of sorts as to why my eyes turned black and I was the way I was. She has been doing a lot of research and believes that my Protector side kicked in. My powers were dormant but activated when I saw everyone dead. It shut down my brain to all that it had seen in order to protect it. I was not able to advance mentally, though. It was in constant alert mode only it wasn't actively sending out mental alerts. She also contacted Head Protector Bryant to get his thoughts. He agrees with her assessment but after he talked with me and asked about my childhood and everything, he believes that my powers were dormant as well but, as far as my inability to learn as fast as everyone else, my mental lag, was not completely that Da spoiled me and wanted to keep me a child but my powers refused to surface and dragged the rest of my brain down, I guess is how to put it, I don't know. But most Protectors' powers show up when they are 10 to 12, mine never did, they were dormant but messing with my brain. I don't know how else to put it. But when I had that episode when we went fishing when all the pain and grief finally hit, my powers finally fired into life, they had been waking up and came in.

"They sent me to a Protector who teaches at Twelve Oaks. When I came back to myself, I came into my abilities, though they are not as powerful because I am only half Protector. I could have taken the courses to train to be a certified Protector but I didn't. I just learned how to send out mental alerts. Jackson Harlow is the Protector for the sector that Greyson House is in. I have no desire to take over his position. I am very happy just being a husband and father. We have talked a few times. He enjoys being a sector Protector and his sons are going to train when they are old enough, so I have no worries about my new family.

"Though I have come a long way with my therapy I have not been able to make myself come here. This is a huge milestone for me and I'm so glad that you all are here to share it with me. And now that I am here, I feel so at peace. I'll come here not out of need but because I want to."

"I'm just glad it's over and those sickos will never harm anyone again."

Jack nodded his head in agreement.

"And you know what?" Jack touched his cheek, his voice soft. "I have my sweet lavender eyed little boy back who could beat the shit out of me at chess and who I could have cheese ball fights with."

Eddie laughed.

"And John loves them too."

"He doesn't do what you used to do, does he, rodent?"

"Sadly, yes."

"So, I need to know, why do you sometimes call him rodent? Eddie never really told me," Tessa asked.

"Never really occurred to me. I call John a rodent just as I was. If it wasn't for the cheese balls I probably wouldn't."

Jack gave Eddie a one armed hug.

"Oh, that goes way back to when he was John's age, maybe a bit older. Michael and Steven had some strange tastes. Cheese balls and nacho flavored popcorn were the two biggest. So, anyway, they were grocery shopping and Michael spies this gallon jug of cheese balls. Begs James to get it. James, ever curious, gets them because he wants to try them. He wasn't struck by them but Michael and John loved them. There were always at least a couple of jugs in the house. So, this one day, Eddie is so fussy, won't eat or drink or even nap. Everyone is at their wits end listening to him cry. I don't know where Michael came up with the idea but he takes a cheese ball and puts it on the tray of Eddie's high chair.

"Eddie stops crying to look at it then, BAM! That little hand came slamming down on top of that poor cheese ball, mushing it. The kid had power. He looked at his hand covered in cheese ball remains and started chewing it off.

"John said 'typical rodent' and it stuck."

Eddie laughed.

"I think I remember that, just slightly. Only thing I can say is I hope they never take them off the market."

Tessa let out a soft breath and lightly touched her husband on the shoulder. There was a 15 year age difference between them but she didn't care. She was deeply in love with him and that was all that mattered. She moved to Unicorn Falls and stayed with him in the cabin and helped him deal with his grief and the intense therapy he went through to help him through his pain and to make life easier for him to deal with.

It made her love him even more when he asked her opinion on the Carstairs properties. Now that he was declared alive and safe, it all reverted to him. But she did not feel angry about it, she felt relieved. They moved into Greyson House. Tessa reopened the studio under her name, took two rooms for herself and rented out the rest. They also reopened the Lounge with Dale as manager. They were all surprised when he retired at the same time Jack did and made the suggestion that if they decided to reopen the Lounge that he would love to work there. It became a big success as it had been when John managed it. She wept when he asked her to marry him and was tender, kind and patient when she helped him to discover the pleasures of making love, since it was his first time. She felt blessed that it was with her. He was always soft and gentle, never rough.

The birth of Jonathan James had been the most exciting day of his life. It hadn't been hard to tell. He was with her every step of the way just as she had been with him. He still had his bad days, that was to be expected, but he never raised his fist to her or their child. It had taken three years to get to this point but it had been worth it.

"Eddie?"

"What I would give just to be able to hug them one more time. To feel Da's strong arms around me in the night when I was scared. Daddy sneaking me cheese balls when Da wasn't around. They stole my whole life from me."

Jack touched Eddie's forearm.

"But they love you and will always be with you in spirit. They are watching over you and I can just bet they are getting the greatest laughs watching their grandchild."

Eddie smiled, Jack was right. Uncle Jack was always right.

"Time to head back."

Jack held his arm out and Tessa took it. They started walking back down the path. Eddie started to follow behind when movement out of the corner of his eye caught his attention. He turned sharply. They stood there, the four of them. They all smiled and gave a quick wave. Eddie turned his head sharply.

"Can you see this?" Tessa and Jack turned quickly, their breath caught in their throats.

But as quick as they were there, they were gone.

Tessa came to Eddie and hugged his arm.

"They came to say goodbye," Tessa whispered.

"Goodbye," Eddie whispered as he allowed his wife to take him home.